Don't You Want Me

A NOVEL

Don't You Want Me

Derlys Maria Gutiérrez

A REGALO PRESS BOOK
ISBN: 979-8-88845-754-2
ISBN (eBook): 979-8-88845-755-9

Cover Design by Conroy Accord

Publishing Team:
Founder and Publisher – Gretchen Young
Editor – Adriana Senior
Editorial Assistant – Caitlyn Limbaugh
Managing Editor – Aleigha Koss
Production Manager – Kate Harris
Production Editor – Rachel Paul

As part of the mission of Regalo Press, a donation is being made to Cuban American Alliance for Leadership & Education, as chosen by the author. Find out more about this organization at: https://caale.org/

This book, as well as any other Regalo Press publications, may be purchased in bulk quantities at a special discounted rate. Contact orders@regalopress.com for more information.

Regalo Press
New York • Nashville
regalopress.com

Published in the United States of America
1 2 3 4 5 6 7 8 9 10

For my daughters, Julia and Chelsea
You two are my dreams fulfilled.

Chapter 1

Just a few more minutes, and his train would arrive.

Lisa sang along with the radio in her loudest shower voice, joyous to arrive at the station to wait for Adam. She had about two hours before her next client meeting, and this afternoon they'd agreed she'd pick him up at the train station for their usual rendezvous on nights she was scheduled to work late. She had not seen him in exactly three weeks, two days, and seven hours, but who was counting?

She was. She always counted.

From the moment he stepped out of her car, she started counting the days until their next rendezvous. Even before he was gone, she already missed him.

On days when they met, they both pretended to work late. Their encounters usually occurred at a stop along the train route on his way home from work, and they'd spend an hour or so talking in her car. When he missed the train home, she'd drive him to the station near his home where he had left the car that morning. Then she'd make the long, lonely way back to her house, often crying, usually resentful. On those marvelous yet rare occasions when they took a day off from work, they'd book a hotel where they'd pretend the outside world didn't exist. There, in that space of wonder, they'd lose themselves—one skin, one heart, one breath. Yet Lisa was always present to the inescapable fact that every passing second was but one moment closer to going their separate ways, back to reality.

Each time he left, she never really knew when she'd see him again. Everything depended on his work schedule, his children, his family, and his wife.

Primarily his wife.

Lisa had a more flexible schedule. Her husband, Marcus, had become even more of a workaholic after their son had died. Now he either didn't care where she was, or how late she stayed out, or he didn't notice. The bottom line was that their marriage hadn't worked for years.

But Adam's wife was insistent he be home as much as possible to help with the children and to be with the family. Since they met two years ago, he had regaled Lisa with stories of how demanding, annoying, mean-spirited, selfish, critical, and unloving his wife was. It was no wonder Adam had told Lisa that, but for the children, he would have divorced his wife years before. Lisa counted on this assurance whenever she felt even slightly guilty about the affair.

As Lisa approached the station, butterflies fluttered in her stomach. She wondered if he had changed in the three weeks since they'd last met. She wondered if he'd still find her pretty. Of course he would. He always called her his "dish." He said he loved her long, brown, wavy hair, her dark bedroom eyes, her lips always ready for a kiss. He complimented her chic taste in clothes, her perfectly manicured long nails, her dark pink lipstick. She knew he had no idea how much time and effort she put into her attire and her looks to please him. He told her he thought she threw herself together artfully, and he was crazy about her. Funny, though, he never told her he loved her, but she knew he did. She could feel it. He just couldn't profess his love because he was scared. He had a family. He had obligations. His children were young.

He was married.

Lisa tried not to dwell too much on this last obstacle. Or that he was cheating on his wife. She rationalized away the fact that she was a participant in this cheating. She even managed to forget sometimes that she was cheating on her husband.

Cheating was such a terrible word. She preferred to refer to themselves as "unfortunate souls who were misunderstood and were not loved by their spouses." Adam's wife did not love him, so he had every right to find comfort in the arms of someone who adored him, of someone who was destined to be with him. He deserved to have her, and she deserved to have him. Their timing was just off.

At the train station, she found a parking spot away from the main staircase, far from intrusive eyes, nestled among the shadows of nightfall where they could forget the world for a fleeting hour or so.

Ten more minutes until he was due to arrive. Just enough time to calm down.

Eye makeup? Check.

Blush? Check.

Lipstick? Check.

Hair just right? Check.

Sweet breath? Check. But better take another mint, just in case.

Lisa settled down with her book. She always brought something to read when expecting Adam because she always had to wait for him. In train stations, in parks, at restaurants, in shopping malls, in bookstores. He usually missed his connecting train, or he got held up in a meeting, or something intervened. This drove his wife crazy. To Lisa, it was just a quirk. She had patience. She'd wait for him forever.

Tonight, the first train arrived without him on board. The next one was due in fifteen minutes. This gave her time to read her work notes.

Yet every minute he was late was one less minute they had together. She dismissed that sad thought. Every second with Adam was worth any inconvenience.

When the next train came and went with no Adam again, she started to worry. What if something happened to him? How strange that he had not called. While he was typically late, he was usually considerate.

Nervous about missing him, she called her best friend. Emily Martinez was the only person in the world who knew about her relationship with Adam. With Emily, Lisa could pour out her heart.

Thankfully, Emily picked up.

"Emily," said Lisa in one continuous rapid breath, "I'm sitting here at the train station, waiting for Adam. He's very late, and I'm getting worried."

Matter-of-factly, Emily replied. "Why? He's always late."

"Well, this is a little later than usual. Plus, he hasn't called."

"You're upset." Emily knew Lisa well.

"No. I'm not upset…. Wait. Yes. I am." The "I am" was muffled by a sob. Three weeks, two days, and seven hours of waiting for him was enough. Another hour was more than she could bear. "Here comes another train."

"Maybe he's on this one." Emily's encouragement didn't sound too convincing.

Passengers walked down the steps, and the train left. No sign of Adam.

Lisa couldn't contain her tears. "I can't believe he's still not here. We were supposed to meet tonight. We talked this afternoon. He said he was coming. I haven't seen him in almost four weeks." Her words were broken by choked tears.

"Lisa Coronado Williams. You're sitting alone in your car, at night, at an empty station, waiting for a married guy who lies, so the two of you can steal some time, and then he can get back on the next train to his wife. Not to mention your husband is probably home, fully confident you're at work. This is the life you've chosen. You can't get so upset when things don't go as planned." Was Emily realistic? Lisa wasn't in the mood for realistic.

"I know, I know," she sighed. "But we'd agreed to see each other tonight. Doesn't he know how to keep his word?"

Emily chuckled. "His word? Look, honey, I'm not trying to be mean. I know you love him, and I know you believe the two of you are meant to be together, but be realistic, Lisa. He's married. The best you can hope for is that he shows up at some point. He's not reliable." Emily paused in her advice column speech.

"What?" Lisa asked, right eyebrow raised suspiciously at the quiet.

"What, what?" Emily stalled.

"What are you saying with the silence?" Lisa insisted.

"Lisa, I've always been honest with you. I love you as a sister. You're my best friend, and I'd do anything for you. But this isn't a good relationship for you. It was fun in the beginning; it was harmless as long as you weren't attached to each other, but this is getting serious with you. I'm afraid you're going to be very hurt, and you're going to hurt other people even more if you don't stop and think about what you're doing."

"I know," Lisa uttered softly.

"He's not good for you, Lisa. He's married; you're married. Against my better judgment, I've stayed impartial about this affair for the last two years, thinking it would help you for a while as a distraction until you found your way back from the crushing sadness with which you've been living since the baby. It's clear though that this has become more than a fling. If you're so unhappy with Marcus, if you don't love him anymore, divorce him and find someone who'll love you back, with no strings or wives attached." Emily paused and took a deep breath. "It's 2008, Lisa. You're a grown, professional, smart, forty-year-old woman. You've been through so much with all the miscarriages, and, after all that, losing your son. You've come a long way from those days. It's high time you live a full life, and stop hiding in shadows."

Lisa cried quietly. Her friend was right: this was no way to live. Ever since her infant son had died, the only thing that had gone well for

Lisa was meeting Adam. Being in love with him helped her forget the pain of her loss, the emptiness of her marriage with Marcus, and the unrelenting sadness that permeated her life. She had initially thought Adam was the answer, but two years was more than long enough to hide in dark train stations. Sending secret emails. Stealing time from work to have lunch. Sneaking off to motels. Never having any stability, lying to everyone, especially to herself. She lived in limbo.

The first day she met Adam had been an ordinary day like any other. Marcus was away on a business trip, so she met friends at a bar in the city. The plan was to have just a couple of drinks, then dinner, then early back home.

She had sat at the bar waiting for her friend Tina. A few minutes and a few sips of Cabernet later, Tina had arrived with some other friends from work—two men and two women. Lisa couldn't even remember anymore who they were. Introductions all around, smiles and handshakes, everything cool for a Thursday happy hour. "Where's Adam?" Tina asked the other coworkers. "Oh, he's running late. You know Adam." They shared a knowing chuckle.

A few minutes later, something told Lisa to turn her head to the door just as a tall, dark-haired man walked into the bar. He commanded attention although Lisa couldn't pinpoint why at the time. He looked around a bit arrogantly as if he were annoyed there wasn't a group gathered at the door to greet him upon arrival.

"Well, he sure is cocky," she muttered to no one in particular. Fortunately, no one listened.

"Hey, Adam, glad you could make it," one of the guys yelled. "This is Lisa Williams, the friend I told you about."

"Hi. I'm Adam Scheiner." He extended his hand. Lisa took it, surprised at how firm his handshake was. She was used to guys giving women a limp handshake as if trying not to hurt their hands. They lingered a bit with the handshake. Not perceptibly, but a second longer than necessary for an introduction. His hands were the softest she had ever held. He mustn't have worked a hard day in his life, she mused.

"You two have a lot in common," said Tina. "Adam went to Columbia too, Lisa." Tina patted the empty stool next to Lisa, smiling all the while. "Adam, sit down and regale Lisa with how you used to ignore the women at Barnard."

He sat down, not taking his eyes off Lisa and asked her what she was drinking.

"Cabernet."

"Sounds good. I'll join you."

Something about the way he said "I'll join you" made her nervous. But he had such a genuine smile, she found herself relaxing.

They started talking. She started feeling comfortable, like she had known him all her life, as if they had been friends forever.

And then it seemed everything around them disappeared. The music stopped, the room got silent, no beers were poured, no waitresses walked around. The only people left in the world were them. They talked of college at Barnard and Columbia in New York City in the '80s, of their jobs, of their families. About their love for The Beatles and classical music, about concerts, pop music, family, and traditions. They could have talked for hours, for days. They could have talked forever.

He looked at this watch. "Oh, shit. I've missed my train." He looked worried.

"Take the next one." Lisa was having too good a time to let him go just yet.

"Next one won't come for another hour." Now he seemed more worried.

"It's OK. I have my car here. I'll drive you home." She hoped he'd say yes. She wanted to talk to him some more.

"Nah. I couldn't impose."

"Sure you could. I'm ready to leave anyway. I have a long day tomorrow." Big fat lie.

"Well, in that case…."

The lie worked.

***

Another train pulled up to the station. The car emptied of passengers.

Still on the phone, Emily cleared her throat. "Well?"

"Nope, no Adam. It's late. I guess I should give up."

"Wash your face, reapply your makeup, and forget about tonight for now. Tomorrow you'll find out what happened."

They hung up. What to do next? Lisa knew she needed to leave this situation, but she didn't know how. She had invested two years on this dream that he would one day leave his wife. But she hadn't done anything to leave her husband either. Sometimes it felt like they were stuck on a merry-go-round—not going anywhere, not able to escape.

If they had met when they were in college, they *might* have taken a class together, or bumped into each other at a concert, or been introduced by mutual friends on campus. There were a million ways they might have known one another when they were young and free. Lisa was certain they would have felt an instant attraction, gone on a date, started a relationship. They would have been inseparable. They would have recognized their souls back then, and they wouldn't be married to other people now.

Her attention was drawn to the radio. Wow, she hadn't heard "Don't You Want Me" in a long time. A blast from the past, it was just as annoying in 1982 as it was now. While she listened, another part of her continued the pretty dream. What would life have been like with Adam and her when they were little more than teenagers? What would she do differently if she knew then what she knew now? Her mind wandered backwards in time.

"Don't you want me baby? Don't you want me oh oh oh oh?" The words were laughable and mesmerizing at the same time.

Opening the window a crack to get some fresh air, she enjoyed the breeze on her skin, all alive and prickly, goosebumps all up and down her arms.

Her thoughts were so vivid. She saw herself and Adam, like in a movie, sitting next to each other on the Low Library steps on the Columbia campus. She imagined a night much like this one, a little cool, not quite yet dark, dozens of kids hanging out, smoking. She could smell the smoke. How could she smell the smoke?

Suddenly she felt cold and hot at the same time, her skin damp and clammy, as if she had a fever. Nausea churned in her stomach.

She tried to change the radio station. No matter what station she tried, the same song was playing.

"What the…?" The song seemed even louder now. *"You know I don't believe you when you say that you don't need me…"*

Above the din of the music, she could hear the thump of her pulse in her neck. She sensed her heart racing. Her breathing quickened, and she felt like she was definitely going to throw up. She reached for the glove compartment, looking for one of the grocery bags she kept there for car trash collection. Her arm brushed up against the radio controls, and the volume went up even louder. She tried vainly to turn off the radio as she searched for the bag.

Then there was silence and darkness.

Her ears were buzzing. She blinked her eyes fast, trying to adjust to bright lights. That song was still playing, but she was sitting on the Low Library steps. She looked around, confused, not sure where she was and certainly not knowing why she was there. People were walking around, dancing, laughing.

> *It's much too late to find*
> *When you think you've changed your mind*

You'd better change it back or we will both be sorry.
Don't you want me baby?

She hugged herself. Yes, she was still intact. She rubbed her stomach, still feeling a dull ache. She couldn't understand. She had just been in the car, looking for a bag. How could she have been in the car and now she was here, on the Columbia steps? It looked like a party was going on.

"This dream is really vivid," she said to herself. Her friend Emily yelled back. "Yeah, it's a real dream."

Lisa looked to her right. Why was Emily sitting here with her? "What did you say?"

"I answered you. You said this dream is really vivid, and I agreed." Emily looked confused. "What's wrong with you? You look like you've seen a ghost."

Lisa stared at her. She thought she was losing her mind. Did she knock herself out in her car back at the station?

Emily looked the same, only young again. Same curly unruly hair down to her shoulders and held back in a ponytail, soft brown eyes, short, with the loudest laugh and a huge smile that showed all her teeth.

"How did we get here?" Lisa asked, afraid of the answer.

Emily laughed. "Why are you acting so weird? We walked over here from my dorm. We're meeting our friends, remember? Georgia, Donna, Elena, and Serge? We're hanging out tonight."

Lisa couldn't understand her friend's answer. She continued to stare at her. These were all college friends. How could they go out tonight? What was going on here?

Emily repeated, "Lisa Coronado, what is the matter with you? Did you hit your head or something?"

"Emily, listen to me carefully. Something strange is going on. What day is it?" Lisa braced herself for the answer.

"OK, you have lost your mind. Today is Thursday. Party night!" Emily looked ebullient. That alone was weird. Emily was never ebullient. She was a serious student. Her idea of partying was getting sandwiches from V&Ts deli and drinking Kamikazes in the dorm. But here she was, on the steps, dancing.

"What's the date?"

Emily didn't get a chance to answer. Just at that moment, Donna, Georgia, and Elena showed up on the pathway, at the bottom of the steps. Emily waved her arms hello, signaling them to climb. A few feet behind them, Serge headed towards them, talking to another guy.

"Hi!" squealed the girls. Emily asked, "Who's the guy with Serge?"

Lisa looked towards Serge and noticed that he and his companion were ambling up the stairs with nary a care in the world. Lisa stood up to see above the crowd. She gasped, instantly knowing the answer to Emily's question. She recognized that face, that build, the way he walked. His hair was dark, of course. Longer, untamed, unmanageable. But there was no doubt it was him.

Serge smiled as he approached the group. "Hey, guys! This is Adam."

Lisa felt dizzy and swayed on her feet. Adam was closest to her and grabbed her by the arm, stopping her from falling down. "Whoa, are you all right?"

She stared at him.

How could this be? she thought.

He repeated the question. "Are you OK?"

She found her voice. "Uh, yeah, yeah. I'm fine."

"Good, 'cause I'd hate for you to fall into my arms before we've barely gotten to know each other." He laughed. She loved that laugh.

He stood there with a goofy sort of smile, a mixture of looking good and acting nerdy. "So, what's your name? I couldn't hear it since you were faint and all." He laughed again. Lisa couldn't stop staring at him. She looked dazed still, as if she were talking to a ghost.

Emily came to her rescue. "Her name is Lisa. She's not quite herself yet tonight. Too much studying before we got here and obviously not enough alcohol. Why don't we head on over to the bar?"

Adam didn't take his eyes off Lisa while Emily was talking. "Yeah, I need something to eat before I start drinking. Want to come with me?" His question was directed at Lisa and Lisa only. She nodded dumbly. She didn't trust her mouth to utter the right words.

Emily came close to Lisa, leaned into her ear conspiratorially, and whispered, "He's cute, but are you really going to pretend to faint around him?" She giggled.

"Shush, he'll hear you," Lisa whispered back.

Before she was able to say anything else, Adam grabbed Lisa's hand and yelled out to the others, "Where are you all going after this? We'll meet you. Lisa and I are going to get a bite first." He gently pulled her with him down the stairs, barely waiting to hear the answer to his question. His hand was soft and warm, safe.

Elena yelled out, "We're going to the West End. You can eat there!" But Adam had his own plans apparently. "Go on! We'll meet you later." He gave no further explanation and skipped down the stairs, his hand gripping Lisa's, pulling her with him. She said nothing, turned her head back for an instant, grinned at her friends, waved goodbye with her free hand, and followed him down the rest of the steps, headed towards the street. She didn't care where they went, how long they'd be there, or if they ever came back.

Chapter 2

Lisa had no idea what time it was. She didn't know how long they had been sitting in this Chinese restaurant on Broadway. The vegetable fried rice and chicken and broccoli were delicious, but she remembered little of the meal. She'd been too busy making sure that she devoured every second being with Adam. She still wasn't sure if this was a dream. Adam had just asked her a question and waited patiently for an answer. She came back to this present.

"Hello...earth to Lisa. Did you hear me?" He chuckled. A goofy smile covered her face.

"I'm sorry. I was daydreaming. What did you say again?" She didn't know how else to disguise her complete infatuation with this boy who was not a boy to her. He had the same mannerisms as her Adam, but everything about him was fresh, new, unsullied by time. There was no tension in him. His voice was not as raspy now, and his face was young, carefree, no creases around his eyes, no gray in his hair. His eyes sparkled, laughter reaching them.

"I asked if you were seeing anyone."

She wanted to answer, "Yes, you," but that wouldn't have made sense to him. Instead, she smiled sheepishly, "No, I'm not."

"Good." He breathed a sigh of relief. "Then I have a chance."

"Are you always this direct?"

"Not really, I'm actually very shy. But something about you. I don't know what it is. I feel like I want to spend time with you, without interference, to get to know you better with no other guy distracting you."

He paused. "Hey, I didn't offend you by taking you away from your friends, did I?"

This time it was her turn to laugh. "Well, it's a little late for that now, isn't it?" She looked at her watch. Two hours had flown. Hadn't it been just a few minutes since they had sat down?

"Should we go find them? They'll think I kidnapped you."

The last thing Lisa wanted to do was to leave this warm Chinese restaurant to find her friends. She was afraid any movement would wake her up, and then she'd lose this new Adam. He didn't know her, but she knew him. She couldn't possibly tell him; he'd think she was crazy.

"I'm sure they'll be fine without me for a while longer. Why don't we go for a walk instead?"

Adam got the check, and Lisa reached into her purse, ready to split the bill. "Put your wallet away," he said. "I've got this." He looked at her, his head tilted slightly, a half-smile on his lips. She wasn't used to this treatment. In the other life, they usually shared costs to deter suspicion in spouses.

"My father taught me that a gentleman always pays when he's out with a beautiful woman."

"Thank you." Lisa hesitated a beat. "For the compliment, too." She leaned her head to the side and cupped her cheek in her hand, delighting in this moment. She was almost hesitant to talk, afraid to break the spell that had brought her here.

"Come on. I'm sure you're used to guys saying things like that to you all the time," he said.

Lisa shook her head. "Not at all. Why would I be used to that?"

They got up from the table. Adam gestured to Lisa, "After you, m'lady," with a fake British accent. As they reached the exit, he hurried in front of her to open the door. The evening was still warm, and the sidewalk not too crowded. Adam reached for her hand and gave it a squeeze. "Which way would you like to go?" he asked.

"Let's head towards Riverside Park. We can see the water from there."

They left busy Broadway behind, walking hand in hand, their pace even, unhurried. Around them, guys were carrying boom boxes, some with hair stuck up in triangles, others with long hair wearing peace T-shirts and combat boots. The women had big hair and faded wide bottom jeans. They passed phone booths with thick telephone books hanging from a hook. The cars were old, yet they looked new even with the bouncing puppy toys on the dashboard. There was not a cell phone in sight, and it seemed everybody was smoking—even inside the restaurants they passed.

"So, tell me about yourself," Adam said. "I want to know you."

"There's not much to tell, Adam. I'm just an ordinary girl, you know. My dad died when I was young, raised by a single mom with a strict upbringing. You know, the usual." She talked quickly, nervously. She tried to gloss over what she knew of her life because she wasn't even sure who she was here. She knew Lisa in her marketing/advertising world, but who was this college Lisa? Had she traveled backwards? How? Was this a dream, and if it was, how long could she make it last?

"There's nothing ordinary about you, Lisa. I've only known you for a little while, and I'm already taken by you." When they reached the park, they leaned on the railing overlooking the river. It was a clear night, so they could see the lights from the buildings across in New Jersey reflected in the water. The hum of cars traveling on the West Side Highway was a constant background noise. The park was busy. Others had the same idea to walk on a warm evening.

Adam put his arm around Lisa's waist, holding her close. She leaned her head on his shoulder, enjoying the warmth of his embrace. They stayed quiet until Adam pulled away and started walking again.

"Let's play a game," he said. "If you're on a deserted island, and you could have one movie to watch, what would it be?"

"Hmmm. A movie?" she asked. "How could I watch a movie on a deserted island with no electricity? There's no logic to that."

Adam laughed. "Use your imagination, girl!"

Lisa scrunched up her face in deep thought. "All right. Favorite movie. *It's a Wonderful Life.*"

Adam sounded intrigued. "Not my choice for an empty island, but I could watch it a few more times. Why that one?"

Lisa smiled. "Because George Bailey gets to see how life would be without him."

"Aha, second chances." Adam pondered. "I think Mary Bailey and that love story were the nicest parts of that movie."

"What a romantic," Lisa said with a teasing note.

He looked down sheepishly, like a dog caught chewing on his master's slipper. "Yeah, I confess. I'm a sucker for romance and the ladies."

Lisa stood on her tip toes and kissed his nose. "You're sweet, you know."

"Aww shucks. You say that to all the guys." He reached down to her face and tenderly moved the hair out of her eyes. They stared at each other, not blinking.

Lisa remembered their first kiss as adults: stolen, dangerous, bristling with the secret excitement that comes from forbidden fruit. Her mouth had melted into his, and their lips became soft, gentle turning ardent. A moan had escaped her throat, and he'd chided her with "Let's not get too passionate. I'm heading to a train," as he had pulled away, opening the car door. She remembered how she had wanted to kiss him for the rest of her life. She had imagined what it would be like, but the real thing had been nothing like the imaginary one.

And now she was here, hoping, anticipating a second first kiss.

"Come here," he whispered. Lisa obeyed; her face upturned. Adam reached for her chin, lifted it gently, and pulled her face towards him. Lisa closed her eyes, the picture of the Adam she knew mixed up with the Adam who was here. She could smell his cheek, that fragrance that was uniquely his—clean, tangy, citrus, summer, spring, and fall. There was no winter in his aroma. She felt odd, remembering him as a grown man, yet feeling their nineteen-year-old mouths together now. No deceit clouded the taste of his lips. For an instant, she disappeared in this new yet familiar embrace. Who was she right now? Her pulse quickened, and the saltiness of his tongue brought her back to the present moment.

He pressed his mouth against hers, tenderly, sweet. His lips lingered, as if getting to know hers with this gesture of affection. Her mouth responded, opening slightly, still relishing this moment. She remembered having told him at least once before, "I love to get lost in your kisses. Time is suspended." And here, in this now, her mind swirled between past, present, and future. She could feel his hands on the small of her back, pulling her closer. Her mind was blank—no words—just feeling a sigh from the beginning of time. Now it was her turn to pull him closer still.

In that embrace, she felt that chemistry between them, that feeling of being home. This is where she needed to be to make things right. She was getting a second chance.

Lost in his kiss, she didn't notice the car that had pulled up to the corner and parked by a fire hydrant. The windows were rolled down, and music blared from the radio inside.

> *You know you don't believe it when you say that you don't
> need me.*
> *Don't, don't you want me?*

She felt that rush of nausea, and the blackness closing in around her. Shutting her eyes tighter, she battled the feeling that she was turning into nothing because she didn't want to lose touch with Adam. She felt a sharp pain in the back of her head and released his mouth. Again, darkness blanketed everything.

When she opened her eyes, she was alone, back at the train station.

Chapter 3

The next day, Lisa decided that whatever had happened the night before was just a figment of her overactive imagination, some sort of a half-conscious dream. She'd been working long hours and hadn't been taking care of herself. She was determined to change her routines and practice self-care. There'd be no more secret rendezvous meetups. She was going to focus on herself and break up with Adam. In her heart, she knew this relationship was wrong, that she deserved better, and that Adam's wife deserved better too. Not to mention Marcus. Without Adam taking up space in her thoughts and heart, she'd be able to think clearly, get a divorce from Marcus, and start a new life away from men who were not available. That was the honorable thing to do for everyone involved.

At her office and in another boring meeting, Lisa's phone buzzed next to her notepad. She took her attention away from the speaker and looked down. Adam was calling. She had been keeping an eye on the phone all morning, wondering when, or if, he was going to explain what happened the night before.

She hit the Decline Call button with the "Can't talk. Busy" message. After her decision to stop the affair, she wasn't going to engage with him anymore until she was ready to speak clearly to him. She was grateful, though, that he wasn't lying in a ditch somewhere. Maybe his not contacting her last night was a sign that she was now going to do the right thing.

She tried to refocus on the meeting. The motivational speaker that her company had hired to inspire them to make stronger pitches to clients was not motivating her away from Adam thoughts.

What was it about him that kept her tethered to him? This relationship wasn't good for her. Emily knew and had been vocal about it. "You spend too much time thinking about him, Lisa," was Emily's usual admonition. "Adam is an obsession. And you're forgetting the impact you're having on others by continuing this ridiculous affair."

Long ago, she had aspired to greatness. She was going to work hard, become a wealthy partner, eventually open her own marketing firm, conquer the world, travel. She was going to do this while raising a family. Things hadn't gone as she'd expected, of course. Seth's death had interrupted her dreams of raising a family in a loving marriage. She and Marcus had become distant, lost from one another as if the baby's death had created a wall between them that couldn't be breached. And although she'd achieved the goal of partner, she wasn't bringing in as much business anymore. She would set goals, but then she was too distracted to meet them. In the back of her head, she still had those big plans, but, somehow, they seemed to belong to someone else now. If she were to listen to this motivational speaker at all, she had not done enough for herself or her goals. She had abandoned her dreams. Nothing seemed to spark her interest anymore unless there was some connection to Adam. And life with him was full of lies. How was she supposed to grow as a person or in her business when her head was occupied with Adam—where he was, what he was doing, when she would see him again. And more often than she cared to admit—when would he leave his wife?

Her phone buzzed again. This time it was Marcus. Her husband rarely texted. She declined his call too. There was nothing to say to him. Whatever he wanted likely involved him being away from home again.

Unavailable men surrounded her. *Why did she attract that?* she wondered.

She refocused on the meeting. Someone was blathering about setting goals and intentions and writing out a five-year plan. The phone buzzed once more. This time Adam was texting. "I'm really sorry about last night. I got caught up at work and then couldn't call. Please forgive me. I really miss you. Meet me tonight for dinner so I can make it up to you."

Her heart raced a little at seeing his message. She was tempted to leave the room to respond, but she was determined to start a new life.

When the meeting was finally over, in the quiet of her office, Lisa texted Emily. "Hey, want to have dinner tonight?"

Emily replied quickly. "What's the matter? Adam is busy?"

Ouch, that stung. After a few seconds, there was another text from Emily. "Sorry, I didn't mean to be snarky. Yes, I'm free, let's have dinner. The usual place?"

***

Lisa and Emily had been dining at Scaramella's for years. It was their favorite Italian spot, hidden in plain sight on a corner of a busy street in Dobbs Ferry, New York. Red and white tablecloths, red napkins, tables big enough to hold the vast plates of food. It was a family restaurant, despite the large bar in the front. Old men sat there watching baseball or football depending on the season. The single guys, the widowers, the husbands who wanted a meal while watching TV without children interrupting ate at the bar. The regulars sat at the bar ordering their usuals. Long ago, Lisa told Emily that maybe they should be eating at the bar. They were clearly regulars by now.

The menu was large and full of daily specials. The staff had been the same for decades it seemed. Vito, the owner, knew them by name. Hostesses came and went as if through a revolving door. They were always pleasant and pretty in black dresses and red lipstick.

Lisa arrived first. She stayed in her car waiting for Emily. She didn't want to deal with Vito by herself tonight. Her phone buzzed with another text message. Adam had been texting all day, and she had been avoiding him. She needed space to figure out what was going on before she saw him again. That dream of him young and in college was too vivid. She couldn't shake it. Emily might be able to help her sort out reality from wild imagination.

Lost in her thoughts, Lisa didn't notice Emily knocking on her car window. Startled, she jumped in her seat, took a breath, and got out of the car.

"Hey, sorry I'm late. Why are you sitting in the car?" Emily asked.

Lisa didn't have an answer. "I don't know. I wanted to walk in with you. Come on let's go, I'm starved."

As usual, when Lisa and Emily arrived, Vito personally took charge of them. While he was taking them to their favorite table in the back, Carlo walked over to the bar to grab a chilled bottle of the Chardonnay they usually drank.

Vito took their jackets. "You girls look good enough to eat. If I wasn't a happily married man…. Madonna, what I wouldn't give to be young and free again." He talked with his hands, laughing at his own joke. Lisa and Emily joined him, giving each other the look that said, *How many times has he said the same thing to us?*

Carlo came over with the wine, and a young new waiter brought bread and olive oil. Carlo was training him well. "So, what will it be today ladies? Did you look at the menu?"

Lisa replied, "What for? You know we always order the same thing. Chicken paisano, Carlo. Why mess with perfection?"

Carlo laughed. "You know that's not on the menu, right?"

Lisa scanned the menu again and snapped her finger on it. "That's weird. It's been in here for the past twenty years."

Emily chimed in, "You're the one being weird, Lisa. I've never heard of that dish. We always order chicken parmigiana. Why would you change now?"

Carlo shrugged his shoulders. "You're such good customers, we'll cook anything for you." He opened their bottle of wine, poured, winked while he said "*Saluti*," and left.

"I don't know what's gotten into me," said Lisa.

Emily raised an eyebrow quizzically. "Well, maybe you're stressed out and forgot. Pay it no mind. A glass of wine cures all memory ills."

Lisa wondered about the mix-up, but brushed it away to focus on her best friend. Here they could talk, laugh, drink wine, and not be bothered by the waiters until it was time to close. It was the perfect place where Lisa could share what she'd been feeling all day, this angst that she couldn't understand, and the unsettling notion that she was losing her mind by thinking she was traveling into the past.

"Well, what's going on? I can always rely on you for some good drama." Emily smiled. She cocked her head to the side and squinted behind her glasses. "Did you do something different to your hair?"

"No, why?" Lisa replied.

"I don't know. You look different. Did you always part it to the side?"

"It usually parts in the middle naturally, but today it parted to the side on its own. I don't know why."

"Huh." Emily tightened her mouth. "But you seem…I'm not sure of the right word. Worried, frazzled, annoyed. Which one is it?"

"I'm all of them." Lisa didn't know how to start the conversation about the daydream last night.

"Did Adam ever show up?"

"No. He never called or texted last night. He called and texted me today, but I didn't respond. I needed time to think and talk to you."

"I don't know what to tell you…." Emily's voice trailed off, then gathered strength. "What do you see in this guy?"

"Lots of things. Plus, I'm in love with him." Lisa tried to sound confident but failed.

"You're not convincing me that you're in love. I think you're just infatuated and bored." Emily continued to stare at her. "Are you sure you didn't do something else? You look different."

"OK, I have to talk to you about this dream I had. I think I'm losing my mind." Lisa told her the story of the steps, of the song "Don't You Want Me" that she'd been listening to just before she was transported to the past. She regaled Emily with the history of the band called The Human League and of its lead singer, Philip Oakey. She told her everything, including finding herself back in the train station. When she was done, Emily was still silent; in fact, she was quiet for a long time. Dinner arrived. Emily picked up her knife and fork and started eating.

Lisa was nervous that her friend would think she had finally cracked. "Aren't you going to say something?"

"I'm not sure what to say. You tell me you went back in time, you were aware of who you were then, and now you remember it all. Sounds like a bad trip on drugs, Lisa. Did you tell Adam about this?"

"Of course not! He'll think I'm nuts."

Emily laughed. "Honey, maybe you are."

Lisa was annoyed now. She'd poured out her heart, and her best friend was laughing. She laid her head in her hands in despair. "I don't know what to think anymore. Maybe I need a vacation."

Emily put down her fork and gripped Lisa's hand. "Maybe you need a break from this guy. This could be your subconscious telling you to let him go. He's no good for you. He's never going to leave his wife." Emily stopped talking and took a deep breath. "Plus, there's Marcus to consider. He doesn't deserve this from you, Lisa. No matter what happened with Seth, you shouldn't keep punishing Marcus. It's not fair."

Lisa's eyes welled up, and she slammed her hand on the table. "Stop talking about the baby or Marcus. You know that subject's not up for discussion." In a stern tone, she continued. "Plus, you don't know what Adam will do. You just don't know him. He loves me."

Emily raised her voice in response. "Well, if he loves you then why am I the one having dinner with you and not him? Why is he still married? And now you're having these delusional hallucinations, or dreams, where you're going back in time. This is your mind playing tricks on you. Why don't you take a break from him and go away for a little while? Maybe a vacation by yourself so you can figure out what you really need." Emily meant well, but she was starting to annoy Lisa. All this good advice was far from good.

Dinner finally over, Lisa turned down Carlo's offer of coffee or tiramisu. "Since when do you pass on dessert?" Emily said.

"I'm just not feeling right. I need to go home and walk the dog. Poor Jojo's been alone for a long time tonight. Marcus left me a voice message that he's going away on a quick business trip to Boston." And maybe, she thought, this will give her a chance to clear her head.

Emily and Lisa walked to the parking lot and said goodbye as usual—a big hug and "Text me when you get home so I know you're OK."

***

Lisa sat in her car after dinner with Emily, checking for text messages and listening to voicemails before she headed out onto the highway. She didn't want to deal with Marcus's recent renewed attempts at closeness, his eyes piercing hers sometimes as if he knew she was up to no good. At the very least, she owed him the courtesy of returning his call, especially since she had ignored his text message.

Frowning, she listened to the voicemail, her guilt adding to the sadness in his voice. "Hi. I called to tell you I have to go to Boston for a couple of days. That deal I've been working on is blowing up. I'm going home now to pack then I'm headed straight to the airport. The company's sending their plane to pick me up. Sorry for the short notice.

I've called the dog walker and made arrangements in case you're home late tonight. I'll call you later." She was right when she told Emily she'd be alone for a few days without intrusions or guilty associations near her. While in the beginning of their marriage, Marcus's work had been a curse with the long hours and responsibilities, now it was a gift of freedom.

He was a lawyer at a large firm representing corporations and foundations. His strength was in creatively resolving problems. At six foot three, boasting a muscular build, dark wavy hair with a shock of white by the forehead, and green eyes, Marcus commanded attention when he walked into a room. Men and women were mesmerized when he smiled and started talking.

Her head shook at the incongruity of her husband's talent. How was it possible that he was such a good communicator with strangers and clients, yet in a relationship he was incapable of understanding her perspective? He worked crazy hours, and she had all kinds of late meetings, so a week could easily pass without them running into one another. Lately she wondered whether he had a woman somewhere. Between his travels and her absences, he certainly had plenty of opportunity.

She listened to his message a second time to make sure she had gotten the details of his being gone. There was a sad note in his voice. She'd detected it in the past but often ignored it. Today, a pang of regret wouldn't let her skip over it. She found herself remembering how good it had been in the beginning. They had been nearly inseparable after Emily introduced them. She had been dogging Lisa for weeks to meet this handsome guy who worked with her. Lisa wasn't disappointed when she relented and went on a blind date with him. They connected, they dated, and she was smitten. And so was he. They wrote each other letters, the old-fashioned type on pretty stationery, mailed with a stamp. She got him into reading fiction. He got her to watch sports. On Sundays they would go to a local bar with friends to have beers and watch football. They had fun together. They had each other.

After about five years, she called him unexpectedly one morning while he was at work. "Hey babe. Want to meet for a drink at Martini's? This afternoon?"

"I have to work late. Don't you?" he replied.

"Come on, live a little. You already know you're going to become a partner. Plus, one drink at Martini's will make you work harder tomorrow." She laughed. "Please?" She remembered intentionally using her silky voice, the one he couldn't resist.

Later that afternoon, she watched him through the storefront window at Martini's. He was nursing a beer and looking at his watch, probably irritated that she was late. She remembered the details of the day as if it had been yesterday. It was one of those picture-perfect Manhattan days when the weather was just a blend of warm and cool, sunny and breezy, the kind of day every movie director wishes she could film. Lisa remembered sauntering in as if she had not a care in the world. "What are you drinking, sailor?" she asked as she put her arms around his waist while he sat on the bar stool. She smiled and batted her lashes.

He smiled back, returning the hug. "The usual beer ma'am. Would you like one?"

"Hmmm…I'd love one, but I can't. I'm drinking for two, you see."

Thinking back to that day, Lisa noticed she had almost forgotten how brightly he smiled when he realized the significance of her announcement.

After announcing to the bartender that he was buying a round of drinks for everyone in the bar to celebrate that he was going to be a father, he leaned over the bar, took a maraschino cherry from one of the containers, popped off the fruit and twisted the stem into a ring. "Babe, will you make me the happiest man on earth and marry me?" He was choked up, tears threatening at the corners of his green eyes. God, Marcus had the greenest eyes. Lisa felt they could see through her.

She had laughed at the impromptu proposal. "Marcus, if you're going to propose with a fruit ring from a bartender's collection, you'll have to get on one knee."

The whole restaurant cheered for them. Life was going to be heavenly.

As if wanting proof that her memory was real, Lisa pulled out her weathered blue wallet and opened the little zippered pocket. In there, bent and dried, was the cherry stem that had once stood as proof of their love. She took it out gently, conscious of its fragile state, marveling even now how it had lasted in one piece for so long. For a brief moment, she actually missed Marcus. She even missed the person she had once been. How did their life get so empty?

Everything with their wedding had worked out as planned, down to the honeymoon in Niagara Falls because Lisa was being careful and didn't want to fly anywhere while she was pregnant. They drove all those hours, singing at the top of their lungs in their best shower voices. They had it all.

Or so it seemed.

Lisa's mother was joyous at the wedding and later was thrilled to become a grandmother. She had started knitting baby clothes as soon as Lisa gave her the news.

Lisa put the phone down a bit too hard, frustrated, and out of sorts. She pulled her hair back into a ponytail. When life was out of control, she could at least control her hair.

Memories flowed in a torrent of despair. She and Marcus had returned from their honeymoon to find out her mother had had a stroke while she was home alone, cooking dinner for her and a neighbor, Bill, a widower who had just moved in next door. Bill found her on the kitchen floor, unresponsive. She was dead by the time the EMT guys arrived. When Lisa arrived the next day to visit her mother, she was already in the morgue. Bill was sweet and explained what happened and helped Lisa with the funeral arrangements.

Her mother had died alone.

Beyond distraught, Lisa had lost her compass and her best friend. Long walks with Emily helped, but only Marcus and the baby growing in her saved her from the stupor of grief.

She was joyous each time the baby kicked. Albeit still grieving, she chose nursery furniture and baby clothes, read all the expectant mother books, prepared herself to be a mother in the absence of her own.

But then more tragedies struck. She lost the baby, and then the next. With each miscarriage, she wondered if she was being punished for not being with her mother when she died. Tensions with Marcus were high. She was committed to being a mother, and he just wanted a happy wife again. Finally, after years of trying everything and failing, she lay in bed for months with her last pregnancy. She was determined that this one would live.

The baby came three months early, in the middle of the night, when all bad things happen. Seth was tiny, little more than a pound of butter, and not much bigger than that. His foot was smaller than the first knuckle of Marcus' thumb. They essentially lived in the hospital's neonatal unit for five agonizing months. Lisa spent all her waking hours by the baby's incubator. She quit her job. Eventually Marcus returned to work, but he was a fixture at Lisa's side during all his nonwork hours.

Seth came home in the summer, tiny and on medication, but improving. Life became a series of adjustments with a sickly child.

Nine months after being home, Seth still had weak lungs. The pediatrician said that Seth would feel better if he had an operation to help his breathing. They did not have to do it now, but the benefits of the procedure increased while Seth was still small.

Lisa hesitated, afraid of putting the baby at risk. Marcus, the optimist, said, "The doctor assured us he'll be fine. Don't you want to ease his breathing problems?"

Marcus was persuasive.

Lisa reluctantly agreed.

The surgery was a complete success. Seth was scheduled for monitoring in the hospital for just a few days. The nurses convinced Lisa she didn't need to sleep at his bedside. Marcus joined in their request. His words were still seared in her memory. "Babe, let's go home and get some rest. He's sleeping well; he's in good hands. We haven't slept in our own bed in days. We'll be back first thing in the morning to take him home."

She relented, bone tired and believing all of them, especially Marcus.

That night, Lisa woke up, cold sweat drenching her nightgown. The phone rang at the same time. Seth was in distress.

She yelled at Marcus to wake up as she threw whatever clothes she could find over her nightgown. They drove in silence, running through every red light, barely slowing down to see what was headed their way.

By the time they reached the hospital, Seth was gone. He had contracted a virus, one of those bugs that live in hospitals, the ones they warn you about. Stay out of hospitals, they say. That's where you get sick, they say.

Her son, like her mother, died alone, without her there.

Even after all these years, she still felt an ache in her chest, like the missing of a phantom limb.

At the hospital a nurse sedated her when she became distraught at the news of her son's death. A coolness descended upon her, like a shroud embedded into her bones. She turned herself into stone, numb to the unspeakable pain.

For weeks, she did not utter a word, not even to Marcus. She communicated by writing on a notepad. Unable to work, to see friends, to do anything other than sit and watch television, she stayed home for months. She refused medication; she refused help; she refused to speak.

Eventually, she let Emily sit with her on the sofa in silence. As the spring days got warmer, Emily would come over after work, and sometimes they'd walk in the park.

It must have been an odd sight to see—two women walking hand in hand while one talked, and the other didn't respond. Behind her back, Emily and Marcus searched for ways to bring Lisa back to the land of the living. The priest who married them tried to help. But Lisa wanted no more platitudes or relentless bullshit that her son was an angel. She had trusted Marcus that they could leave Seth that night. She had believed him when he said the baby would be fine without them.

He lied.

She would never forgive him.

Her son had died alone.

Marcus was responsible.

And so was she for believing him. She would never forgive herself either.

Marcus gave her a puppy he named Jojo, thinking a living creature at home might ease their distance. Even that didn't work. The dog became a source of comfort for each of them but did nothing to bring them together.

After almost a year of silence, she called Marcus at work one late afternoon. In a flat voice, the first words she uttered to him in all that time were, "I'm going on a job interview tomorrow." Without waiting for his response, she hung up the phone.

Once she started working, she started speaking to him again, but their relationship was never the same. She could have divorced him, but she could punish him more acutely simply by staying at his side. Her face would be a daily reminder that he was responsible for her pain. In truth, she was punishing herself also—for her failure as a daughter, as a mother, and as a wife. Without letting Marcus in on her secret, she had committed herself to punishing them both.

Emily eventually cajoled her into trying marriage counseling. It made no difference to her. She was the walking dead, so she could agree to anything. She and Marcus followed the counselor's suggestions to create intimacy so as to find one another again. The counselor urged them to try to have another baby. Marcus thought creating another life would bring them together. Lisa saw him devouring books on how to reconnect. He brought her flowers for no reason, lit candles in the bedroom, and played soft music to create romance. Slowly thawing from her stupor, she remembered physical needs and stumbled into bed with him in a semblance of passion, going through the motions. It felt mechanical, and while they left each other physically satisfied, clearly neither was fulfilled. At times, Lisa pitied Marcus for how hard he tried to breach the wall Lisa had built around her heart.

Emily helped Lisa store in the attic all pictures, all memories, all traces of the baby, as if Seth had never been born. Lisa and Marcus pretended they'd never been parents, that they'd simply gotten married because it was the right time to do so. They lived shadow lives, pretending to be together, not knowing why they didn't separate. Seth's little ghost haunted their lives without anyone acknowledging his existence.

They never spoke about the baby again.

Chapter 4

Lisa drove home listening to the radio, lost in thought. She looked in the rearview mirror when she was stopped at a red light and caught her reflection. Her hair did look different parted on the side. And she hadn't done that on purpose. Because she was busy gazing at herself and wondering what else seemed different, she didn't notice the car behind her coming at a faster than normal speed. The light changed to green, and she still hadn't taken her foot off the brake.

The SUV crashed into her car, hurtling it a few feet ahead into the intersection. She had no control, up against the steering wheel, held back tightly by the seat belt and smothered by the airbag. Her chest was being crushed. As the airbags slowly deflated, she sat there stunned and dazed, and noticed the radio still playing. She took deep breaths to regain her composure. Where did this car come from? Her pounding head caused her to pull down the visor mirror. There was a small cut on her forehead. She grazed it with her finger and heard herself yell ouch like one hears a stranger talking. Her churning stomach added to the ache in her head and the sensation that she was floating near the ceiling of the car. She waved her hand in front of her face as if it were going to disappear. She could hear it then. The radio was playing. That song again? Why was it playing again?

Don't you want me baby? Don't you want me oh oh oh?

Don't you want me baby? Don't you want me, oh oh oh?

Dizzy and nauseous, just like that time before, she touched the cut on her forehead again.

And then there was nothing.

***

He looked at her with longing. "Why don't we get out of here? I have a few hours, and I've missed you."

She pressed a button that she thought was the ignition. Nothing. "Hmm. I don't know what's going on," she mumbled. Something was wrong. She'd just been sitting in her car after an accident, but now everything seemed odd, like she was missing a piece of herself.

The engine didn't turn, but the radio started playing.

Don't you want me baby? Don't you want me, oh oh oh?

Lisa pushed the button again to start the car, but all she accomplished was for the music to go silent.

Adam was laughing. "What are you doing, Lisa? Why are you pressing the radio button?"

Lisa was confused when she saw Adam sitting next to her. He wasn't in the car with her when she left Scaramella's. How was he here now? Not taking her eyes off him, she pressed the radio button again, still sensing something missing. But this wasn't her car. She had an SUV. This was…this was…what was this?

This was her old car—a yellow 1979 Pacer with a radio that had bulging buttons for the tuner and the volume.

Adam continued to laugh. "Are you trying to be funny? Come on, we're going to be late."

Her mouth agape, she stared at Adam. Young Adam. She looked in the rearview mirror. The eyes that looked back at her were younger. Her hair was dark and held back by barrettes she hadn't worn since she was in college. She was wearing bright blue eyeshadow and feather earrings were tangled in her hair. She looked closely. She had a vague memory of a cut on her forehead that had occurred just a few minutes ago.

She wasn't crazy—there had been an accident. She had seen the cut on her forehead that had been bleeding. She could still taste the iron on her tongue from where she had licked her finger. But now there was no cut. Her skin was smooth as silk, and she looked wildly younger.

Adam gesticulated with his hands to get moving as she continued to stare into the mirror. Something else was different. Her hair! Not only was it dark; it was parted to the side.

"Lisa, sweetie, we have to go."

"I'm trying to start the car, can't you see?" Lisa snapped at him. This startled Adam. He wasn't used to her saying anything but in a sweet tone. She reached out quickly and turned off the radio.

"Listen, if you don't want to go out, then we don't have to go anywhere," he said.

Lisa took a deep breath. "I'm sorry. I just have a headache, and this stupid car isn't helping." She smiled. How could she be angry when she had this young Adam with her? He had no obligations in this world. *If this is a dream,* she thought, *then I'm staying here as long as possible.*

She searched for the key, and there it was—in the ignition. She turned it and this time the car started.

They both laughed. "All righty then, where are we going?" she asked.

"Why don't you let me do the driving since you have a headache?" He asked her so tenderly.

She melted into his gaze. Wordlessly, she opened the door and walked over to the passenger side. They crossed paths in the back of the car, and he bent down, grabbed her chin, and gave her a soft, sweet kiss that melted her knees. "There, I've kissed the boo-boo. Better now?" he smiled. He let her go, then moved to the car and took over the driving.

In no time, he had them out of the city and on a highway going north. They were both silent for a while when Adam reached over to turn on the radio. Lisa stopped him. "Don't. Let's just talk. The music makes my head pound."

Adam smiled back. "Sure, whatever works for you."

Lisa was not about to chance that song playing again. She was not sure how

it happened, but every time she had been in and out of this world, that song was playing.

When was here? She couldn't ask Adam. He obviously didn't know anything about the real world because he hadn't been there yet. But if that was the real world, then what was this? A dream? Was she going crazy? Was she already crazy? It was a beautiful crisp fall day. The highway was lined with yellows, browns, reds, leaves of all colors. They were driving, they were free, they were young.

Here, in this shiny bright world where she had Adam to herself, this is where she wanted to stay for as long as possible. Maybe if she got to know him here, she would figure out how to make him leave his wife in the real world. Or was this the real world, and the other one the dream?

***

Lisa listened to Adam whistling on their long car ride. Happy to be here, in this present, she moved forward with her plans to make sure that Adam stayed with her in her actual present day. She still didn't know how this was happening because it didn't make any logical sense. But if she was going to be alive in this time, she was going to make sure that Adam didn't leave her side. This was the answer to her prayers: the ability to change the future. She could make sure Adam fell in love with her now, prevent him from meeting his wife Stephanie, and ensure she'd be the one to marry him. Her plan was perfection at its finest.

After driving for a couple of hours, Adam asked, "Are you hungry?" Lisa nodded with an *uhum*.

He continued, "Why don't we stop and get some lunch? I know a little romantic place with a nice view of the river."

"Food would be grand," she replied.

In truth, she didn't care, even though she had a nagging feeling she was leaving something undone. She had a headache, but she also didn't want to break the easy mood. They were getting along so well, learning about each other.

They stopped at a restaurant off the beaten path in a little town full of quaint shops and cobblestone roads. The hostess offered them a table.

"Could we have that booth instead?" Adam asked.

The hostess led them to a corner booth and placed the menus opposite one another. Adam moved the menus side by side. "No sense sitting across from you when I can sit next to you and feel your warmth."

Lisa's cheeks colored with a rush of joy. This was the same Adam she knew in her real life. He did the same thing there.

Adam smiled mischievously. "So, what are you in the mood for... other than me?"

"I don't know," Lisa replied shyly. Why was she feeling shy when she knew this man so well? "Hey..." she started to say.

"Is for horses," he replied. They both laughed at his stupid joke.

"All right, all right," she smiled. "Enough with the jokes. Let's focus on the menu before I go blind with hunger."

Reading the thousand options in the diner, she rubbed her temples, noticing her head hurting more. Adam was intent on the menu. She could hear a song on the loudspeakers in the restaurant.

I was working as a waitress in a cocktail bar...

She closed her eyes and put her fingers to her ears. Maybe if she shut out the sound, she'd be able to avoid the change. She was sure she had figured it out. This song made her go back and forth, and she wasn't ready to leave Adam here. She didn't know if she'd be able to travel to this time again. She couldn't very well run out of the restaurant. They were far from home, and how was she going to explain that she had to leave when they'd agreed to stop for lunch?

But the song got louder. Now she covered her ears with the palms of her hands and stared at the menu.

I picked you out, I shook you up and turned you around
Turned you into someone new

Adam seemed worried. "Hey, are you OK?"

"Yeah, yeah, I'm fine," she answered, although she wasn't. Her stomach was turning, she was nauseous, and she couldn't stop the blasting song from taking over. The room was full of dark spots, and they got bigger and bigger until she saw nothing but blackness. And then nothing.

***

A woman dressed as a nurse was holding Lisa's wrist when she blinked her eyes open, adjusting to the bright light of the hospital room.

"Where am I?" she asked, disoriented.

The nurse gently lowered Lisa's arm and answered, "Hi there. Don't be afraid. You're in Palisades General Hospital. You were in a car accident last night. You hit your head. I'm your nurse this morning. How do you feel? Does anything hurt?"

Lisa stared at the nurse. How did she get back here? What had happened? She was with Adam, they were about to have lunch, and now she was in a hospital? She remembered a headache; she remembered that damn song. She wasn't about to tell this nurse that she had been in a restaurant just a few minutes before.

She looked at the nurse's identification badge: Stephanie Scheiner.

That was Adam's wife's name.

Stephanie seemed kind as she asked questions. "Hey, don't worry. You'll be fine. We'll take good care of you here. It looks like you hit your head pretty hard in the accident. You have a nice bump to show for it. Do you remember anything about it?" Lisa tried to focus. She remembered being in her car, the screech of tires, and the feeling of being propelled forward. But she also remembered being in a restaurant with Adam, sitting next to him in a booth. They were having such a lovely day. Now, she couldn't figure out where she was when the car accident happened.

Lisa mustered a smile. "I do have a headache. Actually, everything hurts."

"Well, let's see if we can't get you more comfortable. The admitting doctor ordered a CT scan to check that head. You know, make sure your brain isn't too scrambled." Stephanie said this lightheartedly, trying to relieve her patient's distress. "I'll be your nurse today until three. As soon as the CT scan is done, I can give you something for the headache. But we have to see what's going on first, OK? Now, let's see if we can't do something with this bed to make you more comfortable."

Lisa nodded silently as Stephanie straightened the sheets and plumped up her pillows. Her voice was soothing and sweet.

"Did you want me to call anyone for you? We tried calling your ICE number, but no one answered. Is there a husband to call?"

Lisa sighed. She didn't know where Marcus was right now. She should call him and let him know. "My husband is away on business. I don't want to bother him. I'll wait until we get some results from the tests before I call him."

"You don't think he'd want to know you're in the hospital?" Stephanie looked concerned. "I'm sure your husband would cut his trip short to see you."

Lisa laughed. "I doubt it. We don't talk much anymore."

Stephanie was silent for a minute. "Well, I'm sure if you call him, he'll surprise you."

"Maybe, but…I haven't exactly been very communicative either," Lisa replied, wondering why she was divulging the state of her marriage to a stranger. "I see a ring on your finger also. Are you married?" Lisa was curious.

Stephanie replied with a smile. "Oh yeah, happily for years and years."

Was that sarcasm? Lisa wondered. "Excuse me if I'm being intrusive, but that answer didn't sound happy."

Stephanie smiled, as if knowingly. "Well, you know, after a lot of years of marriage, things get…I don't know…flat maybe? How long have you been married?"

"Marcus and I haven't been happily married for years. Things changed when…." Lisa stopped and brushed aside the reason for the change, not wanting to bring up that subject. "Never mind. They changed. But it's fine. He travels a lot for work, and I have a busy career. Sometimes we're just…ships passing."

"I know what you mean," Stephanie replied. She left that answer hanging in the air.

Something about this woman intrigued Lisa. She felt a kindred spirit, and right now she could use a kind person with her. Stephanie's hands were smooth, with long fingers and short manicured nails. Her hair was tied back neatly, showing off a pretty face with dark eyes, long lashes, and thick eyebrows. Her voice was warm and sincere.

Stephanie cleared her throat. "Well, I'd better go check on that CAT scan. The sooner we know what's going on with you, the sooner we can get you out of here, right?"

"Yes, thank you." As Stephanie walked out, Lisa laid her head back on the pillows, closing her eyes, willing herself to sleep. She didn't want to think about Marcus and the guilt she felt at being unfaithful. Maybe if she slept, her head would stop hurting.

Murky thoughts intruded. She still couldn't figure out what was real. This world seemed real, but so did the other one. She remembered having a headache when she was with Adam. And here she was, still in pain. How was this happening, that she could be here in this now, and also back in the past? Which was which? It seemed like her head hurt no matter what year she was living in. And where did she and Adam go when she was here? Where was he?

As she lay back wondering about all of this, she heard the pings of text messages on her phone. She noticed it was on the side table next to the bed. She reached for it and saw that Marcus and Adam had texted her. And there were several missed calls from Marcus. She looked at Marcus's message first. "Hey, where are you? I've been calling. No answer." She ignored that message and went to the one from Adam. "Hey babe. Where've you been? I'm sorry I missed you last night." There were hearts with the message. She smiled. He was worried. She liked that he worried.

Guilt made her look at Marcus's text again. She decided to answer him first. "Had a fender bender. Bumped my head. Ambulance came and took me to hospital. I'm OK. They're just checking me. No worries." She didn't want him to come back from his trip. She couldn't deal with Marcus now.

She switched to Adam. "Oh honey. So happy you reached out. :-) I'm in the hospital. Got into a car accident after dinner with Emily. Scary but I'm fine. They're doing tests. Where were you last night? Not fair to keep me waiting." She hit send then read her message again. It seemed like she was complaining, and she didn't want him to think that. She didn't need to be like his wife, always nagging. She sent a smiley text and waited for a reply. Nothing.

She put the phone down, leaned back and closed her eyes. It was too hard to keep up with a double life.

Just as she was about to hit the call button to find out when she was going for the test, Stephanie came back into the room with a transport guy.

"Hi there. John here is going to take you down for your MRI test. He'll take good care of you in transit." John was a big square hulky guy holding on to the handles of a wheelchair. He looked a little scary, as if he lifted weights for a living but had no smile. Stephanie sounded warm. Her smile felt reassuring to Lisa. "While you're gone, I'll try your husband again if you'd like."

"No need," said Lisa with a quiet smile. "He texted me. I'll catch up with him later. Let's get these tests over with, so I can go home."

Lisa got into the wheelchair, hoping that whatever was going on with her would show up on the MRI readout. Maybe all this back and forth in time was just a short circuit in her brain? Maybe she had finally lost all sense of reality and was just living in a fantasy world. Whatever it was, the tests might give her an answer.

Chapter 5

The transport guy left Lisa alone in the MRI room while the technician finished up with another patient. Wearing her gray and blue hospital gown with matching slippers and sitting in a gray metal chair with a blue seat cushion, Lisa rubbed her arms to find some warmth. The environmental psychologist who designed the color scheme in the hospital must have decided these colors soothed patient nerves. Feeling like she could fade into the background, Lisa wanted to leave a note in the suggestion box that perhaps it would help patients if they didn't freeze every time they had to get a test done. No matter how soothing the colors might be, shivering from cold didn't help anyone's anxiety. She wasn't sure whether the goosebumps on her arms were from the cold or from nerves at having an examination of her brain.

Taking a deep cleansing breath, Lisa leaned her head back against the wall. She focused on the hum of an MRI machine on the other side of the wall wondering how she was going to unravel this pretzeled triangle of people she had unknowingly created.

For so long, she had daydreamed that she could go back to the past to meet Adam before he met his wife. In her musings, she had thought this would be easy. She imagined that she'd see him first, he'd fall in love with her, and the whole Stephanie-is-Adam's-wife thing would be avoided. She hadn't given a thought to the repercussions for the present. And she hadn't anticipated that he'd meet Stephanie anyway.

***

The MRI technician had a soothing voice. "This test won't take very long. Have you had an MRI before? Are you claustrophobic?"

Lisa glanced at the long cylindrical machine with its intimidating hole and flat bed. She knew how they worked but had never been in one. It looked like it could swallow her.

"I'm not claustrophobic, I think, but I'll confess that I'm nervous."

While Lisa talked, the tech reached into a drawer and pulled out a small plastic bag with black earbuds like the ones given out on airplanes. "Do you like music?" he asked as he handed her the bag. "I love eighties music, and I play it for all the patients. The earbuds will help with the noise. You lay on the motorized bed, and I'll move it so that you're inside the cylinder. The songs will distract you. I'll make sure you're OK."

His tone was reassuring, but Lisa wasn't completely convinced as she put the earbuds in. She lay down, closed her eyes, and hoped this wouldn't take too long.

Lisa could hear the knocking of the electromagnetic waves emitted by the machine. She imagined she was listening to drums.

Take a deep breath, Lisa. Just focus. She repeated this in time to the music of the machine. As she slowed her breathing, she heard music.

> *You think you've changed your mind*
> *You'd better change it back or we will both be sorry*

She could hear the words above the knocking of the drums. But these weren't drums, were they? In the distance she heard the voice of the tech guy, "Are you all right?" She wanted to answer but couldn't make words come out. All she could hear were drums and music.

> *Don't you want me, baby?*

It was a loop, over and over. She could feel the blackness taking over her eyes, darker than when her eyes were closed. Her mind was racing. She knew that this would take her back to Adam, but her heart was racing. The drums, the knocking, the words of the song—it all melded into one cacophony. She could hear the sound of her blood pulsing through her veins, every sense heightened, at the same time that the machine, the room, the light disappeared.

Don't you want me, baby?

Empty blackness.

***

"Hello?" Adam snapped his fingers in front of her face. "Earth to Lisa. Where are you?"

The noises of the Hungarian Pastry Shop came rushing at her like wind in a tunnel. Everything was loud, sharp—even Adam's voice—as if she could hear his breathing from her side of the table. She shook her head and looked around, wondering for a moment where she was and how long she'd been here.

"You looked like you went away somewhere," he said.

She inhaled sharply, trying to regain her composure. "Away? How silly. I've been here the whole time."

"Didn't feel like that. I've repeated the same question, and you just didn't answer. You kept staring at that picture on the wall."

Lisa looked around, pretending to be looking at the picture he pointed to, but really, she was just trying to figure out where she was… and when. There was a crude painting of a black circle in the middle of a yellow canvas. The circle was jagged, as if painted by a child who defied the rules of staying in the lines. Little black spots randomly dotted the edges of the painting, some almost falling off the canvas.

"It's a very interesting painting. I hadn't noticed it before."

Adam didn't seem curious at all. "I think it's pretty ugly. Any kid could paint that. Even me." He laughed at his own joke.

He continued to stare at her. "I was asking if you were ready to go."

Lisa returned her gaze to him. They were still in the pastry shop. *How long had they been here?* she wondered. "Yeah, I'm ready," she said as she stood up. She could see a young woman who looked like Adam's wife, Stephanie—her nurse—behind the counter staring at them. Or staring at him, really. She wore braids tied with cartoon characters at the ends. Were those blue mushroom people? Emily used to love the Smurfs. She had them all over her dorm room. Lisa couldn't understand what was going on, but everyone was wearing either lots of spandex and colorful leggings or were clad all in black.

Adam headed to the cash register to pay. Lisa moved slowly, still reeling from the transport. She was getting better at this. She remembered she had been in the MRI machine. She wondered what *that* Lisa was doing now. She could see Adam, smiling broadly, laughing with Stephanie. She could see him writing something on a piece of paper that he pushed towards Stephanie. A square pillar holding up the ceiling blocked Lisa's view. As she craned her neck a little to see better, Stephanie grabbed the paper, read it, and put it in the pocket of her apron. Even from this distance, Lisa could see the girl blushing. And giggling. *I've come this far for nothing. He's met her anyway.*

Lisa hurried to the register. She put her hand on Adam's back, letting Stephanie know that this was her man. *Don't even think about it, girl. He's mine this time.* Adam finished paying. As they walked away, Adam in front, Lisa turned her head to catch Stephanie watching Adam. Lisa flashed her most fake version of a smile and saw Stephanie's fall away.

They walked for a few blocks holding hands in silence while Lisa figured out what to say next. "What was that paper you gave that girl?"

"Oh, nothing. Just the address for the party tonight."

"What party?"

"I told you. There's a frat party. You're coming with me, aren't you?" Adam pulled her closer while he said this.

Lisa stepped out of his embrace. "Of course I'm coming, but why did you invite her?"

"Come on. She's a nice girl." He hesitated. "You're not jealous, are you?" He pulled her closer again.

"No, but I just don't see why you have to invite a random waitress you just met. She wasn't even that good of a waitress. The coffee was cold by the time she brought it to the table." Lisa heard herself sounding shrill but couldn't stop.

"You are jealous!" Adam held the *r* like a pirate and laughed. Again, he pulled her close, only this time he poked her in the ribs. "Come on, babe. She was nice and has no friends. I was just inviting her to a party with hundreds of other people. No reason to be mad at me." He pouted like a child. Lisa stopped on the sidewalk, staring at his eyes. He gazed back at her, lips curled up with charm. She focused intently, looking for some form of truth. She hadn't been able to stop him from meeting Stephanie, but maybe this party was where she was supposed to accomplish her mission.

***

Back at Emily's dorm room, Lisa scoured Emily's packed closet for something to wear to the party that night. Emily sat on the lower bunk, an open psychology textbook on her lap, twirling a purple pen between her fingers. Lisa muttered to herself, not realizing she was speaking out loud, "I can't believe we wore this stuff." There was spandex in bright colors on every hanger, ruffled blouses with black lace, outrageously big shoulder pads on blouses and jackets.

Emily raised her left eyebrow. "What do you mean, wore? Half the stuff in that closet is yours."

Lisa stopped pushing hangers around. "You know what I mean. I can't believe we have nothing here that I can wear to a frat party." She hoped that covered up her gaffe.

Emily closed the thick book with a thud. "Well, Lisa, that's because we're not the type that goes to frat parties."

"What type goes to frat parties, Em?"

"The type that run off with a guy they don't know and disappear for days only to return to their friend's room looking for clothes for a party!" Emily's words lingered in the awkwardness between them.

Lisa sighed and then turned around to see her friend staring at her.

She stepped away from the closet and sat down next to Emily. "Look, Emily, this guy, I know I don't know him that well, but…."

Emily interrupted abruptly. "Don't know him that well? Lisa, you don't know him at all. You met him three days ago; you've disappeared, and honestly, I don't know what's gotten into you. I haven't seen you in days, you even cut Shit Lit, which I know you love, and then you barge in here, looking for something to wear to a party that you would never go to if it weren't for him. What the hell is wrong with you?"

Lisa stared at her hands during Emily's outburst. Her words stung, but Lisa couldn't explain. How could she? "Emily, I'm sorry I barged in here. And I'm sorry I disappeared. But, look, you know me better than anyone. Don't I look different to you?" Lisa paused for effect then crossed her eyes and stuck out her tongue.

Emily stared at her. "You look stupid, that's what you look like. And your grandmother would tell you not to do that. Your eyes are going to stay that way." *Maybe I could confide in Emily about the time travel?*

Emily broke the silence. "Fine. If you like this guy so much, then go for it. But be careful. You say there's something special about him, but I say he's just a player. I have this gut feeling that he's going to break your heart, and I just don't want to have to pick up the pieces when that happens." Emily reached for Lisa's hand and gave it a squeeze. Lisa opened her mouth to speak, ready to tell the truth, but while she hesitated, Emily let her go, sighed loudly, stood up, and, heading for the closet, said, "But he makes your eyes sparkle, so let's see how we can turn you into some frat girl for tonight."

***

The party was in full swing by the time Adam and Lisa walked in the door. The music was loud, the room full of smoke, beer cans everywhere, people dancing, laughing, guys and girls crushing themselves into one another's space. *How did we breathe with all this smoke?* Lisa wondered. Adam pulled Lisa by the hand, making his way through the throng, looking for his friends and beer. "Isn't this great?" he yelled into her ear when they finally stopped by the keg. She could barely hear him above the din. Plus, she was looking for Stephanie. She was hoping not to see her, but she had seen the intensity on Stephanie's face at the pastry shop. Lisa knew she'd come to the party.

She turned to Adam with a smile that belied her worry. "Yeah, babe, this is great!"

Adam leaned down to kiss her. "I'm so glad you came with me. I'm the luckiest guy here." The world disappeared in that kiss. Adam was the first to pull away. "I like the way your lips fit mine," he whispered. Lisa had no words while they stared into each other's eyes. For a moment, she felt they were alone, back home, in the present, in the future, sharing one of those lazy stolen afternoons in a hotel. She started to mutter something she thought would be profound when Adam broke the spell.

"Hey, look who's here!" Unbalanced, Lisa turned to see Stephanie standing there, arms at her sides, wide grin on her face. Adam reached over and grabbed her hand to pull her closer.

"You said to come, so I did," Stephanie added.

"I'll get you a beer," Adam smiled cheerfully while he strode away, leaving the two of them alone.

Lisa seized the opportunity. "So, do you live around here?"

"With my parents in the Heights. I go to school downtown, but I work part-time at the Hungarian Pastry Shop." Her voice was soft, as if she were shy. She seemed gentle, maybe a little scared. She looked around, clearly out of place. She was wearing simple jeans and a light blue collared blouse, her hair held back with a plastic barrette. Lisa chuckled to herself that Stephanie here was dressed in her future colors.

They both looked back to where Adam was talking to some guys. Stephanie took a step towards Lisa.

"Is he your boyfriend?"

"Yes." Lisa's answer was a sharp thud, like a nail hit by a hammer.

"Oh." Stephanie stepped back again, busying herself with looking around the room.

Lisa decided to use the opportunity.

"Don't play coy. You know he's my boyfriend. You waited on us today." Her words sounded sharper out of her mouth than they did in her head. Lisa knew who this woman would become. She knew her. She was a caregiver; she was kind. Lisa felt a blanket of guilt wrap itself around them, pushing them closer together. "Look, I'm sorry. I'm not trying to be mean."

Stephanie reached over to whisper in Lisa's ear. "I just wanted to make sure. He asked me to meet him later tonight. That's why I was asking you. I don't want to break you guys up."

Adam showed up just then. "Hey, hey, glad you guys are getting to know each other." He handed each of them a plastic cup. "My buddies hooked me up with the good stuff, not just plain beer." Lisa couldn't stop looking at Stephanie.

"Drink up, drink up, ladies. We're here to party!"

Lisa touched Adam's arm. "Babe, is there any food anywhere here? I'm really hungry, and I'm sure Stephanie is too."

Almost too happy to leave them alone, Adam saluted Lisa. "Your wish is my command, m'lady. I am on the case."

Both women looked at him as he sauntered away, greeting people as he passed like some kind of politician.

Lisa's eyes were black with fury. "What do you mean he asked you to meet him later?"

"Listen, don't get mad at me. I'm being honest with you. I wasn't sure if you were serious or just friends."

Lisa didn't know what to say to that.

Stephanie kept talking. "Maybe he's not as nice as you think. Have you known him for a long time?"

How could she answer that? Lisa thought. "If this is your idea of a joke, it's not funny, Stephanie."

"I'm being honest." Stephanie's voice trailed off as Adam approached with a bowl of potato chips in one hand and another beer in the other, grinning widely.

"Miss me?" he asked both of them.

Lisa and Stephanie looked at Adam, then back at each other. The music seemed to be getting louder since they had arrived. He stood there with a goofy smile. He put the beer and the chips down and stood between the two, one arm around each shoulder. "Man, you two are so beautiful."

Stephanie pulled his arm off and turned for the door. The DJ interrupted her thoughts with the sound of scratching records. "Yes, yes, here I am for you all. DJ Baby, here to rock you all night long, wanting to know, needing to know, don't you want me, baby?" That's when Lisa heard the lyrics again.

> *Don't you want me, baby?*
> *Don't you want me, oh oh oh?*

Adam yelled out to her. "Hey! Don't leave. We just got here."

Lisa struggled with her words. The song was getting louder, and she wanted to get an answer before it happened. She could feel it coming now. "Adam, why did you invite her to this party?"

"What do you mean? I thought she'd have a good time. She's sweet." Adam kept looking towards the door and towards Lisa.

The five years we have had have been such good times
I still love you

"Adam, please. I need you to be honest with me. Why is she here?" The room was getting darker. She put her fingers in her ears, trying to block out the music.

"I am being honest. Damn it! You're a jealous freak! I don't have to put up with this shit." As he stormed off, the darkness kept growing.

But now, I think it's time I live my life on my own
I guess it's just what I must do

Lisa fell to the floor as Stephanie walked back towards her. Lisa felt Stephanie kneeling at her side, screaming, "Lisa! Lisa! Somebody help!"

***

Lying on the MRI bed, struggling to wake up, Lisa saw Stephanie and a doctor running towards her. She held her head in her hands, shaking a little. She opened her eyes and looked up at the concerned faces. "What happened?" she asked no one in particular.

Stephanie was the first to speak. "That's what we'd like to know." In her confusion, Lisa noticed Stephanie's concern but couldn't figure out where she was. A guy in a white coat was talking, asking her questions, but she couldn't understand what he said. It sounded like he was in a bowl of water and all that came out of his mouth were gurgling bubbles. He was balding with little round black glasses that made his eyes look small. His brow was furrowed. His name was embroidered above the pocket on the left side of the coat. The small details, like the neat blue stitching of his name and the ink stain on the point of the pocket captured Lisa's attention. The shape of the letters mesmerized her, as if this were the only thing that mattered right now. The name was in cursive and ended in M.D. *Cursive writing is a lost art,* she thought. *Hmmm…Robert Pons, M.D. I guess this guy's a doctor. Stephanie's here too; she looks different. We were at the party, and now we're here. Did she come back with me?*

Dr. Pons was still talking, making her open her eyes wide while he looked at them with a pen light. He kept flashing the light, switching from one eye to the other. "Follow the light, Lisa." *How did he know her name?*

While Dr. Pons continued his examination, Stephanie reached her left hand for Lisa's right and gave it a little squeeze. Lisa took her eyes away from the doctor and focused her gaze on Stephanie's hand. The wedding ring jolted her back into the present. This was Adam's wife. She half listened to the doctor's explanation.

"It doesn't look like anything abnormal is going on. It's concerning that you seem to have fainted while undergoing the MRI, but let's see the results first before we jump to any conclusions. We should have the results later today or tomorrow, and then we can talk. I think it's best if we keep you under observation until we can figure out next steps. How does that sound?"

Lisa turned her attention to Dr. Pons. "Yes, uhm…I suppose that sounds fine."

With a perfunctory goodbye, he turned on his heel and walked out the door, leaving Stephanie and Lisa still sitting on the MRI bed. They were quiet for a few seconds, just staring at each other. The MRI tech cleared his throat, catching Stephanie's attention. "Shall I call for transport for the patient, or will you take her back to her room?"

Stephanie stood up, pulled on her scrub shirt to straighten it, and replied. "No need for transport; I'll take her back."

The women were unusually quiet as Stephanie pushed Lisa in a wheelchair to her room. Even in the elevator they said nothing. Lisa was lost in thought. *What was going on in the past while she was here? What was Adam doing now? Stephanie? Were they together right now in college in 1982? Did they take her to a hospital when she passed out at the party?*

Their arrival at the room brought Lisa back to now. Stephanie walked her towards the recliner. "Did you want to lay down or stay up for a while? You've had quite the afternoon."

"I'll sit for now, thanks."

Out of the corner of her eye, Lisa watched Stephanie inch toward her while she grabbed a throw blanket. "Are you cold?"

"No, but I could use the comfort."

Stephanie looked pensive. She gave Lisa the blanket and helped her tuck it around her waist. "You know, Lisa, I had this weird sensation when I was holding your hand earlier, on the MRI bed, that I know you from before you came to this hospital. I hadn't had that feeling until now. Isn't that strange? Have we met before?"

Lisa wasn't sure how to respond. She had more questions than answers. How could she tell Stephanie that she knew her when she was young and a waitress? How could she share that she had just been with her, younger, carefree, in college, not knowing what lay ahead in their lives?

In what seemed like years ago, she had daydreamed of going back in time to ensure that Adam didn't meet Stephanie. On all those nights when she waited for Adam to show up, she fantasized that she could change the past and the future. By some miracle, her fantasy had come true, and she was able to fly backwards in her life. But now the past seemed determined to continue as if she had never set foot in it. Lisa was in a boat on a river of time, aiming for a particular dock, and no matter how hard she rowed, or where she stopped, she kept hitting upon the same obstacles. Regardless of how hard Lisa tried to thwart Stephanie from meeting Adam, she always showed up. And now, if

Stephanie was sensing she knew Lisa from before, did that mean traveling was also impacting the present?

Returning from her reverie, she focused on Stephanie, the nurse, the caregiver. She opened and closed her mouth a few times, trying to find the right words. "What do you mean that you feel you know me from before?"

Stephanie averted her eyes, and her cheeks flushed a little. "I don't know how to explain it. When I held your hand, I got a sense that I met you before, that we were connected somehow." She paused and took a deep breath. Lisa listened intently, urging Stephanie to continue. "Go on. What else did you see?"

Stephanie laughed nervously. "It's not so much that I saw something, but more like a feeling, like when you have déjà vu."

She kept talking, rushing her words. "I don't know. It sounds kind of crazy because I also got this feeling that you know my husband, and I know you don't because we never met until you got admitted to my floor, but somehow my husband—his name is Adam.... I have this feeling in my gut that Adam and you and me are connected in some odd way."

Lisa stared at Stephanie in silence. A million thoughts crashed into each other at warp speed. *What do I do? Do I tell her? She'll think I'm nuts. How does she know me? She wasn't there, not this Stephanie. It's the other Stephanie who was there. This is a mess. How do I sort this out?*

Stephanie smiled with a furrowed brow. "Crazy, right?"

There was no point in hurting this person who was so kind. Lisa found her voice. "I don't know what to think, Stephanie. Maybe you had a dream or something. I read in a magazine that happens with people who are caregivers. They take on the problems of their patients. Maybe that's what's happening here. You know I have a medical issue. And you're afraid you can't help me." Even to Lisa's ears this sounded like gibberish, but she didn't know what else to say.

Again, Stephanie lingered in an awkward silence. She covered up the moment by smoothing out the blanket on Lisa. "This is all crazy nonsense. I'm probably sleep deprived. You just get some rest. It's almost the end of my shift, and I have a ton of work to do. I'll check in on you before I leave." Before Lisa even had a chance to say anything, Stephanie marched out of the room.

Alone again, Lisa grabbed her cell phone and checked for messages. Nothing from Adam and nothing from Marcus. Figures. Men continued to be unreliable. She didn't want to think about all this. Her head was going to explode with all the possible permutations. She was in the present, going to the past, changing the present, presumably changing the future, and she had no idea how she was doing all of this.

She wanted to call Emily. Maybe Emily had some wise words that would help her sort out this situation. How would she open the conversation? She hadn't even told her about the time travel. Emily didn't even approve much of the affair. How was she going to handle Lisa traveling back to change the future? *Hey girl, I've been traveling back in time to when we were in college, and yeah, I wanted you to know that it's making everything weird.* Emily, with her logic and blunt answers would tell her she was crazy. She wasn't ready to hear that. She still had hope that she could make things work for her and Adam. But Emily was the only person she could trust with this mess, whether or not she created it. But did she create it? Was any of this in her control? Did any of this have anything to do with these strange headaches she had? Nothing made sense anymore, not that it did much before anyway.

She dialed Emily's number and got voicemail. It was too much to leave in a message. She hung up, hoping Emily would notice the missed call and try her later. In the meantime, she felt jittery. She turned on the television hoping the news or a boring daytime show would help. Unwittingly, she landed on a music channel.

Don't you want me baby? Don't you want me....

Darkness and nothing…

***

Lisa opened her eyes to the sight of Emily sitting in a chair next to the lower bunk bed, staring at her, a cup of water in her hand.

"Ah, her majesty wakes up." Emily sounded sarcastic.

Lisa tried to talk, but her voice cracked, like she hadn't used it in a while. "Where am I?"

Emily handed her the cup. "Drink. It's water. You remember that, don't you?" Lisa sipped, still groggy.

Sounding angry, Emily continued. "And as to your question, where are you? Where do you think you are, princess? In our room." Her voice was high pitched, and she paced in the small space between door and desk, emphasizing her words with each step.

"You know, it's not bad enough that you leave here to go to some frat party with some guy that you barely know. No, that's not enough. You then disappear for hours, and I have no idea where you are or if he's killed you or something." Each word pounded into Lisa's head.

"But even that's not enough. You then show up at the door, still drunk, not knowing how you got here, no Adam dreamboat around. Instead, it's some girl named Stephanie with you hanging onto her. She said she was at a party with you, and she didn't want to let you walk home alone. She was so nervous that she stuttered. She gave me an envelope, left you in my arms, and ran off. And then you sleep for hours, looking comatose, and you wake up and ask *where am I?*"

Emily's voice rose, shrill and insistent. "The better question is where have you been?"

By now Emily was red in the face, looking like her head was going to explode. Lisa sat up gingerly, not sure what to think or what to say. *I seem to be in this position a lot lately,* was the only thought that surfaced.

Apparently not done, Emily reached over to the desk, grabbed an envelope and handed it to Lisa. "This is what she left for you."

Dazed, Lisa asked, "What is it?"

"Genius, what does it look like? It's sealed. It has your name on it. I didn't open it." She sat down in front of Lisa. "Look, I don't know what's going on, and I seem angry, and I am, but mostly I'm really worried. You're acting all kinds of strange. Are you in some kind of trouble?"

Lisa turned the envelope over and over in her hand. The handwriting on the front was neat and precise. Her name was in cursive. Lisa remembered being mesmerized by the cursive name embroidered on the doctor's white coat in the future.

No one would ever understand all this. Everything was so mixed up. So, what was the worst that could happen? She handed the envelope to Emily. "Open it. Read the letter to me. I also have tons of questions. Maybe this will answer yours. And mine."

Emily hesitated, then opened the letter and read slowly.

> *Lisa, if you're reading this, you're feeling better. I'm glad of that. Meet me today after work. My shift ends at 10 tonight. Come to the pastry shop alone. Don't bring Adam. We need to talk about him. Please come alone.*

"It's signed, Stephanie," said Emily. "What is going on? Who's this Stephanie?"

"She's the girl who brought me here."

"No kidding, I know that. I mean who is she to you? And what does she know about Adam? Why does she need to talk to you alone?"

"I have no idea."

Emily stood up abruptly and slammed the letter on the desk. "Well, you can't go alone at night to meet some strange girl you don't know to talk about some strange guy you don't know. I'm not letting you go alone."

The truth was that she was afraid of facing Stephanie alone. She wasn't sure why. Maybe because her plan to derail her marriage to Adam was getting derailed itself? She didn't know what Stephanie wanted, but she was here again, so she needed to see this through. "Fine. Come with me."

Emily pointed her finger in Lisa's face. "And don't think I'm going to like it, or that I'm going to approve of any of this." Emily's harsh tone softened when Lisa jumped out of the bed and hugged her.

Emily tried, in vain, to push her away. "No, no, you're not going to cajole me into agreeing with you about any of this."

Lisa kept holding on to Emily as if she were a life preserver. Emily tightened her grip on Lisa's back, and the room became quiet and still. The posters of The Cars and The Go-Go's stared back at Lisa, accusing her almost of being an interloper, a fake. She didn't belong here anymore, barrettes in her hair and a long white shirt that reached her thighs, with shoulder pads that made her shoulders broad and a wide black belt that cinched her waist to look tiny.

Emily continued softly. "Listen, I have this scary feeling in the pit of my stomach that something's wrong. That you're in some kind of trouble, and I won't be able to help you out of it later."

For the first time in a long time, Lisa felt like she had an ally. "Actually, I expect you will be able to help me. I'm just not sure with what. Then again, you always say you like rollercoasters. Wanna go for a ride?"

Chapter 6

Lisa and Emily killed time at one of the outside tables of the pastry shop. Sitting there, in the shadow of the Cathedral of St. John the Divine, Lisa marveled at how much had changed since she'd last been here. Thinking about the future in which she lived and sitting here in the past, which was her current now, almost made her head ache. In the time where she actually lived, the giant sculpture of a battle of good and evil stood in the garden next to the cathedral, its countenance glaring at the customers of the Hungarian Pastry Shop. Here, in this past, the garden was filled with only trees and flowers.

Music from boom boxes blasted as kids walked along the sidewalk, some sporting penny loafers and others combat boots and punked out hair. Lisa recognized a song from Men at Work and reached for her cell phone to see if she could find out the name when she remembered there were no cell phones in the '80s. She pretended to look for tissues in her oversize handbag to avoid describing a cell phone to Emily.

Stephanie had waved to Lisa a few minutes earlier and had motioned for her to wait outside. Emily fidgeted with the rings on her fingers. Lisa, tapping her foot, felt more nervous watching her. "Will you stop fidgeting please? It's not helping."

"I'm not fidgeting. You're fidgeting. How many times are you going to look at your watch? She's in there. She knows you're here. She'll come out when she's good and ready."

Lisa stuck her tongue out at Emily. She hated when Emily was right. And she was right a lot of the time. That was always a problem in the future too.

Emily continued. "What could she possibly want to say to you anyway?"

Lisa raised an eyebrow. "Really? Haven't we been through this already?" Before Emily had a chance to respond, Stephanie pushed open the glass door and stepped outside. She looked at Emily and Lisa and directed herself to Lisa. "I thought I asked you to come alone. Who's this?"

Emily opened her mouth, prepared no doubt with a retort, but Lisa interrupted her. "She's my best friend. Whatever you have to say to me, you can say in front of her."

Stephanie looked Emily up and down with a glare reserved for enemies. "I prefer if we talked alone, but she's your friend, not mine. Let's go find a coffee shop where we can sit. I've been on my feet for hours."

They walked a few blocks to an all-night diner. Stephanie sat in a booth across from Emily and Lisa. The place was seedy, with tiled floors that hadn't seen a thorough scrubbing in decades. The grout was as gray as the tiles. The booths had red plastic cushions with tears on the seats that looked like gaping mouths spilling once-white but now yellowish-brown stuffing. The women had to sit carefully to prevent their bare legs from getting scratched on the seats. Their coffees came in thick, yellowed porcelain cups that had seen many years of hot dishwashing. The pattern on the cups had once matched the pattern of the tiled walls and floors. Now they just seemed tired, accompanied by equally tired, flat spoons.

Stephanie stirred sugar in her cup, appearing to Lisa as if she were delaying the conversation that she clearly was afraid to start. Lisa covered up her nervousness with bravado. "OK, you have me here. What's with the drama? What do you need to say that's so important?"

Stephanie put down the spoon and lifted the coffee to her lips. She took a sip, put it down and stared at Lisa. "How well do you know Adam?"

Lisa wasn't expecting this question. *How well did she know Adam?* "What kind of a question is that?"

"It's a simple question. He's your boyfriend. How well do you know him?"

"Why are you asking me that?"

Stephanie spoke at a rapid clip, her words dropping like stones on a cement path. "Because I'm an honest woman, that's why, which is less than I can say about you. Look, I like him. A lot. I met him a few weeks ago. He came to the pastry shop, and we started a conversation. Even if I don't look it, I'm kind of shy around guys. Something about him let me feel comfortable around him. He kept coming back and always found a way to sit at my table. He'd made it clear he was interested in me. I had planned on saying yes to him on the day that he showed up with you. But then he pretended not to know me. I was kind of angry, and to make matters worse, he was obviously flirting with me, and he asked me to come to the party as if he didn't know who I was. I showed up thinking that he was playing a joke, or that this was some kind of romantic way of going out with me, that maybe you two were just classmates. Or that maybe he was trying to make me jealous, so I'd finally say yes to him. I don't know. But then I saw you guys at the party together. And now I'm confused because I think I was there first with him, but now you're in the picture, and I'm just not sure."

Stephanie paused and took a gulp of hot coffee as if she were looking for strength to continue. "Plus, after you fainted at the party, he came looking for me again. He said that he really liked me, that he just wasn't that into you."

Lisa rolled her eyes. "Oh, come on."

Stephanie motioned to let her continue. "There's more. He said that he couldn't keep waiting around for me to decide. I told him I wasn't sure, that if you were his girlfriend, I didn't want to interfere. He insisted you were nothing to him. So, what actually is the deal? I wanted to talk to you because I don't believe in women backstabbing each other. If you're his girlfriend, then I need to know, because up until a few days ago, I thought I was going to be his girlfriend, but then you appeared, and now you're in the way, but it feels like it's all twisted, so…." Her voice trailed off.

Lisa's eyes opened wide as she grasped all this information. Stephanie's words rang in her ears. *"Now you're in the way."* Did this mean that she was actually changing the past? Was this evidence that her traveling was making an impact? This was her opportunity. All she had to do was tell Stephanie that Adam was her boyfriend, and she'd have what she wanted all along.

This was it.

Emily coughed. "Well, Lisa, is he your boyfriend?"

Lisa stared down at her coffee cup looking for an answer that made sense. She had this chance of a lifetime, and she didn't know what to do with it. She had Stephanie sitting in front of her, and she had this terrible feeling that whatever she did was going to have an impact that was larger than she had imagined. What if she said *Yes, he's my boyfriend?* Did that mean that Stephanie would get out of the way? Did that mean that they wouldn't get married? It had all been well and good in her imagination, but what if she was actually able to change the future?

Lisa remembered Stephanie the nurse. She was so kind, so dedicated. She was so unhappy with her marriage, but she loved her family. She talked of her daughters and how she adored them. If Lisa said yes, what happened to them? Would the daughters disappear?

The coffee swirled in the cup while she stirred and stirred. *What's the right answer? What's the right thing to do?*

Her gut told her that everyone's life was in the balance. The circles in the coffee mimicked her thoughts. Round and round and round she goes; where she stops, nobody knows.

And then she knew.

"You're damn straight he's my boyfriend. Has been for weeks, and you're in my goddamn way. How dare you try to take him away?"

Lisa spit bullets like machine-gun fire. "And this phony-baloney story of how you met him before is ridiculous. Who do you think would believe that bullshit? You said so yourself that he didn't know who you were when I was in the pastry shop. He may have invited you to the party, but he was trying to be nice because he felt sorry for you. He told me when we left. That he thought you were pitiful, so he figured he'd throw you a bone."

Lisa stopped to catch her breath, her heart racing. *Did she just say all that? Who was she?* Emily was staring at her, mouth gaping. Stephanie sat there, quiet, face immobile. Lisa looked her in the eyes, defiant, her face pretending to be certain about her decision. But this was her chance. This was what she had dreamed about. She couldn't back down. She couldn't consider the consequences for everyone else. She needed to do what was best for her and for Adam. And she was the best one for Adam.

The silence at the table was palpable. A single tear fell down Stephanie's cheek. She brushed it away with her index finger. She reached for the rectangular paper napkin on the side of her coffee cup, wiped her finger and then her mouth. She pulled out her wallet and took out two single dollar bills. She turned them, so they were both facing in the same direction, laid them neatly on the table, under her cup saucer. She slid out of the booth and stood for a few seconds next to the table, looking at Lisa. She opened her mouth to speak and nothing came out. She took a deep breath. In a voice barely above a whisper she said, "Fine. You can have him. Good luck with that." She turned towards the door and, in a few long strides, exited.

Lisa lowered her eyes, intent on her coffee. She knew Stephanie was gone when she heard the jingle at the door as it opened and closed.

After what seemed like an eternity, Emily broke the silence. "That was special."

Lisa didn't answer. She motioned to the waitress for a refill, wanting an excuse to delay saying anything. After adding more sugar and milk to the cup, she took a sip, swallowed hard and turned to Emily. "That was the truth. She needs to stay out of the way."

Emily reached out and placed her hand on Lisa's arm. "I hope you know what you're doing. I have a bad feeling about this, but, hey, if this is what you want, then I'm with you."

Taking a deep breath, Lisa put her hand on top of Emily's and squeezed her best friend. She noticed how smooth Emily's skin was, how unblemished from the sun, how soft. In that instant, she noted the passing of years, how they had been friends for so long, how she didn't want to disappoint Emily ever, and how she felt that whatever decisions she made here were bound to be a disappointment. She took a deep breath again and uttered words she'd been thinking for years. "This is exactly what I want."

***

At the end of her first class the next day, Lisa intended to find Adam and give him a piece of her mind. Still reeling from her decision the night before, she wanted to let him know, in no uncertain terms, that he was to stay away from Stephanie completely. She wanted to leave nothing to chance.

The professor of her geometry theory class droned that day. She remembered she usually enjoyed his funny lectures, but today she couldn't concentrate. Perhaps the realization that nothing from this class would be useful in the future made her look at her watch repeatedly. Each time that she thought at least fifteen minutes had passed, she looked and the minute hand had moved twice. Finally, after an eternity, she ran out as soon as class was dismissed.

Not watching where she was going, she tripped over her own feet and landed right in Adam's arms. "Whoa! Where are you going so fast?"

Here he is, she thought. "Oh, I've missed you so," she whispered to herself, not realizing that he could hear her.

"Oh yeah, you've missed me, huh? Well, maybe you need to take better aim." He leaned down and kissed her tenderly. It felt like a first kiss, the kind that stays in the memory banks she'd return to when the loneliness of life threatens to swallow her whole.

She was the first one to separate. She leaned back to look up at him and remembered where she was headed minutes earlier. "I was on my way to see you."

He laughed. "It's a good thing I showed up then, otherwise you would have missed me even more." He stared at her, eyebrows quizzical. "What's up with you? You look like you're on a mission. Feeling better from last night? Or still hungover?"

She remembered her resolve, and the words tumbled out. "I'm fine, but you must promise me that you're not going to see that girl Stephanie anymore. I don't want her near us. She's a nutcase."

Adam frowned, forehead scrunched. "Who's Stephanie?"

"Don't play games with me, Adam. You know who Stephanie is. That girl from the Hungarian Pastry Shop. The one you invited to the party last night."

"Oh, that girl. Is that her name? I barely remember her. Why would I want to see her again? What does she have to do with us?"

Lisa thought for a moment. *Should she say anything more or just drop the subject?* She pressed on. She needed to make sure that this Stephanie business was squashed completely. "She met me last night. She had this idea that you were seeing her."

Adam wrapped his arms tightly around Lisa's back. He leaned his face into her neck, nuzzling her, as if they were not in the middle of a hallway outside of a classroom. Lisa noticed students glancing at them, but she didn't care. She smelled the skin on his neck, transfixed by his fragrance. "Lisa, I don't care about anyone other than you. There is no one but you."

His words melted her. Nothing mattered. No portents of doom, no stubborn conscience or guilty feelings, nothing was going to get in the way this time. He belonged to her.

A professor stood in front of them, *harrumphing* to get their attention. Lisa looked up, eyelids half shut with a dreamy feel, and realized they were being a bit inappropriate. "If you lovebirds don't mind, I'd like to close the door, so I can start my class."

***

Back in Adam's room, hours later, they lay on the bed, legs wrapped around each other, a thin sheen of sweat covering them both. The day had passed quickly. Time was a harsh taskmaster. When she needed it to move slowly, it ran at the speed of light.

She reached up and ran her fingers through his thick curly hair. She remembered the grays that had started to crop up in the future. She wondered what he was doing right now, not here, but there. She hadn't seen him in a few days. Was he missing her?

Adam positioned himself even closer to her if that were possible. "I like when you touch my hair like that."

"Hmmm…yes, you've always liked that," she answered.

"It makes me sleepy," he whispered.

"Then take a nap."

She had barely gotten the words out before she heard a soft snore. She smiled. It would be louder in a few years. She didn't mind. It meant he was spending the night with her.

Unable to sleep, she turned on the radio to find soothing music, so she could relax. She was torn between wanting to spend the night watching Adam sleep and realizing she needed rest. Who knew what adventures tomorrow would bring? As she fiddled with the dials, she heard the familiar tune and the words.

I was working as a waitress in a cocktail bar....

And there it was...the nausea, the darkness, the nothingness.

***

Lisa woke up from what she thought was a nap, sitting upright in a hospital guest chair. Still a little groggy from sleep, she picked up the phone as it rang. "ICE—cell," said the screen.

ICE? Who was IN CASE OF EMERGENCY?

She answered with hesitation. "Hello?"

The familiar voice greeted her. "Hey, babe. How're you feeling?"

Adam.

He was ICE.

It had worked.

Chapter 7

Lisa didn't know how to answer Adam's question. How did she feel? She looked around the room to make certain she was sure of her location. Yes, still in the hospital, but she felt different. The caller ID on the phone was evidence of a change. Was it possible that she had been successful? Goosebumps covered her arms. Her throat was tight as she opened and closed her mouth several times trying to find the right words. She wasn't sure how much Adam knew or what had happened.

This was a new world, one where Adam was her call in case of emergency. That meant he was more than a lover. But what exactly had happened?

"I'm feeling better. Where are you?"

"I'm still at work, but I'll come by when I'm done. I wanted to know if you needed anything. And did you talk to any doctor today? Did they do the MRI? Do you have results?"

Lisa still didn't know where to start. Adam laughed. "Sorry. Too many rapid-fire questions, huh?"

"No, that's fine. Sounds like you're worried."

"Of course I'm worried, sweetheart. My wife is in the hospital for undiagnosed head trauma that makes her black out. How could I not worry?"

My wife. They were married. Lisa looked down at her left hand and saw empty fingers. She wondered momentarily why there was no ring. Maybe she took it off for the MRI. She got up from her chair and found her purse. There, inside the coin pocket of the wallet was a pair of rings. A gold engagement ring with a single small round diamond and a simple gold wedding band.

She didn't recognize these rings. She had never seen them before, but they were in her wallet, obviously hers. She lovingly put them on her finger, trying to emulate what Adam would have done on their wedding day. But she had no memories of this wedding. She noticed that she remembered every detail of her wedding to Marcus. But her wedding to Adam was a blank page.

Adam broke her reverie. "Hello? Are you still there?"

Lisa returned her attention to the call. "Yes, yes. Still here. No word yet on test results. What time are you coming?"

"I told you. As soon as I get out of work. I've arranged for Zelda to stay late with the kids tonight, so I can stay with you as long as you need me."

Lisa scrunched her face, struggling to remember details she didn't know. "Who's Zelda?"

"What do you mean, who's Zelda? Our nanny. What's the matter with you? You don't remember the name of the woman who's been taking care of the girls since birth?"

They had children. Daughters. She had no memories of this. She didn't know any details of this life she had created from her travels to the past. She had created the future she had dreamed about, and apparently had lived it on some plane, but she hadn't participated in it at all. Now she had to figure out how to navigate this new world.

Lisa returned her attention to the call. "Of course. Sorry. My brain's gone mushy with all these tests. Hospital food doesn't help." She tried to keep her tone light. "So, what time will you be out of work?"

Adam snapped. "I told you already. I'm not sure."

Lisa was jolted by his response. She wasn't sure how to react. She didn't know *this* Adam. He was neither past nor present that she knew. His voice got softer. "I'm sorry I snapped a little. It's been hectic at work, and with you not around, it's been crazy at home. I'll probably get to you around six or so."

"No apology needed. I'm not going anywhere. Maybe I'll have some news by the time you get here." She added that last piece just to have something to say. She felt so disjointed not knowing the routines of his life.

After they hung up, she examined the phone for the first time. There, on the welcome screen, was a picture of two little girls with identical faces. They had long hair with soft brown curls. Their eyes were deep brown, large and expressive. They were laughing, hugging each other, in polka dot white and blue summer dresses with blue bows pulling their hair back from their foreheads. They looked like they were about five or six years old. They had sweetheart lips and chubby cheeks. They were beautiful. And apparently, they were hers.

Lisa scrolled through the phone, looking for more pictures, feeling like she was snooping on someone else's life. She wanted to see what she was like now. But when she clicked on the Photos icon, she was surprised to see that it was empty.

Not one picture to show for all these years of her life. It was as if she had sprouted into this world from the nothingness of the universe. She could remember her past, the one she had come from where she and Adam were lovers, where she had pined away for him and where she had traveled to her youth to meet him, so she could change the future.

Now she was here in this strange new world where she had everything she had dreamed of—children, Adam as her husband, a family. She had succeeded. But she knew nothing about this life.

Where did they live? Did she have friends? What were her children like? She didn't remember their childhoods. Had she been pregnant? What did that feel like? It looked like they were twins. In her past, she had experienced pregnancy and childbirth with disastrous results. This time she was a mother. But she knew nothing about it. She felt the pang of loneliness with that realization.

She looked at the photograph of her daughters again. They were so lovely. How old were they? What foods did they like? Were they good students? Did they sleep well at night? Were they affectionate, playful, energetic? Did they like to read? These children, and this life, were strangers to her, and she was going to have to learn everything. How was she supposed to do that without giving away her secret?

Lost in these thoughts, trying to calculate her way out of this mess, Lisa didn't hear Stephanie at the door. A cough brought her back from her reveries. Stephanie stood at the at the threshold with a computer on a cart, charting notes, her eyes fixed on her work, not looking at Lisa. "Hey, how's my favorite patient? Feeling more rested?"

Lisa was shocked to see Stephanie here, still her nurse. She wasn't sure what she had expected, but seeing Stephanie brought her back to the reality that everything had changed, yet some things had not.

Man, I can't get rid of this girl. "Your patient is feeling very well, actually."

Stephanie walked towards her. "Good to hear. I was worried about you after that MRI debacle. The technician told me that you scared them so much they put your test at the top of the list for review. They should have results later this evening. They had to send the test to a radiologist who specializes in pineal gland issues."

Stephanie walked over to the windowsill, leaned down, and smelled the flowers Lisa had received earlier in the day. With all of the day's excitement, Lisa had forgotten them. "Your husband Adam is so romantic, sending flowers and telling you he loves you. So sweet. I wish I had a husband like that." Stephanie audibly sighed, her back to Lisa.

For the first time since the discovery of her time travel abilities, Lisa felt guilty, as if she had stolen Stephanie's life. She was the one who now had daughters. And she was the one who was married to Adam. *What does Stephanie's life look like now?* She didn't need to wonder for long.

When Stephanie turned around, the look on her face was not wistful or sweet. Her smile seemed plastic, and anger coated her voice, like the dark, crusty film on milk that has been boiled too long. "I've never been able to find a guy like that. I met one once, in college, that I thought might be the one, but he disappeared. And I've had no luck since then."

Lisa's hands had turned cold. There was something clearly off with this Stephanie.

"I'm sure that someone wonderful will show up in your life. It's just not been the right time."

"Maybe. What I've found is that all the nice guys are married."

Lisa had no response. What could she say? Just a little while ago, she would have said the same thing, but now, in these shoes, her mind was too confused and jumbled for any witty repartee or sage advice.

Stephanie straightened her back and focused her attention on Lisa. "Nothing to be done about men, right?" She took a deep breath. "So, while we wait for these results, you get some rest. Hopefully, you'll have answers soon that will help figure out what's going on with your headaches. I'll come back later to check on you again."

Left alone, Lisa wondered how she was going to learn about her new life. Adam was coming to see her in a few hours. She couldn't face him with a blank slate instead of memories. Could she confide in him? What would she say? *Oh, honey, you know, I went back to college when we could have met, and we did, and I made sure that I got rid of your girlfriend who would have been your wife, so now she's not, and instead I am, but I have no idea what happened between the last time I saw you in the past when we were eighteen or so, or now in this new present when we're fortyish, so be a dear please and fill in all the blanks of the last twenty years or so?* That approach wouldn't work very well. For sure, they'd put her in a straitjacket and leave her in a padded room.

She needed a better plan. Maybe someone could give her an update of her life. Someone she could trust. She grabbed her cell phone again.

Other than Adam, there was no one listed in the contacts. Her phone, and her life, had been blanked out with a restart and both required a new software installation. Lisa got up and paced the room from one end to the other. She stopped at the window and looked out at the Hudson River. She was fortunate to be in one of the few hospitals in New Jersey where one could see the Manhattan skyline. At least that hadn't changed much from her other past. Until now, she had taken all this for granted and hadn't even bothered to notice the view.

She stood there for a while, lost in thought, trying to figure out the timeline on her own. "Her other past." Even the language she was using made no sense. The past, the other past, the present, the future. Everything was jumbled. A whole new language had to be invented to explain what, where, or which when she was in. She hadn't even been able to figure out how it worked. It was as if she were two separate people floating on boats in parallel-flowing rivers. Her choice of vessel determined which life she'd lead.

But what happened on the other route while she was here?

When she was Marcus's wife, she knew she stood in the present. There was a clear demarcation of past, present, and future. She knew what she wanted: to be with Adam. She loved him. She wished and wished, and then her wish came true. She started traveling to the past. But it wasn't the real past she remembered. It was a new past. And in that past, she remembered her present—the one where she was married to Marcus. That was a solid marker. It was secure and fixed like a true north.

Until she changed the past. When she encountered Stephanie and decided to take Adam from her, everything altered in the future. So here she was, in this new future/present, and she was Adam's wife. They had a family.

I have daughters. I am a mother.

That thought should have made her happy. She would have been delirious with joy in the past if she had had that thought. But now, what now? In this moment, she remembered nothing of how she got here. She had the life she had been wanting, but she had missed it all. She had no memories.

Lisa leaned her hands on the windowsill, gripping the edge to keep her balance. She felt her body heavy with a deep sadness that weighed her down. How was it possible that she had what she wanted, yet she wasn't happy?

She knew how to handle problems in the past, but she felt rudderless here. She lost track of how much time she had stood at the window. As she chewed on her lower lip, still searching for an answer, she noticed the wind picked up, turning the clouds into long fluffy oblong shapes with gray undersides. They looked as if they were painted on a pale blue canvas. Staring at them, Lisa's face broke into a big smile. Out of nowhere, the thought came to her. *Emily!* Her ride or die friend. Emily would know what was missing.

Lisa went back for her phone. She looked in the contacts again, but she realized she didn't need any help. She dialed the number she had been dialing for what seemed like more than one lifetime.

Emily picked up almost on the first ring. "Oh my God, Lisa, where the hell have you been?"

Laughing, Lisa plopped herself face down on the bed, happy to hear the familiar reprimand. "Why do you care, you haven't called me."

"Oh. My. God. What is the matter with you? I've been calling you for days, the phone goes to voicemail, and then I get the message that your mailbox is full. I thought you deliberately blocked me."

Lisa sat up abruptly. *How could Emily not know I'm in the hospital?* "Why would I block you?"

"I don't know, but I was literally about to start calling hospitals to find out where you are. I was starting to panic when you didn't even call me to find out about Jojo."

Lisa wasn't sure how to respond. She didn't know what she was expecting, but an angry Emily hadn't crossed her mind. How was she going to get Emily to tell her the whole story?

"Ummm. Emily?"

Aggravated, Emily responded. "What?!"

"Who's Jojo?"

"You're joking right?"

"No, I'm not."

"Jojo is your dog. Did you hit your head or something?"

"Well, kind of…." Lisa let the words trail off as she tried to figure out how to broach the subject of her memory. "Look, something big has happened, and I need to talk to you. I'm in the hospital. I had a car accident, remember? And stuff has happened that is confusing me, but you're the only person I can talk to about this. I really can't talk to Adam, and anyway, you're my best friend. Right?" That last word rang in the air for Lisa. It dawned on her that she didn't know if Emily was still her best friend in this dimension. *Oh God, what if Emily isn't close to me anymore? Then what'll I do?*

Emily sighed loudly. "You must have hit your head hard to ask such a stupid question. We've been through the ringer and back, and now you wonder if you can talk to me? What did you do? Kill someone?"

Lisa stayed silent. *Kind of….*

Emily spoke again. "Where are you? I'll come see you."

"Palisades General. Fourth floor. Adam will be here in about three hours, and I need to talk to you before he gets here. Can you come over now?"

"On my way."

Chapter 8

Tears escaped Lisa's eyes as she hugged Emily. Her whole body shuddered from anticipation, nervousness, and relief. Emily patted her back, murmuring, "Shhh...it's OK, Lisa. It's OK. I'm here, and it's all going to be all right." Lisa's crying softened. Looking for tissues, she let go of her friend's embrace. Emily grabbed the box first. "You never have tissues when you need them. What the hell would you do without me, huh? You never had any money in school, you never have a good babysitter for the kids...or the dog, and now you can't find tissues that are right under your nose." Gratefully, Lisa blew her nose, trying to figure out where to start.

"We have to talk. I have a lot to say, but I need you to..." Lisa paused to measure her words. "I need you to believe me no matter how crazy my story is. We've known each other for a long time. You're the only person I can trust with this, but it's going to sound crazy, so suspend judgment until I'm done and then...well then, we'll see what you think. Agreed?"

Emily raised her right eyebrow like she always did when she was skeptical. "Start talking. I promise to listen and to leave my judging for the end."

Lisa took a deep breath and smoothed out her hospital gown. "I had that car accident, remember?"

"Of course I remember. Right after we had dinner. I knew about that, then I didn't hear from you again."

"Yes. That night. Well, they've discovered that I have something wrong with my pineal gland."

"Your what?"

"Pineal gland. It's a little gland in the brain. It's about the only thing I remember from that biology class we took together. I'm not sure what it does normally, but it controls memories, and somehow, it's also called the 'third eye.' Mystics and gurus have been doing all kinds of wacky stuff with their third eye for centuries. It gives you power to see things, to have visions. Because I had the car accident and hit my head, they did a CT scan, and they found that mine's enlarged."

"So, what does that mean? Are you having visions? Do you need surgery?"

"No, I don't think so, no surgery. But that's not my point. There's something else, something bigger, going on."

"Visions?"

"Not exactly. More than that." Lisa paused. She took a deep breath. *Here goes nothing.*

"I've been traveling back and forth in time."

Emily said nothing. Her face was blank. Lisa wasn't sure if that was intentional or if she hadn't heard correctly.

Lisa continued. "Did you hear me? I said I've been time traveling."

"I heard you. I'm waiting to hear the punch line of the joke."

Lisa sat back down next to Emily and took her hand. "I'm not joking. For a few days now, I've been back and forth between the present and the past. Actually, our past. I've been going back to college. I've seen you and me there and all our friends. We're all young, like sophomores. And I met Adam there."

Emily leaned away from Lisa. "Honey, how hard did you hit your head? I know you met Adam in college. I was there, remember? On the Columbia steps. You took off with him, and I was really mad at you because you had abandoned me."

Almost afraid to hear the answer, Lisa pressed for detail. "What else happened?"

"You met him, you started dating, he graduated, the next year we graduated, then you got married. You bought a house. You waited years to have babies. You had a miscarriage. Then you had two kids, one after the other. Then you got a dog. And now we're here." Emily rushed all the words out as if she were trying to say them before she lost her nerve. Emily stopped. She noticed the bouquet on the windowsill and headed to it.

"Flowers?" Emily yanked the card from the bouquet and read it out loud. "'My darling wife. I hope you feel better. I love you more than ever. Adam.' Hmm. Sweet." Emily spoke in a flat tone. She looked back at Lisa, her jaw just the slightest bit clenched.

"He is sweet. But listen, we don't have time to talk about the flowers. Let's focus. My story's more complicated." Lisa wasn't even sure how to explain it logically. She tried again. "This reality we're in now, this time we're in, is not real."

Emily leaned away from her, her eyes scrunched together, that right eyebrow up again. "What are you saying?

"Em, in my real life, I never met Adam in college. I met him at a bar with friends at a happy hour, after I was already married to Marcus. When I met Adam, we fell in love and started having an affair. Well, at least I was in love. I kept wishing that I could go back in time to meet Adam in college since our time at the school coincided, but we never met. I was waiting for him at the train station one night. Do you remember? I called you, and you told me I was being silly waiting for a married man. Then we met for dinner at Scaramella's? Do you remember that, Emily?"

Emily rolled the words out slowly. "Yes, I vaguely remember we had dinner. I seem to remember you were upset, but I don't know why."

Lisa stared at Emily focusing on her eyes. It seemed Emily was believing her, but Lisa wasn't sure. "You must think I'm stark raving mad. But I'm not, Em. I can remember all three lives. The real one with a real past—the past that I traveled to—and now this one we're in. This one is a new future." Frustrated that she couldn't express herself clearly, Lisa pushed herself off the bed and paced across the small room, gesturing wildly. "All this, all this, Emily, none of this is real. I've been here for a couple of days, and I can tell you I've been back and forth to 1982. The last time I was in this very room, I was married to Marcus, and Adam was my lover. That's the life when you and I had dinner. He was married to a woman named Stephanie, and they had two daughters. I wished and wished I could go back and prevent them from meeting, and my wish came true. I went back. I stopped them. Then when I got back here, I'm the one married to Adam, and Stephanie isn't."

Emily cocked her head to the side. She remained quiet for a minute, then shook her head. "Stephanie, huh? Let's pretend for a moment that I believe this insanity of yours. How do you know Stephanie? If you're the one married to Adam, how do you know Stephanie?"

"Because she's my nurse."

"Your nurse? Here? Now?" Emily seemed incredulous. Lisa tried to explain.

"The same Stephanie that used to be married to Adam in the real life, the same Stephanie that I met in college and stopped from dating Adam, she's my nurse in this hospital. She's my nurse in the real life, and she's my nurse now. I can't get away from her." Lisa, exhausted, plopped herself on the bed, picked up a pillow and covered her face with it. She screamed quietly into the pillow.

Emily stood up and walked the few steps to the window. She stared at the skyline for a little while, saying nothing. She turned around just as Lisa put the pillow down.

"Lisa, I believe you."

Excited, Lisa jumped up from the chair and clapped her hands. "You do? That's fantastic! I'm so glad! I need your help in figuring out what I've missed." Emily's face didn't reflect back Lisa's enthusiasm. Lisa could tell something was off. "Wait. Why do you believe me?"

Emily reached for her friend's hands and took them in hers. "I believe you because I've heard you tell me many times that you think Adam is having an affair with someone named Stephanie. And you've told me you think this Stephanie is a nurse."

"You must be mistaken Emily. Stephanie is a common name. It's just a coincidence."

"You're right. Maybe it's a coincidence." Emily headed to the window.

The sky was starting to darken. Clouds were turning pink, and the buildings in New York City had that glow from the lights of the approaching sunset. The golden hour. Lisa felt a punch to her gut when Emily told her that she suspected Adam was having an affair. That wasn't possible. This was the perfect life. This was the life that she had dreamed of.

Emily stared at the view. "Lisa, as you're talking, I remember us in a diner: you, me, and a girl. You argued with her. You told her something."

Emily came back towards Lisa who was leaning against the back of the chair, still as a statue, waiting for her friend's reaction. "It's kind of hazy. Like I'm looking at an old sepia photograph with the edges all blurred out."

Relieved and scared, Lisa reached for her friend again. "Yes, you were there. I can't believe that you can see that. You remember. How is this possible?"

Just as Emily was about to answer the improbable question, they heard a knock on the door, and then it opened. Standing there, in his dark blue suit and white shirt, tie hanging loose around the collar, was Adam. "Honey, I'm home!" His smile lit up the room. Lisa beamed at the same time that she was terrified. She needed more time with Emily. She still didn't know the facts of her new life.

Adam reached her in three strides. "Babe, I've missed you so much. It feels like a lifetime since I last saw you."

Chapter 9

Adam wrapped his arms around her, leaning his cheek onto her head. He hugged her. She hugged him back tightly, holding on to him as if this were the first time that she was caught in his embrace. Like a long-lost lover, she welcomed him home. In his arms she felt the weight of disappointment, exhaustion, and confusion melt away. She stayed there, basking in this feeling that she didn't even know how to name. This wasn't a first embrace. She knew him.

Adam raised his head and leaned back slightly. He touched her chin, bringing her face close to his. He reached down and kissed her gently, tenderly.

This was a new first kiss. It was soft, a whisper really, as his lips brushed hers lightly, his eyes closed. Lisa kept hers open in wonderment. Still, as she willed herself to yield to this momentary bliss, her mind was racing. This kiss was different from all the others they'd shared. This kiss came with no regrets, no guilt, no reckless thoughts that in a few moments he'd have to leave. This kiss belonged to her. She had rights to his lips now. She closed her eyes and allowed her emotions to sweep her away. She floated, a disembodied ghost, watching herself kissing Adam, enjoying the scene, realizing that this kiss was her first as his wife. Like the scratch on a broken record, that thought jolted her back into her body. She stepped away from him, keeping her hands on his arms.

She opened her mouth to speak but uttered no sound. Adam laughed. "What's the matter, honey? My kiss still leaves you speechless, eh?" Lisa didn't know quite what to say. *Hi, I'm so glad you're mine now.* Those weren't exactly the words one said to one's husband. She stayed quiet, trying to figure out the next move.

Adam spoke first, sarcasm dripping from his voice. "Oh, hey there, Emily. I didn't see you standing there; happy to see me as usual?"

"Yes, it's always a pleasure."

"How's my dog?"

"Your dog is fine. Waiting for you to pick him up."

"I'll go over after I leave here tonight. As you can see, I'm busy visiting my wife." Adam turned his attention back to Lisa. "I didn't know you had company. I would have come later."

Lisa found her voice. "Emily isn't company, honey. She's family."

Adam took off his jacket. "Is there anywhere to hang this? I don't want it to get ruined." Lisa pointed to the tiny closet in the corner made for a patient's few belongings. She didn't remember him being fastidious, but then again, she didn't know him as a husband. Late night or afternoon trysts don't leave much room for finding out one's lover's neatness habits. The other Adam she knew was from the few visits to college. As she realized that she didn't know this man who was now her husband, Adam had hung up his jacket and sat down in one of the visitor chairs.

"So, what did I miss?" he asked no one in particular. He had a wide smile, but Lisa noticed that it didn't reach his eyes.

Emily spoke up first. "Not that you asked, but Lisa is feeling better."

Adam blinked and laughed nervously. "Of course I want to know how she's feeling. I assumed that since she was standing, obviously waiting for me, that she was feeling better." Adam turned his attention back to Lisa. "How are you feeling babe?"

Before Lisa had a chance to answer, Emily added, "Lisa and I were just talking about the children. Who's watching the girls?"

Adam crossed his legs and brushed a piece of lint off his trouser. "Thing One and Thing Two are both at choir practice. The nanny took them, Emily. You know that."

Lisa thought she detected a hint of annoyance in Adam's voice but wasn't sure. She felt as if she had been turned inside out. She dismissed the thought. She needed to focus. She was in this new reality. She had Adam, she had Emily, and she had daughters, even if she still didn't know their names. She wasn't going to let fears and insecurities dampen her joy.

Then a thought entered her mind. What if this wasn't permanent? What if it was only a dream? What if she traveled again? She could lose everything she had just gained. She shuddered involuntarily and rubbed her hands on her arms. She would analyze and obsess later after everyone had left, and she was alone.

She turned her attention back to Adam and Emily. She had to figure out a way to get information from Adam without divulging her secret. So far, he seemed fairly the same as before. Then again, she didn't know much about him as a family man.

"I've been in this hospital for so long, I feel like I don't know my daughters anymore." Lisa thought this sentence might be a good ruse to get some information. "What are they singing lately, honey?"

"Come on, dear. You know. The usual choir songs. Religious stuff, classical songs, whatever the school's choir director thinks is a good idea to teach third graders. I don't know. I don't pay much attention to that stuff. That's your domain." Adam reached his arms out to Lisa and gestured with his hands that he come to her.

"Come here. Sit down with me; I've been sleeping without you for years it seems. We can talk about the kids another time." Lisa walked over and sat on his lap. He ran his fingers through her hair and spoke tenderly. "Now, when are you coming home? What did the doctors say today?"

Before Lisa answered, Emily cleared her throat. "OK, well, since you're here now Adam, Lisa's in good hands, so I'm leaving."

She gathered her things and turned to Lisa. "Listen, buddy. You get some rest tonight. I'm going to go home and walk your dog." She pointedly looked at Adam with these last words. "We'll talk in the morning, OK? If they discharge you tomorrow, I'll come get you, and we can have lunch."

Lisa could tell that Emily had more to say but didn't want to speak in front of Adam. Emily walked a couple of steps to get close to Lisa to say goodbye. Lisa tried to get up from her perch on Adam to hug Emily, but he held tightly to her. A slight struggle ensued. It was imperceptible to anyone who would have been watching, but the air was thick with a vague discord.

Someone tapped on the door and opened it while speaking, "Hello, anybody home?" Stephanie appeared and stood in the threshold. "Oh, I'm sorry. I didn't realize you had company." Her face looked crestfallen when she saw Lisa sitting on Adam's lap. Emily moved her gaze from Stephanie to Adam and back like a ping pong game. Lisa, feeling inexplicably embarrassed, jumped up and walked away from Adam. "Come in, come in, you're not interrupting."

Adam stood up. Lisa noticed that he didn't take his eyes off Stephanie. He walked towards her, hand outstretched. "Hi, I'm Adam."

"You must be the famous husband. I'm Stephanie." They shook hands, but it seemed to Lisa that they held hands just a tad longer than customary. "I've heard so much about you from your wife."

"I hope she's telling good stories about me."

There was a familiarity to their banter that nagged Lisa. Did they recognize each other from the real past? She wasn't sure if it was her imagination or if they did have something between them. Stephanie seemed shy, but Lisa dismissed that idea. *You're making yourself crazy. This is all in your head. He's yours now; don't ruin this. This is a new beginning. You're the wife now. Not Stephanie. She's nobody.*

Emily joined in the introduction. "I'm Emily. Lisa's best friend." Emily seemed to emphasize "best" like a cat marking her territory.

Stephanie replied simply. "Hi, Emily."

Emily continued. "You look very familiar. Have we met before?"

Lisa shot her a dirty look, which Emily ignored.

"I don't think so, but you do look a little familiar."

Emily continued with a forced smile. "Well, maybe you have one of those faces that looks like others. But I just feel like we know each other. I run along the water in Hoboken. Do you run?"

Stephanie shuffled her feet and rubbed her hands together, definitely looking uncomfortable to Lisa. *Emily, stop it. What are you doing?*

Adam came to the rescue. "We're all of that certain age where we look like everybody else. But you must have come here to see your patient—right Stephanie, not to be interrogated by her best friend."

"Ummm. Yes, of course. Lisa, I wanted to tell you that the neurologist called a few minutes ago to say that he can't stop by tonight, but he'll be here in the morning to go over your test results."

"Did he tell you what's going on?" There it was. Time traveling and creating a different future hadn't changed the medical issues. Or maybe they had. Lisa wondered if the problem in this world was still an enlarged pineal gland, or was it something worse?

"He didn't say. He'll discuss it with you tomorrow." Stephanie smiled warmly, appearing more like the nurse that Lisa had gotten to know in her real life. "I also wanted to tell you that my shift is over, and I'm headed home. Good night. It was nice to meet you all."

With an odd feeling of relief that Stephanie was leaving, Lisa said, "Hey, have a great evening, and thanks for all your help. Got big plans for tonight?"

"Oh, no big plans. It's just me and my cat. I have leftovers and a good book, so it will be a great night." As she said this, Stephanie looked at Adam. They exchanged a brief look, so slight that it would have gone unnoticed except that Lisa was hyperaware. Emily glanced at Lisa and raised her eyebrows but said nothing.

Right after Stephanie walked out, Emily said goodbye. "I'm headed out too. You guys need time to yourselves, and I have a dog to feed and walk." She glared at Adam. "Don't bother to pick him up today. Wait until Lisa gets discharged. She could use good company at home."

"You're funny, Emily. I'm going to the bathroom. I'll let you two have your private chat behind my back."

After Adam walked out, Emily kissed Lisa on the cheek. She whispered, "I've got a feeling that he's messing around, and you need to stop being blind to him."

Lisa grabbed Emily's hands tightly. "Emily. Please. Don't do anything stupid. This is my chance to be happy. Finally. You know that in my world I've been wanting Adam to be mine alone for years. Don't ruin it for me."

Emily sighed. "Fine. I'll keep playing dumb for your sake. At least until we can talk more about this time traveling thing you're doing."

When Adam came back, Emily was already gone. "Oh, thank God, we're alone. I thought she'd never leave." Adam grabbed Lisa by the waist and kissed her on the neck, pretending to be devouring her.

"Why can't you get along with Emily?"

"Because she hates me, and I don't know why. She's the only woman I've ever met who doesn't like me."

He paused.

"Maybe she's a man-hating lesbian."

Lisa laughed, forgetting her worries. "Maybe you're an idiot, and she can see through you."

Adam fondled her breast. "When are you getting out of this hospital? You seem fine to me. Maybe we can just lock the door and...." He left the words hanging. Lisa was tempted. She stood on her tiptoes and kissed him, grabbing the back of his head, pushing his face towards her. The door opened, this time with the night nurse.

"Oh, my! Well, this isn't the place for hanky-panky, folks." They separated to opposite corners, like teenagers caught by the teacher at school.

Adam gathered his belongings while the nurse took Lisa's vitals for the evening. "Babe, I'm going to head out. I'm starved, the kids should be home soon, you know. I'll see you tomorrow." He looked at his watch.

Lisa was disappointed that he was leaving so soon, but she had a thermometer in her mouth. She mumbled, "Do you have to leave?" He kissed her on the top of her head and walked out. *Where is he off to in such a hurry?*

L isa tried calling Adam again on his cell phone. *Where could he be?* When she called the house, the nanny told her the kids were asleep already. Lisa was relieved. She wouldn't have known what to say to them if they were awake. *Hi, this is your mom who doesn't know you?* But Adam had rushed off.

Between time traveling and the excitement of realizing she was now Adam's wife and that the future was new, she was exhausted. She put down the book she had been pointlessly trying to read, *Time and Again.* Funny—someone in the time-space continuum had a sense of humor. She rearranged the pillows on the bed and lay down. *Maybe I should call Emily and talk to her some more?* But she was afraid of the answers Emily might have for her. Lisa had a nagging feeling that Adam's not answering the phone involved Stephanie. Maybe the pineal gland problem made her intuition more acute now. Maybe she was just paranoid. *Or maybe, I just know infidelity well enough to recognize it in others.*

She tossed and turned, and, after what seemed like hours, she decided to call Emily.

"This better be an emergency that no one at the hospital can solve." Emily whispered. "Have you fallen and can't get up?"

Lisa laughed. Even in the middle of the night, her friend had a sense of humor. "No, but I can't sleep. I thought you could help me?"

"You're funny. At this hour, I'm in bed too, but I'm sleeping. Or was, until you rudely interrupted my delicious dream."

"I'm sorry; I didn't mean to wake you."

"You have an odd way of showing that. Hold on. Let me get up. I don't want to wake…." Emily didn't finish her sentence.

The abrupt ending piqued Lisa's interest. "Em, who's there that you don't want to wake up?" No answer from the other side. "Em?"

Lisa could hear padded footsteps. "No one. I just don't want to wake up the cat. She'll get all crazy if I disturb her beauty sleep."

"When did you get a cat? I thought you were allergic to cats?"

"What gave you that idea? I love cats." Lisa heard the phone crackle while Emily walked. "I can talk now. Never mind my cat though. You said you need help? With what? I'm in the kitchen. Shall I make you a cup of tea?"

Lisa decided not to mince words. "Come to the past with me, Em."

"Ah, you did fall! And obviously cracked your head." Emily paused. "First, you tell me you time travel, and I indulge your fantasy, even though it's preposterous. Now you want me to go back in time with you. You've lost your mind."

"Maybe. But I think it would help."

"Help with what? Lisa, I've given you the benefit of the doubt when you say you went to the past, changed the future, and now Adam's your husband. Aren't you happy with that? Even if you could, why would you want to go back? Plus, if I were to believe this crazy story that you travel in time, wouldn't you be worried something could get messed up?"

Lisa could understand Emily's questions, but she was so focused on making things perfect with Adam that she wasn't really listening to the undertone of her friend's voice.

"It's always possible that life might change if I go back again. I don't know how it works, so I can't predict anything. I just know that I went back and forth a few times, and things have changed drastically. Now here I am, Adam's wife with two children, but our relationship still isn't right. I think there's a chance that if I go back again, I can get Stephanie out of our lives permanently. Or something else may change. But that could be good, don't you think?"

Emily was silent. Lisa tapped her fingernails on the bed rail while she waited. Then she heard a sigh.

"Lisa, you're my best friend, and you know I'd do anything for you, but I think this fantasy of yours that you travel back and forth through time is going a little far."

Emily's words were a punch in Lisa's stomach. "You...you...don't believe me?" she stammered.

"Honey, don't be upset with me. I know this isn't what you want to hear."

Lisa interrupted. "You're damn right I don't want to hear that my best friend doesn't support me."

The two women were silent until Emily spoke up again. "Lisa, it's the middle of the night, and neither of us is in any condition to make decisions, much less big ones. I'll visit you tomorrow, we'll get your test results, and we can figure out a plan for when you get out of the hospital. I'll even bring you a large chai from your favorite tea shop. I make no promises beyond that."

Lisa paced back and forth from the bed to the window, her steps loud in the quiet room. She hesitated in responding, realizing this wasn't the way to convince Emily to travel with her. Maybe she needed more time. To an outsider, of course, it was a crazy idea, but if she could only show her. "You're right. We'll talk in the morning, and I'll prove to you that I've traveled back in time."

Emily audibly sighed. "Please go to sleep. We'll sort it out tomorrow."

"You're right. Everything's better in the morning. Have a good night. But Em?"

"Now what, Lisa?"

"I still like chai."

"Well, that's a relief."

***

Stephanie arrived at the hospital with just a couple of minutes to spare before she started her morning shift. She was usually half an hour early, but today it was difficult to tear herself away from Adam's warmth in her bed. To her surprise, he had stayed the night, taking advantage of his wife being away. She meant to ask him what he told the children—then thought better of it. It wasn't her business how he handled his family life, was it? Maybe they didn't notice him gone, but didn't he help get them ready for school? That's what she would have liked in a husband if she had had one. Maybe the nanny is the one who takes care of the kids in the morning.

Stephanie shook her head to banish all these guilty thoughts. The truth is he spent the night, so they barely slept. With last night's passion, no one remembered to set the alarm clock, so they ran out of the house without breakfast, and she rushed, barely arriving at work on time.

But just remembering her amazing night kept her walking on air. She had exploded into a zillion little lights, and his arms were the only thing that made her whole again. The thought of those feelings made her smile as she walked towards her nurse's station.

The fact she'd see his wife in a few minutes wasn't going to get her down. As she read the patient charts for today, she noticed Lisa's MRI results had arrived and felt compelled to look at them. Nudging her was the suggestion Adam had made that it would be convenient if his wife stayed in the hospital longer. Would these results grant him that wish? She scrolled through the report. "Cross section analysis of brain...using contrast...no tumors or cysts...all normal...pineal gland enlarged...twice normal size...no other abnormalities noted."

Stephanie got a sour taste in her throat as she pictured the happy family reunited after Mommy had been in the hospital for so many days. Despite her best intentions, she couldn't help but feel she was going to be in this situation for the rest of her life—unless she took action to change it. Adam had promised so many times that he was working on a plan, but she was starting to suspect he was simply toying with her. Maybe all those women's blogs were right: *They never leave their wives, you know.* She could almost hear Oprah saying that.

The sound of another nurse's voice brought her back to reality. "Hey, Steph, you going to be long? Mind if I use your computer for a few minutes?"

Stephanie grinned at her coworker. "No problem, I'm done." With that, she started her morning rounds. No matter how many deep breaths she took, though, a large piece of her dreaded going into her lover's wife's room while she could still feel his hands caressing her.

***

Lisa sat up in bed, listening intently to the doctor explain her MRI results. Why did doctors show up at what felt like the crack of dawn? She had barely slept last night, tossing and turning with thoughts of going back to the past with Emily. And here was this guy telling her that her pineal gland was enlarged.

Lisa's voice rose audibly with concern. "Enlarged? What does that mean?"

"It means exactly that. It's a small gland in the back of your brain. Scientifically, it has no function, like an appendix. In prehistoric humans perhaps it had a purpose, but we don't know of any now. However, yours is twice the normal size. Now, an enlarged appendix could mean trouble. Usually those have to be removed surgically before they explode. But this? We're not sure what the enlargement means." The doctor paused with a grave look on his face—or so Lisa thought. "So, we need to keep an eye on it. Check it periodically to make sure there are no changes. Do you understand what I mean?"

Out of the corner of her eye, Lisa saw that Stephanie was standing in the room now, near the door, listening to the conversation. "Doctor, you're telling me that I have a gland in my brain that's double the normal size, and you have no idea why that's happened? Is that why I'm having these intense headaches?" *And is that why I can travel backwards and forwards in time?* she wondered silently.

"Mrs. Williams," the doctor paused again. "We don't have an explanation right now. Nothing else seems abnormal. It's possible that the headaches are caused by this enlargement, and it's possible that the enlargement could be benign cysts, but without further testing, we don't know. Unfortunately, while I can look at your scan, I think it's best that you seek the opinion of a specialist. I've already done some research, and there are several throughout the country. With your permission, I'm going to reach out to them and send them your medical records to see if any of them would be willing to examine you and follow up. Of course, we'd like to continue to see you, get another MRI here in three months, and see if there have been any changes."

Lisa wasn't sure what to think of all this. She was still trying to understand what this doctor was saying in comparison with her very real knowledge that she was moving across time. *Maybe this last trip caused my pineal gland to enlarge? Or maybe that's why I'm traveling in the first place? What came first?*

The doctor was talking again. "So, what do you say, Mrs. Scheiner? Do I have your consent to send the records?"

Lisa came back to reality. *Scheiner?* "Yes, yes, of course."

Stephanie jumped into the conversation. "Um, Doctor, I can have Mrs. Scheiner sign a consent form and send it to your office."

"Perfect," said the doctor. "Mrs. Scheiner, there's no reason to keep you here, so I'll sign the discharge orders, and you can go home. Please make sure that you schedule a follow-up test. Your nurse will give you all the instructions you need before you leave today. Do you have any questions?"

In a span of a few minutes, that was the second time that Lisa had been called Mrs. Scheiner. The significance of it didn't strike her until she heard it from Stephanie's mouth. She was Mrs. Scheiner now. The enormity of that made her smile broadly. "No questions; thanks for your help."

The doctor ended the conversation abruptly. "You're welcome. I'll see you in a couple of months. Your nurse will tell you how long it will take to get you ready to leave. You know hospitals—once we have you, we don't want to lose you." He laughed at his stupid joke and walked out.

Stephanie spoke first. "I'll take care of all the papers, and you can probably be out of here in an hour." She paused. "More or less. Probably more. I know, it takes a long time, as he said." Stephanie smiled. "At any rate, you'll be home with your family today. I'm sure you've missed them a lot."

Lisa noticed this Stephanie was just as kind as the one she met when she was first admitted to the hospital, which seemed like a lifetime ago. This time traveling was causing some strange twists that were hard to describe. Lisa's travels had taken Adam away from Stephanie. She had this uncanny feeling that this Stephanie might be sleeping with Adam, but she had no proof, just a hunch. A piece of her felt responsible for changing this woman's life so drastically, for taking away her entire family. If Lisa hadn't gone after Stephanie's husband, then Stephanie would have him now. Who was the real cheater, after all?

When she talked to Emily the night before, she wanted to go back and permanently get rid of Stephanie. But here, this morning, with the light of the sun streaming through the window, Lisa couldn't help but feel guilty. So maybe if Stephanie and Adam were having an affair, that was the price Lisa had to pay for being married to Adam. She had done something heinous, and now she was paying for it.

Maybe.

"I'll be back in a little while. Do you need anything?"

Lisa wondered whether the way to get to the bottom of what was going on with Adam and Stephanie, if anything, was to get closer to Stephanie. "No, Stephanie, thank you. You've been very kind. I was thinking just now that I'm going to miss you. I've gotten used to seeing you every day and having our little chats."

"Oh…no, don't…umm. I'm not kind. Believe me. I'm going to miss you too."

Lisa continued. "Maybe after I'm discharged, we could grab a coffee or lunch one of these days while my kids are in school?"

Stephanie raised her eyebrows as she listened to Lisa. "Well…" She hesitated. "Sure. We could do that, once you're no longer a patient, there's no problem in getting together. Just give me a call."

Lisa smiled. *This was definitely the way to get more information.* "I'll do that. After I'm home and settled, I'll get in touch. I don't have many girlfriends. It'd be nice to have another woman to chat with, you know, about life and everything."

Stephanie smiled again. "Absolutely. That'd be great. One can never have enough friends." She turned and walked out the door without another word, almost bumping into Emily, who had appeared from nowhere.

"Good morning, ladies! What a beautiful day, right?" Emily was at her most annoying when she was joyful in the morning.

"Excuse me," said Stephanie and left abruptly.

"I guess that's the one you wanted to erase last night?" Emily whispered as she approached Lisa's bed.

"Stop! Someone will hear you say that!" Lisa giggled nervously. "Come in. I'm being discharged today. Your timing is perfect. You can get me out of here, and we can go talk somewhere privately, so I can convince you I'm telling you the truth."

Emily closed the door as Lisa started changing into her street clothes. Emily walked over to the tray table and put down the cup she was carrying. "I brought you tea."

Lisa had her back to Emily as she got dressed. "Thanks, that's so sweet of you."

"Why are they discharging you? Did they figure out there's nothing wrong with you? That you're just bat-shit crazy?"

"What are you talking about? I'm not crazy. And yes, I got the results. My pineal gland is super huge; they don't know why; I need to follow up with a specialist. But I don't know if I want to do that. I don't want it changed. I think that's the reason I can time travel."

Emily plopped herself down on the chair and took a sip of her own tea. "No, Lisa. You have to follow up. You can't walk around with something wrong with your brain."

"Em, I can time travel. I will prove it to you. I just don't know how yet. But for now, just get me home. Help me figure out my family. You're the only person who knows that I don't know anyone or anything in this new world. Whether you think I'm insane or not, at least you know that. So, give me a hand, will you?"

Emily took another sip of her tea and stared at her friend. She sighed, and stood up, helping her to pack her few belongings. "OK, but somehow I'm afraid that this helping you figure things out is going to get me in trouble."

Lisa laughed, for what seemed like the first time in a long time. She was headed home to *her* Adam and *her* new family. Thoughts of a possible Stephanie and Adam slipped from her mind for a minute. This was her new chance.

Chapter 10

R iding in Emily's car, with the top down, Lisa's eyes teared up from the loveliness of a gorgeous sunny day with its impeccably blue sky. Emily had an extra hair band, so that Lisa's hair could stay under some control as the wind whipped it around.

She tried yelling. "Emily, I need your help. I have questions."

"What?! I can't hear you."

Lisa put her hand on Emily's. "Pull over." With gestures, Lisa was able to make herself understood. There was a field nearby, and Emily drove into it, parking the car in a nearby spot.

"All right, Lisa, what do you want to talk about? Going to the past again?"

"Yes...no...I mean. I need your help. I don't know what I'm headed into. I don't know my daughters' names. I've never been to this house. I don't know anything, Em. Do you understand that?"

Emily looked incredulous. "You mean you were serious when you said that before?"

"Of course I was serious! Why would I make that up?"

"I don't know. I've never had a friend who comes back from the past." Emily swallowed hard and grabbed Lisa's hand. "Why don't we go for a walk, and I can answer your questions."

As they got out of the car, Lisa felt a rush of relief. Was Emily was believing her now?

The park Emily had picked had a man-made lake in the center. In the middle of the lake, a water fountain intermittently spouted a stream high into the air. An asphalt path with a stone border circled the lake, surrounded by woods full of tall oak trees. The ground was covered in wildflowers of all types: daisies, sunflowers, hyacinths, pansies. It looked like someone had run around with seeds and strewn them everywhere to create a painting of riotous colors—blues, purples, yellows, pinks—no organization, no pattern, just joyful colors and scents. Not a single cloud interrupted the bright blue of the sky.

Emily locked arms with Lisa, like they used to do in college, and they walked along the path. "OK, girlie. What do you want to know?"

"Well, for starters, tell me about my daughters. What are they like? I have only one picture of them in my cell phone, but I don't know how old they are, their names, their school. I know nothing about these children that I supposedly gave birth to. Why don't I have pictures?" Lisa's lip trembled as the enormity of what she didn't know hit her again.

"How am I supposed to know why you don't know any of this? I'm not the time traveler. Isn't there a manual for that somewhere?"

Emily was trying to joke, but this was no laughing matter. "This isn't funny. I need serious help." One solitary tear rolled down her cheek. "Please. All I ever wanted was Adam and a family with him. Finally, I have it. And I know nothing about it. It's as if I've been living my life somewhere else, and now I'm back here and don't remember anything. I don't want to screw up anything to lose it. As it is, I'm already scared that he's cheating on me."

Emily took a deep breath. "I'll tell you as much as I know. But remember that I'm not there all the time. There will be inside jokes and things you all share that I know nothing about. If you really can't remember, you may have to ask Adam directly. If he wonders why you don't know, then just blame it on your brain episodes. Deal?"

She nodded her head in agreement. "Now let me have it."

As they walked, Lisa noticed several women pushing babies in strollers. One pair of friends talked animatedly while their toddlers ran ahead, gleeful as children tend to be, carefree and joyous. Lisa tried to pay attention to Emily but repeatedly got distracted by the sight of so many mothers and their children. As they neared the playground, Lisa saw a woman pushing a young boy on a swing. She could tell she was his mother by the way she kissed the top of his head each time she caught the swing to push him back. He squealed with delight at the affection, threw his arms in the air and yelled, "Again!" In front of them, a man who seemed to be the father, took pictures. He laughed when he heard the boy's cries.

Lisa stopped to watch them. The boy was about four years old with curly brown hair and ruddy cheeks. His little fists pumped the air, and he threw his head back as the swing moved back and forth. "Higher! Higher!" he yelled.

The wind picked up, and blew Lisa's hair into her face, momentarily obscuring her sight. Her thoughts swirled, and her feet felt unsteady, as if she were spinning, but she knew she was standing still. She realized she'd been feeling like this since joining this version of reality. That's how this felt, like a different reality, as if nothing were normal. Unsteady and needing something solid to tie her to this present, Lisa gripped Emily's hand and pointed at the child. "Isn't he cute?" Emily said.

Tears trickled down Lisa's cheeks as she watched the tender family scene, and the words came unbidden. With a trembling voice, she said, "That could have been Marcus and me if our son had lived."

With eyes wide open and a questioning look on her face, Emily turned towards her friend. "Who's Marcus? What son?"

The questions jolted Lisa. How was this happening? Her entire life had been erased, so now who was she? She had memories of a life that apparently hadn't occurred. She had been sure that Emily would remember also. But who was this Emily then? And what was she walking into by going to her new house? She didn't know these children that she now had. The memory of her baby boy came alive and pulled her like a magnet. She felt a pain so strong she doubled over, wrapping her arms as if trying to hold her insides together while she sobbed inconsolably.

Emily held her and moved them away, towards a bench on the other side of the park. They sat there for a while until Lisa stopped crying. Tenderly, Emily asked, "Better?"

Sniffling, Lisa searched for a tissue in her purse while she tried to find the words to tell her friend about the enormity of what she had realized. "Yes, I'm better now. Just terrified." She didn't think that this Emily would understand the depth of her feelings. How could she? This Emily didn't even know Marcus or the baby. Lisa took a deep breath and exhaled. "I don't remember anything you know, and you don't remember my past life even though you were a part of it. I've lost my compass." She paused. "I'm scared, Em."

Emily grew serious. "You'll be fine. You've always been a quick study, and this is no different than taking an exam. The only thing is that you'll have live subjects as part of the tests."

Lisa could tell that Emily was avoiding the subject of a past she didn't know. She decided not to pursue it for now. Later, after she acclimated herself to this new world, she'd talk to Emily about it again. In the meantime, she had to move forward. She stood up, blew her nose, adjusted her hair, and steeled herself to face this storybook life. She poked Emily in the arm. "You think you're so funny. Not!"

Emily looked at her watch before opening the car doors. "Let's get you home, and we can figure out the rest. The girls will be back from school soon. The bus drops them off at the corner. The nanny usually picks them up if you're not home, but maybe today you can get them. I'll be with you, so you'll know which ones they are." Emily paused in her explanation as she started driving. "I can't believe I'm having this conversation with you. Are you sure it's not that you just hit your head in that car accident, and you have amnesia? Should I take you back to the hospital?"

***

Emily drove down a pretty, suburban street lined with trees. There were big and small houses, nicely spaced apart with ample room for gardens and trees. The lawns were impeccable with row after row of colorful flowers. Lisa thought it was beautiful but at the same time had a nagging feeling that it was all too manicured and perfect, like when she was a child and her mother returned from the hairdresser with a can of hairspray in her hair to ensure not one strand was out of place for days. Something felt off, but Lisa couldn't put her finger on it.

As if reading her thoughts, Emily said just then, "Don't be nervous. It will all be fine."

Emily pulled into a circular driveway leading to the biggest house, featuring light brick with mustard yellow shutters and a red front door. Lace curtains adorned the windows, each curtain parted perfectly so. The roof was made of burnt orange Spanish tiles. From the outside it looked like a center hall colonial with a huge attached garage that fit three cars. One garage door was open, revealing a spotless space painted light yellow, with carpet on the floor. The garden, like all the others on this street, looked like it was tended to by professionals. Not one thing was out of place.

Lisa stayed in the car for a minute or so, staring at the house, at the driveway, taking it all in. "What's with the carpet on the garage floor?"

"That's Adam's garage for his Corvette. It is too precious to sit on mere concrete. Your housekeeper vacuums it every time he leaves the house in that car." Lisa could hear the note of disapproval in Emily's voice.

As they walked to the front door, Lisa realized she had no key. "What do we do now? Ring the doorbell?"

"We'll just say that you lost your keys in the hospital. I'm sure the help has a spare."

Lisa raised both eyebrows. "The help? Emily, are we rich?"

As she answered, Emily pushed the doorbell. "Not we, dear. You and Adam are rich. You're just slumming by being my friend."

A short woman with a neat bun of dark hair answered the door. She was slim and wore a simple black dress as a uniform. "Oh, Mrs. Scheiner, you're finally home! I'm so glad you're well again. We were so worried." She stepped aside to let them into a massive foyer. "Please, let me take your bag to your room. Hello, Miss Emily."

"Hello, Zelda. Nice to see you again."

As Zelda ran up the stairs, Emily led Lisa around the first floor of the house. She looked at her watch quickly. "It looks like we have about half an hour before Zelda picks up the girls. Let's just give you a quick tour of the house, so you know where to find things. If you get lost, just blame it on the headaches."

Lisa nodded without speaking. She was dumfounded by the sheer height of the ceilings, by the pretty light wood throughout, and by all the antique furniture. Each room was painted a different color—some bright, some pastels. All the ceilings were white, giving—at least this floor—a sense of connectedness. The living room was pale green with a large Persian rug that dominated the center. Double doors led to an enormous dining room with a table that sat at least twenty people.

"Do we entertain that much that we have such a large table?" Lisa asked.

"No. I've never eaten in this dining room. You don't like it. Your decorator made you buy that furniture. She's the one who decided you needed a multi-color house that doesn't match the Spanish exterior."

Lisa ignored the sarcasm dripping from Emily's voice. "I have a decorator?"

"Mhmm. Monique. She goes by one name. Very posh, or at least she thinks so. A family of four could live for a year on what that dining room table cost."

From the dining room they walked into a bright, airy kitchen. It connected to a den with comfortable couches, a large television set, and plants in every corner. Toys were scattered around. Clearly this was where the children spent their time. The windows looked out onto the backyard with an indoor pool, an outside kitchen, a tiki bar, a fenced grassy area with a swing set, and a wooden castle. Lisa couldn't believe how different this was from her former life. Obviously, they spared no expense in this house. The kitchen was state of the art with white cabinets, blue and yellow tile, and dishes that matched the walls. Who has dishes that match the walls?

Lisa stood in the middle, mouth wide open, unable to fathom that this is what she had come into. She didn't even know where to start. But she turned from staring out the double doors that led to the backyard when she heard wild squeals and running steps. "Mommy, Mommy, you're home!"

Two blonde girls ran into her, hugging her waist at the same time. They squeezed her and jumped simultaneously, both about the same height, faces turned up to look at her. She almost fell back from their impact. Her heart thumped wildly and sweat ran down her back. She couldn't understand why she felt hot and uncomfortable. She watched these children in disbelief wondering who they were, momentarily forgetting she was supposed to be their mother.

That's what this all felt like—as if she was supposed to be living in this world, but she was merely a visitor. Maybe not even that, more like an intruder. The clock on the kitchen wall ticked loudly. Every sound was amplified. With the girls still holding on to her, Lisa contemplated whether she should touch them. These children were strangers, but they seemed to love her. The only other adult in the room was Emily, and she looked mildly amused with a tinge of wistfulness. Lisa felt as if she were supposed to be doing something, responding somehow to this outpouring of affection but she didn't know where to start. She held her arms in the air like airplane wings as if wishing hard enough would help her fly away from these unexpected and unknown emotions. Her face whipped from one side to the other, desperate for some direction.

Emily came to her rescue with a quick step. "Suzette, Natalie! Be gentle. You're going to push your mother to the ground!"

The girl who answered to Suzette was the older one, a little taller than her sister with bright blue eyes and curls escaping from the lopsided barrettes on each side of her head. "But we've missed her, Auntie Emily! She was in the hospital, and Daddy wouldn't take us to see her, so we want to just love her." Natalie ignored Emily and continued to hold on to Lisa. In her slight lisp, she whispered, "Mommy, I missed you. I love you so, so much."

The child's words tore at Lisa. She lowered her arms and rubbed Natalie's back. In a trembling voice, hoping this is what mothers did, she said quietly, "Honey, I missed you too." Lisa watched herself as if she were an actor playing a part. She didn't know how she was going to do this, but this is what she had wanted, right? She closed her eyes for a moment, losing herself in a tenderness that was so new to her. She opened them when she heard Suzette scream, "Daddy!" Smiling, Adam bent down, picked up his daughter, and walked towards Lisa and Natalie. He kissed Lisa's cheek. "Welcome home, babe."

Lisa froze with the realization that she was here and had no clue what to do next.

Chapter 11

In unison, the girls chanted in singsong, "Mommy, Mommy! Snack time! Snack time!" Suzette wriggled out of her father's arms, forcing Adam to put her down, so she could run to Lisa. "What are you making today? My favorite, please!" Her little voice was shrill in that high octave of the young before their voices change to accommodate growing up. Lisa's heart beat so fast she felt it was going to pop out of her chest. She looked around at the adults in the room, hoping for a clue of what she was supposed to do, but Zelda had left the kitchen earlier. Emily only shrugged her shoulders, and Adam didn't seem to notice her silent plea. Lisa could hear the clock ticking as if it were on a high-fidelity speaker. Beaming at his daughter, Adam bent towards Lisa and whispered in her ear, "Don't you think you should get started, dear?"

Lisa felt all four pairs of eyes on her while she struggled to decide what to make. She didn't know where to start or how to be a mother, much less surprise children with a snack after school. She tried to remember her own childhood. What would her mother have done?

She tried to calm herself. She had yearned for family, and children needed to be fed, so she was going to make this work. With a determined step, she walked towards the refrigerator to see if its contents would spark an idea. Holding the door wide open, pretending to be in charge, nothing jumped out at her. There was the usual: vegetables, turkey, mayonnaise, ketchup, milk, cheese. Everything you'd expect in a typical fridge. She looked back at the family that seemed weirdly frozen in expectation when an idea came through. With a broad smile, she took out the jar of mayonnaise and bottle of ketchup and placed them on the counter. She wanted to find saltines, but this kitchen was so huge, she had no idea where to start looking. She decided she'd play the "I just got out of the hospital" card and put her hands to her head.

Arms loaded with still-warm kitchen towels from the laundry room, Zelda walked back into the kitchen towards Lisa. "Mrs. Scheiner. Are you all right? Let me help you. You've been through a lot lately. What are you looking for?"

Bless Zelda for coming to her rescue. "I'm sorry. I seem to have forgotten where we keep crackers? How silly of me, right?"

Zelda, with her straight-backed primness and confident efficiency, marched like a soldier with a mission towards a cabinet. She opened the door to reveal an assortment of crackers and snacks that rivaled an aisle in a supermarket. Lisa stood behind her and pointed to the box of plain saltines. "Those, that's what I want."

Both girls ran over. "We want to help! We want to help, Mommy!"

Lisa looked at Zelda again, eyes begging for more help. Like a saint, Zelda pulled out a bowl, spoons, and plates. "Here you go, Mrs. Scheiner. Is there anything else you need?" Unlike her dour appearance, her tone was gentle and kind. "I can do this for you if you give me directions, so you can take a rest."

"No, thank you, Zelda. I think I have everything."

Feeling as if this were a test on how to be a mother, Lisa faced her daughters. "Girls, sit down, and I'll surprise you with my favorite snack that my mother made for me."

"You mean Grandma?"

Lisa swallowed hard. Grandma? Lisa hadn't thought of her mother in a long time, and never as a grandma. She'd been dead for so long that Lisa was used to thinking of her only in the past. Did this odd world contain a mother for her? Best to play it safe until she had more information. "Yes, your grandma made this for me when I was your age. Now go, go, and wait for me in your favorite chairs."

Lisa grabbed the mayonnaise and ketchup, mixed them in a bowl, spread the mix on saltines, and made little sandwiches. While she did this, Zelda placed small plates on the counter for her. She turned to the table and set placemats before the girls. "Now remember that we have manners, so we keep our elbows off the table and wait for your mother to finish." Like little soldiers, the girls sat up straight, grinning from ear to ear, waiting patiently for Lisa to finish.

As her first mother job, Lisa was so proud that she had thought on her feet. She brought over the two plates and set them before the children. "Here you go, my lovelies. Yummy sandwiches!"

Suzette and Natalie looked down at their plates, frowned and stared at Lisa. "What's this?"

Suzette picked up a saltine, examining it closely by twirling it in her fingers, then sniffing it. She made a sour face and declared loudly, "This is disgusting."

Natalie chimed in. "Don't be rude Suzie. Mommy made this with love. You have to eat it. Remember we eat everything that's put on our plate, right, Zelda?" Zelda nodded somberly. Still smiling at Zelda, Natalie leaned over to her sister and half covering her mouth with her chubby hand whispered, "Even if it's gross."

Feeling like she had to salvage this moment, Lisa smiled brightly, though her heart was sinking. "Why don't you try it before you decide?" She took a cracker sandwich and bit into it. "See? Delicious!" She turned to Adam, eyes pleading for help.

Adam took his cue. "Wow, this is wonderful, babe." He munched with a smile, but Lisa could see him grimace. "Girls, try it. You'll like it."

The girls didn't look convinced. Lisa left the kitchen, tears streaming down her cheeks. She walked into the unused dining room, with Adam on her heels. He took her in his arms, kissing her tears away. "Babe, don't be upset."

Silently, she sank into his warm arms, grateful for this respite, for a sense of normalcy. Adam was all she knew. She snuggled her face into his neck while he held her, closing her eyes and forgetting the awkwardness of the kitchen scene. Wishing this moment could last forever, she drifted off into the fragrance of his skin. The embrace was broken with a tug on her skirt that she tried to ignore. The tugger, however, was insistent.

Suzette's persistence snapped her to attention. "Mommy, I don't like your surprise snack." Lisa tore herself away from Adam, disliking this tiny voice that was sorely interfering with her dream. Reluctantly, she bent down to the child. Something softened in her when she saw the little girl's lips quivering. "It's yucky. I don't like it, Mommy."

Lisa crouched down onto her heels and wiped the tears from the child's face, realizing that this was supposed to be her daughter. She searched inside herself and found empathy for this child looking for solace. "Oh, sweetheart, I'm sorry. Why don't you tell me what you'd like, and I'll make it for you?"

Disappointment apparently forgotten, Suzette skipped off towards her sister in the kitchen. "Nope. Too late. I'm going to play with Natalie." She turned around mid-way and yelled out. "But, tomorrow, Pop-Tarts!"

Adam burst out laughing, grabbed Lisa's arm and helped her up. "Babe, you can't win with kids. Don't worry." He hugged Lisa tightly, kissing her temple and caressing her hair. He felt so strong and safe. She was starting to like this life again when he pulled away from her with a sharpness that felt like a needle scratching on a record.

"I hate to do this to you, hon, but I have to get ready to go. I have a big client dinner tonight. I know it's your first night back, but you understand, don't you? Clients come first, right?" He smiled with that toothy grin Lisa loved, but she couldn't believe he was leaving her already.

"Wait. I just got here. Can't you reschedule?" She hated the pleading sound in her voice.

"Lisa, it's a big client, and I can't say that my wife needs me to stay home to keep her company. You have the kids to keep you busy, and Emily's here. She can give you a hand if you're not up to it."

Emily was talking to Zelda. Adam yelled out, "Hey, Em. You don't mind staying for dinner with Lisa, do you?"

Emily glared at Adam, opened her mouth as if to say something, closed it, took a deep breath, and said, "Of course. My pleasure."

As Adam walked off, Lisa felt more lost than ever. The girls were playing in the backyard, and Zelda had turned her attention to chores and to making dinner preparations. Lisa stood in the dining room, staring off vacantly, wondering how she was going to make this marriage, this family, work. She was drowning in an unexpected emptiness. Where was the happiness that she was sure she'd find when she was married to Adam? True, she hadn't anticipated children so quickly, much less a fully formed family, but she figured this would be easy. She loved him. Isn't that all that was needed? Maybe this was a mistake? Maybe she had done this wrong? Maybe she should go back and make it better? But how? As her mind swirled with these thoughts, she felt a hand take hers.

That's when she noticed Emily at her side. "Hey, buddy, are you OK? Do you need to lie down?"

Her friend's hand in hers brought her to the present like a rush of wind. "I'm fine. I'll be fine. I'm just...totally lost right now." A solitary tear ran unbridled down her cheek. "Oh, Em. This isn't what I expected."

"You're tired. These have been long, difficult days. Why don't you lie down and get some rest? Zelda's got dinner and the girls under control. I'll stick around until Adam comes home." Under her breath, she muttered, "If he comes home."

Lisa heard her. "What do you mean?"

"Nothing, honey. I meant nothing by that. You're just confused with all this homecoming stuff. Let me show you where the bedroom is. I'm sure some quiet time will make you feel right as rain."

Like a child weary from a tantrum, Lisa let her friend lead her upstairs.

***

The stairs to the second floor were grand and sweeping with dark wood that gleamed from persistent cleaning and waxing. Lisa marveled at the shine, not a speck of dust in sight, as she caressed the polished wood on the banister. How could anything be this spotless? As if she could hear her thoughts, Emily said, "Don't worry. You're not responsible for this. A cleaning crew comes once a week."

They walked into a spacious hallway with several identical white doors. Not knowing which one was her bedroom, Lisa gave Emily a questioning glance. Emily shrugged her shoulders and moved her towards a door that was slightly ajar. From inside they could hear Adam singing in the shower.

Pointing in the direction of the sounds, Lisa said, "I guess that's my bedroom?"

"That's your man there, babe. I'll be in a guest room if you need me." As she walked away, she added. "Last door at the end of the hall."

Hesitantly, Lisa pushed open the door and entered a huge bedroom that looked more like a living room than sleeping quarters. The walls were painted a grayish pink. A four-poster, wrought iron, king-size bed reigned in the middle of the room with a comforter and sheets that were golden hued and silky, strewn about carelessly as if lovers had just walked away from it. To one side was a sitting area with mahogany bookcases and a teak coffee table with a now cold porcelain teapot, an empty cup, and a plate with crumbs, evidence that Adam had eaten breakfast there at some point. A crystal vase of white peonies vied for attention at a spacious writing desk near a large window that overlooked a tall oak tree. A short hallway with more doors opened to the left of the desk. Lisa ventured towards them, opening each door to discover walk-in closets the size of her former life's bedroom. One was filled with dark suits, collared shirts, and men's shoes, the other with a dizzying array of dresses, skirts, blouses, designer bags, and high-heeled shoes. Lisa wandered in her closet, touching everything until Adam's voice startled her. He stood in the threshold, still wet from his shower, wearing only a pale blue towel around his waist. His hair sleek from water, she noticed his corkscrew curls escaping where he had tucked them behind his ears. She wondered why she noticed such a detail, even while mesmerized by the opulence around her.

His voice was smooth. "Going somewhere tonight while I'm out?" he asked.

She cocked her head to one side, momentarily forgetting that until now she didn't know her surroundings. Like an explorer in unknown terrain, her senses felt more acute than ever. His face was closely shaven, and he smiled at her with a satisfied look. Behind him, the door to his closet was open, and she noted that he had hung a dark blue pinstripe suit and crisp white shirt on a hook, apparently what he was wearing to his dinner meeting. His dark eyes were bright with a dash of mischief. She could smell his delicious cologne, musky, aromatic. Like an animal with heightened senses, she could also smell deceit.

She shrugged her shoulders in response to his question. "I'm just looking around to see if anything's changed while I was gone." He approached her, pulling her to him and kissing her neck. "I'm going to miss you so much tonight. Forgive me that I'm leaving you?" he murmured tenderly.

Lost in his embrace, she responded softly. "Of course I forgive you. But do you really have to go? When will you be home?" As she said the words, she heard herself sound whiny and pleading.

He stepped away and went to the closet. As he started to dress, he threw out a casual reply, "I'll be home as soon as possible, but this client likes to eat and drink, and the client comes first. So, knowing him, I'll be home very late. Don't wait up for me."

Feeling oddly shy while he dressed, Lisa stepped away and sat on the sofa by the coffee table. "Don't worry about me. I'll find something to do."

He laughed. "Are you kidding? With those two kids, you're always complaining that your hands are full!"

Lisa shrugged, not sure how to respond. She casually turned the pages of a photography book on the coffee table. Who was the photography buff? Her or Adam? She was a mother now. She should know she'd be busy with two young children in the house. There was probably homework to be done. And dinner. And chores? In this house with a bevy of servants, did those girls even know what a chore was? How was she going to take care of all this? She hadn't known these children when they were babies, and it had been forever since she'd changed a diaper. Motherhood is learned by experience, with trial and error, and she'd had next to none. How was she supposed to know what to do?

Her mind wandered to Marcus. A snarky voice in her head told her he wouldn't have left her alone on the first night of coming back from the hospital. He would have known what to do with children. He was one of four siblings. She remembered that he had been so excited about the baby; he had made lists and plans. She wondered if she could find him in this world. Maybe she could call him and ask him? She shook her head at the silliness of this thought. Still, it persisted.

"Adam, do you remember Marcus?"

She could hear Adam mumbling in the closet. He walked out with a pair of socks and shoes in his hands, grimacing. "That nerd you dated once? Why are you asking about him now?"

Lisa continued to feign interest in the book as she mindlessly turned the pages. "I just wondered if you knew where he was. He popped into my head recently, and I just…you know, wondered what had become of him."

"I have no idea where your ex-boyfriends may be, Lisa. What kind of stupid question is that?" He sat down in a chair to put on his shoes. "And why the hell are you wondering about an ex now?"

Lisa could hear the note of frustration in his voice. Not wanting to start an argument, she changed the subject. "Never mind. Just silly thoughts."

Dressed and ready to go, Adam kissed Lisa on the top of her head. "Why don't you stop thinking of old flames and just take a nap. The kids will only be entertained but so long with Zelda. Pretty soon they'll be clamoring for your attention, and then you'll start complaining as usual."

With that, he turned and walked out the door.

L isa sighed deeply. She'd been in this house for less than two hours, and already she was lonely, if not regretful. Turning to the unmade bed, she decided to heed the advice and lay down on the side closest to her. As she curled into the soft covers, she drifted off to sleep, wondering again what Marcus would say if he were here.

***

The first thing Lisa did when she woke up from her nap was look for a clock. She felt like she had been sleeping for hours, but the sounds of laughing children in the house told her it wasn't as late as she thought. She lay back and wondered what came next. She should get up and figure out the dinner routine. Zelda had been helpful with the snack fiasco, so maybe she could continue to play the amnesia victim to learn about her family from the housekeeper.

She started by trying to figure out which side of the bed was hers. One quick look at the nightstand next to her answered her question.

It was stacked with books filled with bookmarks with drawings by the kids. There was a teak meditation clock, assorted pens, a notebook, and a small vase with tissue flowers, also clearly child-made. In contrast, the other nightstand held nothing but a coaster made of cork holding a half-empty glass of water. Obviously, she had lain on her side of the bed. As she was about to hunt in the drawer for more clues, she was interrupted by the door banging open and a rush of children's arms and legs tossed on her, jumping wildly on the bed, bending down with each bounce to kiss her face and her hands. They laughed and squealed with delight, carrying her away in a smothering of love. Lisa joined them, adding a tickle fight to the melee. Emily stood near the door, watching with arms crossed, smiling. She made her voice loud to be heard above the fracas. "See? I told you a nap would make things better!"

"Mommy, get up, get up! It's dinner time. Zelda made the best!"

More tickles ensued while Lisa asked slyly, "Oh yeah? What's the best?"

Both girls screamed in unison, "Chicken nuggets!"

Lisa looked at Emily and mouthed, "What?"

Emily laughed and came closer to grab one child from the bed. "Don't worry. The chicken nuggets are for the kids. Zelda made something better for the grown-ups."

Natalie kept tickling Lisa, and Suzette tried to make Emily join the fun. "Who says we're grown-ups?" Lisa asked between spasms of laughter.

***

Dinner over, Lisa had the girls help clean up the kitchen, then sat with them to finish the last bits of homework. Emily joined them in the family room to watch a Disney movie before Lisa got them ready for bed. There were baths, pajama selection issues, and story time. Then tucking in and kisses goodnight and, "One more kiss please, Mommy," and, "One more drink of water, please." Lisa felt she had been working a full day by the time she got downstairs and joined Emily with a glass of wine. She looked at her phone and saw that it was past nine o'clock already with no word from Adam as to when he was returning.

Emily sipped her drink quietly while Lisa stared at the phone. "Maybe I should find out what time he'll be home?"

Emily cleared her throat. "Didn't he tell you not to wait up for him? That you have me here to entertain you?"

"He was serious about that?"

"Didn't I tell you I have a guest room in your house? Did you think I was joking?" Emily looked at Lisa closely as if seeing her friend for the first time. "You really don't remember anything about your home, your marriage, and your children? Is it the pineal gland thing you have?"

Lisa rubbed her hands on her face, searching for the right words. They came out in a breathless rush as if speed would make Emily believe her. "Emily, I wasn't kidding about the time travel. Maybe the pineal gland has something to do with it. I don't know. It sounds like a lot, but it's true. I remember my old life. I was married to Marcus, but I was having an affair with Adam, who was married to Stephanie. They were the ones with two kids. I went back to our college days, interrupted Adam and Stephanie, and you were with me. And now I'm here, in this new life that has everything I ever wanted, except Adam's just as elusive now as he was when he wasn't my husband." She paused. "And now I feel guilty about Stephanie being all alone, and Marcus. I don't even know what happened to him."

Emily put down her glass and draped her arm over her friend's shoulder. "I don't know how to help you." She paused, brows furrowed in thought. "I do know that Adam is out a lot. He spends most days out of the house, returning late. You complain about that to me all the time. I spend a lot of time here with the girls, but you've been a good mother, even if a bit indulgent."

She paused again, took a deep breath and continued. "I don't know if I understand this time travel thing you keep talking about, but I will believe you and try to help you. But know this, Lisa. Whatever you thought you'd have here with Adam, I can tell you from what I've seen, it's not that good. You've even told me you've considered divorce, but the girls keep you here." She added more softly. "And the money."

Lisa listened intently, trying to absorb her new reality to reconcile it with the past. She picked up the phone and dialed Adam's number. It rang then went to voicemail as if he had declined the call. She repeated this a few times, until the call went immediately to voicemail. Now it seemed he had turned off the phone.

She had just as little control here as she did in her other life.

Chapter 12

Lisa put her phone down in exasperation, convinced Adam had turned his off. She recalled he did that in the past when his wife, Stephanie, called repeatedly. She didn't know what explanation he concocted back then when he returned home. Now, she was the one with no idea when he'd be back or even where he was. The telltale signs were clear.

The ice in her glass clinked as she twisted it. "I think he's with Stephanie. He used to turn the phone off when he was with me."

Emily stood up and gazed out the window, staring into the night. "You talk as if you knew him in some past life."

Lisa slammed the glass on the table with more force than she intended. "Don't you see? That's exactly what I've been saying to you. This is the same pattern only now, it's reversed. I'm the one waiting for him at home."

The house was quiet. With the girls asleep, Zelda had also retired, having left the kitchen spotless, ready for the morning's onslaught of children and the busyness of preparing for school. Somewhere a clock ticked loudly, although Lisa couldn't discern from where the sound came. There were so many rooms in this unfamiliar and strange land-scape, and she still hadn't explored the entire house. Like a visitor from another country, Lisa glanced around, trying to discover where she fit in if she did at all. With trembling hands, she reached for the glass once more, hoping the wine would calm her. Emily was a consolation, but

Lisa still felt as if she were drifting aimlessly from the shore, floating farther and farther away with nothing and no one to ground her.

Her mother's face appeared just then, looking the same way she did on the day she told Lisa her father had died. She remembered every detail as if it had happened yesterday.

Lisa was in Mrs. Tarantino's fourth grade class. The children were returning from lunch, still giddy with excitement from the games at recess. Mrs. Tarantino's gentle, firm voice ordered them to settle down, and as they were finding their seats, Lisa felt a shiver, looked up, and saw her mother standing in the classroom's doorway. She looked disheveled, her hat crooked, wisps of hair strewn about her face. Her usually perfect makeup was streaked with blotches of mascara around her eyes, and her nose was red. Lisa stood stock-still at her desk. The only time she'd come to school during the day before was if Lisa felt sick, but she didn't feel sick now.

Mrs. Tarantino walked to the door and met with her mother in the hallway for a few minutes. Lisa didn't move from her spot, frozen in place, knowing that something was awfully wrong but not sure how to articulate it. She gathered her books for homework. She knew she was leaving, and she didn't know when she'd come back. As she was putting her pencils in the little pink polka dotted bag, she felt Mrs. Tarantino's soft hand on her back. "Lisa, honey, here's your coat. You need to go home with your mom now. Don't worry about the homework for tomorrow. We'll talk about that when you return." Lisa felt she was moving through wet sand as Mrs. Tarantino helped her with her coat. The class was silent, as if everyone could tell something terrible was happening. In her stupor, she forgot her books, leaving them neatly stacked on the desk. Her reading buddy, Georgia, ran to her in the hallway with the book bag while Lisa stood silently watching her mother, waiting for a decision where they should head. In slow motion, Lisa grabbed the bag from Georgia, who gave her a hug, and ran back into the classroom.

It seemed Georgia's appearance broke Lisa's mother from her stupor. She took Lisa's hand without saying a word, and they marched out of the school to drive home in silence. Lisa didn't know when she should speak, so she stared out the window. Whatever this was, she knew instinctively it involved her father. Once home, she found out he was killed in an automobile accident the night before while he was on a business trip.

"Dead on impact," her mother had said. Lisa didn't know what that meant, really. Was it good? Was it bad?

Holding her tightly to her chest, Lisa's mom repeatedly whispered, "We're going to be all right, don't worry. We're going to be all right." Lisa never knew who was supposed to be comforted by those words—her mother or her.

With her father gone, grief became a steady household member. For a long time, Lisa and her mother played their respective roles of daughter and mother, but the cloud of sorrow permeated even the drapes. As time passed, routines returned. There was school, homework, activities. Lisa's mother tried to be cheerful and make sure that things were as normal as they could be, but changes were inevitable. Her father had been a force to contend with, and now it was just the two of them.

When they moved to a smaller house, most of their grief stayed behind. The new place was theirs only, and they became inseparable. Lisa trusted in her mother completely and consulted her for everything. Among her friends, this was corny, but they only had each other. Her mother never dated, never even mentioned remarrying. She now devoted her life to Lisa.

When Lisa introduced her to Marcus, it was like her mother had just found a son. She liked him instantly and encouraged them to marry. Her mother's screams of delight welcomed the announcement of a baby. She started buying baby clothes the day she found out she'd be a grandmother. Lisa remembered thinking that, finally, life was perfect again. And it was for a little while.

When she and Marcus returned from their honeymoon, the first place they stopped was her mother's house. That's when the neighbor next door, Mr. Elder, met them at the door with the news that her mother had died the day before.

Choking back tears, Mr. Elder held her small hands in both of his giant ones, calloused from construction work. "I found her on the kitchen floor, Lisa, already gone. I tried to revive her, but I couldn't. I'm so sorry, honey."

Emily's voice brought Lisa back from her reverie. "Tomorrow's Wednesday. It's Zelda's day off. Your mom comes on Wednesday to help with the girls. Do you remember that?"

Lisa froze. Her mother was alive? How could that be? "What do you mean, my mother comes here on Wednesdays?"

Emily smiled warmly. "She'll be here tomorrow, Lisa. Your girls love her, and she loves them just as much. Why do you look so surprised?"

Tears streamed down Lisa's face. The more she tried to wipe them off, the more they came. "My mother's been dead for years, Emily. You were at her funeral. You helped me through those dark days. And now you're saying she's alive? She's in my life?"

Emily opened and closed her mouth several times before she could speak. "Lisa, I don't know what you've been through, but all I can say is that your mother will be here tomorrow, in the flesh, bringing chocolates for the girls, the forbidden food, totally ignoring your rules. It's an ongoing joke with the two of you."

Lisa crooked her head to the side, silent for a moment. "This is all too much. I can't handle much more." With that, she stood and headed for the stairs. "I'm going to bed. I'll figure it out in the morning." She left Emily sitting on the couch, desperate for time alone to think.

***

Upstairs in her vast, yet empty, bedroom, Lisa lay down on the soft sheets, eyes wide open, staring at the ceiling. It was late. Adam should have been home if he'd really been out to dinner with a client. She reached for the phone to call him once more but decided against it. What was the use? He wouldn't answer; he was busy. She knew where he was. She had meddled with time, and this seemed to be the price. She was now the woman waiting at home. All afternoon she had wondered what she was doing here. The daughters and the house and even the housekeeper were a product of her creation by playing with the rivers of past and future.

But her mother being alive was a cruelty beyond comprehension. Her mother had cared for her, nurtured her, loved her. Her mother was the one person she loved most until she had her baby, Seth. When he died, it was her mother she missed the most because that's when she needed her comforting words, her understanding, her soothing touch. Without her mother, she had been rudderless in the storm of silence that appeared in her house with Marcus. Until now, she hadn't realized how empty life had been for her without someone who loved her unconditionally.

***

Noises from downstairs woke Lisa up from a restless sleep. It was still dark outside, but she could hear someone struggling at the front door. Dazed in unknown surroundings and only half awake, she ran to the hallway outside her bedroom, leaned over the railing, and saw Adam creeping into the house. He stumbled around heading for the basement door. Should she follow him?

The wood steps on the staircase to the first floor felt cold on her bare feet. She tiptoed, not wanting to disturb the sleeping house or to alert Adam that she was up. She hadn't been to the basement yet. The laundry room was just off the kitchen, and the children's playroom was also on the first floor, so there'd been no reason for her to venture into Adam's private domain.

The door was closed. She touched the brass doorknob, hesitated, and pulled her hand away. The imprint of her sweaty palm left a mark. She wiped her right hand on her nightgown, and touched her stomach with her left to calm the knot that twisted her insides. With eyes closed, she took deep breaths but paused when she heard an archaic "tick tock" sound coming from the living room. No one had clocks anymore. Why was there one here? She shook her head to refocus, reached out again, and turned the knob with icy fingers, careful not to make a sound.

She poked her head in the crack of the doorway and saw a wood floor landing at the top of the stairs. The ceiling lamp above the landing was dark, but the lights from the room below illuminated the stairs. Voices from the television mixed with drawers banging open and closed. She heard what sounded like ice against glass, pouring liquid, and then feet shuffling. She was at the bottom of the stairs, still in the shadows when she saw Adam plop himself onto a large sectional black leather sofa. He was on the end that reclined and she watched him put his feet up, tumbler with a gold liquid in hand. He swirled the drink so the ice cubes rattled then brought the glass to his lips. She watched him down the drink all at once like a man dying of thirst, eyes closed, head back, then exhale a loud "Aaah…that's better," as he pounded the glass down onto a side table. The noise startled a gasp from Lisa, and Adam abruptly turned his head to the stairs.

"What the fuck are you doing down here?" He yelled. Lisa had never heard him raise his voice before. She was mute at the fury she heard. He repeated the question, rising from the chair in one smooth arc, his athletic body poised like a spring. "I asked you a question, didn't I? What are you fucking doing here?"

She was frozen in place. She opened her mouth, but unbidden tears choked her. Her hand gripped the banister like a vice, keeping her from moving forward or retreating. Adam was in her face in three long steps. His face was inches from hers, his lips twisted into a sneer. She could feel his hot breath. He smelled of whisky, cigarettes, and sweat.

"What's the matter with you? Are you deaf or stupid or both?" He yelled with such force that spit landed on her cheek. Instinctively, she bent her head, covering her face with a free hand. She knew she should leave, but the muscles of her legs didn't interpret the command to move. It was as if her brain were short circuiting with each word Adam brandished.

For a few seconds, Lisa cowered in fear. She had altered time to be with this man, the love of her life, and here he was, hurling curses at her face. This was not the plan. And this was not the man she had loved back then, before, later, or wherever this time travel led her.

She released her grip on the banister and stood still for a few seconds, incredulous as she stared at him, trying to figure out what had happened.

"You really are a dumb slut, aren't you? Didn't you hear me tell you to get out?"

She turned and ran back up the stairs as fast as she could. She stumbled near the top, missed a step, and smashed her shin against the wood. She regained her footing and continued running until she was inside her bedroom. She slammed the door shut and leaned against it, breathing heavily. She stood there, trying to catch her breath when she heard heavy footsteps. She tried to press the lock button on the doorknob, hopelessly fumbling, when she heard Adam's gruff words from the other side, "Don't bother locking the door. I have no interest in you and your constant complaints. Stay in there and don't come downstairs again, do you understand me? Never." Mute at this additional onslaught to her senses, she stared at the door and listened as Adam retreated to his den. When she heard the slam of the basement door, she breathed in relief and stumbled onto her bed. She buried herself under the covers and cried herself to sleep. What had she done to deserve all this?

***

The bed seemed to be rocking as if she were on a ship. Lisa opened her eyes to see Natalie and Suzette jumping up and down, nearly crushing her. "Grandma's here! Grandma's here! Mommy, wake up. Grandma says we can't have breakfast without you." Lisa blinked repeatedly.

She had barely slept after her horrible encounter with Adam. For a moment, the voices of the girls made her smile. They were so sweet. Then the memory of Adam's tirade assaulted her and lay there like a boulder on her stomach. It wasn't all a dream then. She was here in this new world, with these daughters, and a husband who was a stranger to her. And now her mother was downstairs, just a few feet away.

Her mother. In each moment of sadness or loneliness, she had wished she could seek her mother's counsel. When Seth, her baby, had died, she remembered talking to her mother at her graveside, looking for comfort and words of advice from the air, knowing that her mother couldn't help her anymore. When she had met Adam and thought she had found warmth and sunshine again, she had wished she could confide in her mother. She knew her mother wouldn't have judged her, or maybe she would have guided her better than she was guiding herself.

She had missed her every single day for the past twenty years.

Lisa was equal parts afraid and excited, not knowing what to expect. What if her mother was not her mother? This world she had created through her traveling was nothing that she'd ever imagined. Adam was certainly different now. So maybe her mother was a new woman, someone she didn't know? But the girls' giggling, their sweet, unabashed joy, provoked Lisa's heart to fill with warmth, as if there had been a hole in it that she didn't know existed before, and now it overflowed. Impetuously, she grabbed the girls and hugged them tightly. They smelled of soap and new teddy bears.

***

With one girl on each side of her, holding hands, they went downstairs. When they reached the first floor, the children darted off, leaving Lisa alone to walk the last few steps to the kitchen. She could hear two women talking to the girls, so she stopped just short of the threshold to listen. She recognized Emily's voice above the din of chairs scraping the floor. "Who's ready for delicious pancakes made by Auntie Emily?"

Natalie, or maybe Suzette, yelled out, "You're so silly, Auntie Em! You didn't make those! Grandma made pancakes for our day off from school!" Both girls chanted, "Grandma! Grandma!"

That's when Lisa heard her voice. "Everybody settle down or else we can't enjoy these delicious, amazing, super-duper Mickey Mouse chocolate chip pancakes, and I'll have to give them to the dog!"

"Noooooo!" came the chorus of voices. "The dog can't eat chocolate!"

She heard Emily say, "Gladys, please, give me the platter, and I'll start serving the girls."

"Thank you, dear. You're such a help. Now, where's Lisa?"

Frozen in place like a statue, Lisa stayed in the hallway listening to her mother in the kitchen. The timbre of her voice, the throaty laugh quick to join the fun, it was all the same. She didn't realize how much she missed that voice until she heard it again. Goosebumps covered her as she stood there, wondering how she could find the strength to walk in and face her. She was so scared that the woman in the kitchen was an imposter. Lisa knew she wasn't real, that this woman, this mother, was only created from traveling back and forth, yet to be in her presence again, to have her near, to touch her and feel her warmth was almost more than she could bear.

Lisa closed her eyes, mustering courage to move her feet. She was startled by the voice. "There you are! Oh, sweetheart, Emily told me only this morning you were in the hospital. I go away for three days, and I'm left clueless that you were not well." She took Lisa into her arms and hugged her. Lisa grasped her around the waist and buried her face into her mother's neck. She had no words. This woman smelled like lavender and jasmine, her skin was soft, and in her arms, Lisa was safe once again. She hadn't felt this secure since before her mother had died. Her mind swirled uncontrollably as she stood there, holding on to her mother like a child who's been lost and has just found home. All the years of wandering in loneliness and despair, the heartbreaks, the disappointments bubbled up and spilled out of her eyes. Her cries were guttural, from deep within, held back until the dam broke apart. Wracking sobs poured out. Her shoulders heaved up and down as she cried more inconsolably than the day her mother died. Back then she was mute and frozen in shock. She was appropriate and polite. She thought being a grown-up meant shoving all her feelings inside, shaking hands, smiling, and soothing others as they gave her their condolences.

But here, in her mother's arms again, the carefully built walls tumbled down. She was brokenhearted and joyous at the same time, incredulous that this could be real, yet knowing in her bones that it was only temporary. Her mother just held her, saying nothing, stroking her hair, rubbing her back and holding her tight.

When Lisa's sobs subsided, her mother whispered to her, "I'm very angry no one told me you were in the hospital. Not you, not Adam, not even Emily." She turned her head and gave Emily her most disapproving stare. "If I'd known, I would have been there for you."

Lisa sniffled, not wanting to talk but yearning to keep listening to her mother's voice. "It was just a short visit. I didn't want to worry you." The lie sounded convincing enough.

"Well, don't you ever do that again, young lady. Imagine my shock when I arrived here today and found out you had been hospitalized with no mother to check on you as if you were some kind of abandoned orphan."

Lisa hugged her mother tighter. "I won't do it again. Promise."

"Are you OK?"

"Yes, Mom, I'm OK now."

Her mother kissed her head. "Now, let's get to breakfast. You can explain to me what happened later."

Lisa followed her mother into the kitchen. Her hair was sprinkled with gray, and her face had aged with soft wrinkles, but her blue eyes were sparkling as always. She was as slim and immaculately dressed with pearl earrings to match her necklace. Lisa remembered that her mother prized those pearls that Lisa's father had given her. She marveled that she still wore them. She wore a pale blue dress beneath a blue and white gingham apron with yellow flowers scattered throughout. Bumblebees spread their wings and spelled "Grandma" in a semicircle in the center.

Lisa sat down next her. That's when she noticed her mother's left hand. There was a wedding ring on it. She couldn't remember if she had still worn a ring after her father died. "Mom, that's such a pretty ring."

Her mother smiled. "Thank you honey, but I've been wearing that ring since Jeff and I got married. Now's when you notice it?"

Lisa cleared her throat. "Jeff?"

Emily chimed in, leaning in conspiratorially towards Lisa and her mother, "Gladys, remember the bump on her head. She keeps forgetting things."

Gladys raised her eyebrows, "So this little hospital stint wasn't as simple as you'd want me to believe, huh?"

Natalie walked over to Gladys to get more pancakes and smirked at Lisa. "Mommy, you're acting crazy. Grandpa's name is Jeff. Remember? We did a family tree for school?"

"Lisa, darling, Jeff is my husband. Has been for the last twenty years. You mean you don't remember him?"

As Lisa was about to answer, Adam waltzed into the kitchen, followed by a taller, older, gray-haired man. He was handsome, with a huge smile above a neat gray goatee. Adam yelled out, "Look who I found wandering in the driveway?"

Both girls jumped out of their seats at the same time, "Grandpa!"

Lisa turned to her mother and saw her face light up. "Jeff, you're early. I thought you were going to be gone all morning, love."

With one girl hanging on each leg, Jeff walked over to Gladys and kissed her softly on the lips. "I was very lucky. The service department at the car dealer was quick today." He turned to Lisa and put his hand on her shoulder. "Your husband told me that you've given us a bit of a scare, young lady. Why didn't you call us, hmmm?"

Before Lisa could respond, Gladys chimed, "Don't bother. I've already pulled her ears on this one." She stood up, still talking, "Jeff, honey, sit down. Have some pancakes."

Almost as an afterthought, Lisa heard her add over her shoulder, "There's some for you too, Adam."

"Thanks, mother-in-law dearest."

Lisa stared at Adam while the awful words of the night before flooded back. Hot tears of anger and disappointment spilled, and she brushed them aside not wanting anyone to see her crying again. She contorted her face into a smile. "What?" he asked harshly. "What are you looking at?"

"Just wondering what time you got in last night," she replied.

"Bad memory, huh? You know the answer perfectly well. Why don't you tell me?"

Gladys returned to the table with a plate in each hand. "Why don't you two take that conversation elsewhere?" Jeff reached for syrup and busied himself with the food. Lisa thought he looked embarrassed. Emily and the girls got silent, almost holding their breath.

Adam rose from the table and grabbed his plate. "It's too crowded in here. I'll be in the den."

Lisa followed him with her eyes. As she was about to get up, her mother put her hand on Lisa's shoulder and nudged her back into her seat. "You stay there and eat. You need your strength. He can wait."

Gladys insisted that Lisa sit at the table and do nothing while she and Jeff cleaned up in the kitchen.

While Lisa wondered what her next step was, Emily leaned into her, bumped shoulders to catch Lisa's attention. The she turned with a big grin. "I have a grand idea!"

The girls squealed in unison, "Auntie Emily's ideas are the best!"

Emily continued, "Why don't the three of us have an Auntie/Nieces Day today? We can get dressed, go to the park, and then play 'yes' day! What do you think?" The kids sprang into action, running off to their rooms, racing to see who'd get there first.

Emily put her arm over Lisa's shoulder and whispered in her ear, "You don't seem yourself. I'll keep them out of your hair, so you can spend some time with your mom. Is that OK?"

Lisa nodded, unable to fashion words of gratitude. As usual, Emily knew what to do without being asked.

Dishes done and the kitchen spotless, Jeff twirled the kitchen towel with a flourish and bowed. "M'ladies, your faithful servant has completed his duties. I'm off to run the errands my wife so generously added to today's list." He made a big show of kissing Gladys on her hand, then conspiratorially winked at Lisa as he exited the kitchen.

Finally alone with her mother, Lisa basked in her warmth. It was like watching a home movie, except this one was flesh and blood. While she was going through the ups and downs of her marriage with Marcus, she often wondered what it would be like to have a mother to confide in, to love her unconditionally. She had missed this more than anything else. And now, unbelievably, she had it.

Gladys brought them each a cup of herbal tea and sat in a chair next to Lisa.

"Mom."

"Yes, dear?"

"What do you think of Adam?"

Gladys stared at her cup before she spoke. "I think that's a question that only you should answer, honey. It's not my place to give you my opinion about your husband."

"Not if I'm asking you for it. I need to know what you think."

Gladys turned to Lisa. "This isn't the place to talk about this. Finish your tea, and we'll go for a nice walk."

***

Out in the sun, things didn't seem as strange as they did inside the house. They turned left; Lisa didn't know where they were headed, but she trusted her mother.

They walked a few blocks until they reached a large park with tall stone columns like the guardians of the gate to a fortress. Beyond the entrance, Lisa could see a path that circled a lake. Even from a distance she could see runners weaving in and out among the mothers with strollers and toddlers.

Gladys squeezed Lisa's arm. "So, what's on your mind sweetheart? Why the questions about what I think of Adam?"

"I'm just curious. You two didn't seem to like each other much today."

"You know we've never been close." Gladys stopped at a bench by the water. "Here, let's talk." The back of the bench had an inscription. *For Laurie, with all my love, Michael.* Lisa was struck by the permanence of Michael's love for Laurie. Here it was, etched for all to see forever, or as long as the bench lasted. Upon closer inspection, sun and visitors had started fading the wood planks from a deep brown to a splotchy beige.

Lisa sat close to her mother, holding her hand. "I'm so happy to see you again. To be here with you."

Gladys smiled at her daughter, eyes bright. "That's sweet to hear, but you just saw me last week, honey." Gladys tilted her head as if examining her daughter's face. "I sense there's more to this being happy to see me."

Lisa laughed. "You always knew me so well; I thought you could read my mind."

"I always told you since you were little. I know…" Lisa joined her in the last word, "Everything!"

As they laughed at their old inside joke, Lisa decided to confide in her. Maybe if her mother knew about the time traveling, she'd have an idea of how to fix her marriage to Adam. She opened and closed her mouth several times, seeking the right words.

"Out with it, Lisa."

"You'll think I'm crazy."

"Try me. I'm your mother. I've seen it all."

Lisa gazed at her mother's eyes. They were so blue, unlike her own brown ones. When she was a little girl, she used to think her mother was really a fairy, not a human. Right now, she hoped there was more fairy to her; maybe that way, she'd believe the magical story.

***

Just as Lisa stopped talking, a breeze picked up, making her fold her arms around herself, although she wasn't sure if she was cold from the wind or from her mother's lack of response.

After what seemed like an eternity, Gladys spoke. "So, you're saying that you travel back and forth through time, from here to college and back, and that now you've changed the future, but that it's really the present? That's what you're trying to say?"

"Something like that." Lisa had omitted her death. How do you tell someone they're dead?

In a voice filled with frustration, Gladys asked, "But Lisa, while we've been here, living our lives, with you, where has the other you been?"

"I don't know how it works, Mom. Maybe it's a freak of quantum physics, or it's this pineal gland problem I have that so far, no doctor knows what to do about or what it means. All I know is that in my time I was married to a man named Marcus, we had no children, I was Adam's lover, and he was married to a woman named Stephanie. After going back and forth, now I'm here in the same year that I left, except that now I'm married to Adam, I have two daughters, and I'm pretty sure he's having an affair with Stephanie. And I have no idea where Marcus is. It's like everything got turned upside down. And Mom, one more thing…." Lisa's voice trailed off.

"More? Isn't that all strange enough?"

"Well, this bit is more complicated." Lisa covered her eyes with her free hand to continue speaking. "In my real life, you're dead."

Gladys stayed quiet for a few minutes. Lisa shook her leg up and down, waiting for her mother to react.

"Dead, you say?"

The wind picked up again, harder this time, rustling the leaves and making ripples in the water. Lisa turned her head in the direction of children's laughter as they fed Cheerios to the ducks and geese that congregated by them like churchgoers anxious to hear the day's sermon. Before answering her mother's question, Lisa swallowed hard.

"Yes. It happened long ago. That's why it was so hard to see you again because I've missed you for years and years."

"I see."

Lisa felt her throat tighten as she herself strained to understand, and explain, the inexplicable. "And now that I'm here, you're here too. I didn't expect that. It wasn't part of my thoughts. I had daydreamed that going back in time I could find Adam before he got married to another woman, but I hadn't counted on what would happen to the other people in my life. It's as if whatever I do affects everyone else."

"A butterfly effect of sorts," added Gladys. "Each movement, no matter how small, affects everything else."

"Yes. Maybe. But now that I'm here, this isn't what I had wanted at all. Adam is...." Lisa left off the end of the sentence.

"Adam's what?"

"He's not the man I thought he'd be as a husband. He's cold, dismissive, cruel even. And I'm certain he's having an affair with the same Stephanie that he was married to in my other life."

Gladys rubbed her back, just like she did when Lisa was sick as a child. They sat like that for a while until Gladys spoke again.

"Well, honey, you have to admit that your story is a bit...I don't know how to say this without upsetting you. It's farfetched. Like the science fiction novels you liked to read when you were a teenager."

Lisa jolted up from the bench, her eyes a mixture of glowering and disappointment. "Are you saying you don't believe me?"

"It's not that I don't, sweetheart, it's just that...." Gladys sighed. "Lisa, back and forth in time, from the present to college and then to the future. And not even a real future!"

Lisa turned to face the lake. She was angry, disappointed, almost ashamed.

With arms crossed and her feet slightly apart, Lisa stood tall, seeing nothing but the confusion of her feelings. Then a duck in the water caught her eye. This mother duck swam in front with five ducklings following in a straight line, not deviating for a second. The mother never looked back as if she trusted her ducklings to follow without question. Lisa realized this is what she wanted from her mother now, to take her word on faith even though the whole conversation seemed preposterous. Her thoughts were interrupted by the sound of a nose blowing. Lisa turned back towards the bench, disappointment still burning her.

But when she saw her mother crying quietly, her stance softened. She knew she wasn't crazy, so she wasn't about to waste precious time being angry.

She returned and put her arm around her mother's shoulders. "Mom, I'm sorry. Please don't cry."

Gladys breathed deeply and faced Lisa. "I don't really know what to say about the whole time traveling thing, but you know I adore you; you're my life, and I just want to help."

"I love you too, Mom."

"I just don't believe that this is happening for real, Lisa. I think you need professional help. Maybe it's the stress of abandoning your career, raising the girls, such a big house. I don't know. It wouldn't surprise me that Adam behaves badly. I never really liked him, but you insisted that he's the love of your life, so I supported you in that. But this, honey, this is more than anyone can be expected to believe." Gladys's voice trailed off.

Lisa bit her lower lip. "Mom, I swear. It's true."

Gladys took Lisa's hands in her own. "Honey, you're my daughter, and I love you. I will do anything I can to help you. So, let's just agree that I'll believe you for now. I don't want us to have a fight."

"Mom, please don't patronize me."

"I'm not doing that, dear. I'm just trying to help."

Lisa stood up again and headed towards the lake, away from her mother. She could hear Gladys following her. "Wait, Lisa. Wait! Don't walk away."

Immersed in her own thoughts, Lisa heard nothing. There had to be some way to prove her story. Emily and her mother had to see she was telling the truth. This was crucial to her; it would help her figure out how to handle her problems with Adam. If she returned to the past, she'd be able to fix whatever went wrong there. She glanced behind her and stopped to let her mother catch up. As she did that, she noticed two trees in the distance, rooted farther apart from other trees, claiming their own separate space. Tall and majestic, their branches reached up, appearing to pierce the fluffy clouds that dotted the sky. The breeze blew Lisa's hair into her face blocking her view. As she pulled her hair back, she noticed the branches of the two trees outstretched in the middle, towards one another, touching, mingling leaves, so she couldn't tell which ones belonged to which. They swayed in unison with the wind, an ethereal dance of praise to the sun.

What if there were some way for her to bring her mother or Emily back to the past? That would show them she was telling the truth. But how could she do that when she didn't even know how she did it herself? She didn't even know if she could go back anymore. What if she were stuck here now?

Gladys put her hand on Lisa's shoulder. "Lisa, please, don't make me run after you. Let's talk about this like people who love each other."

Lisa reached her hand up and touched her mother's. "Don't worry, Mom. I'm not mad at you. I'm just analyzing how I can prove to you I'm not crazy." They stood there for a bit, Lisa enjoying her mother's touch.

Lisa then turned, eyes wide and filled with tears as she stared into her mother's piercing blue eyes. She now had everything she had wanted, yet nothing was right. Maybe this was her punishment for trampling on time? Her heart ached at the thought of losing her mother again, of going back to her prior lonely life.

"Mom, in this world I have a family, I have a house, I have money." She then whispered. "I have you."

Gladys put the palm of her hand on her daughter's cheek. She pulled her towards her and kissed the other cheek. "I love you sweetheart. You can always count on that."

The cell phone buzzing in her pocket interrupted them. The number was unknown, so she sent it to voicemail, but the same caller insisted for three calls. "I'd better answer this," she said to Gladys. "Maybe it's the doctor or the hospital."

"Hello?"

"Hi. Is this Lisa?"

"Yes. Who's this?"

"Um...this is Stephanie Karch, your nurse. Remember me?"

Lisa glanced at her mother with eyebrows raised in curiosity and shock. "Of course I remember you, Stephanie. How are you?"

"I'm not doing so well, so, um, I wondered if you'd like to have a cup of coffee or something one of these days? We said we'd keep in touch." Lisa noticed a tremor in Stephanie's voice.

"Sure. I'd love to meet. How about lunch tomorrow, while my kids are in school?"

Lisa heard Stephanie's soft intake of breath before she spoke. "Perfect. There's a diner across from the hospital. Meet you there at twelve thirty?"

Chapter 13

Gladys called Lisa late the following morning. "How are the girls?" Lisa battled with the long-sleeved T-shirt she was pulling over her head while holding the phone to her ear. She didn't want to be late to her meeting with Stephanie, but she also didn't want to miss the opportunity to talk to her mother—in case this world vanished. She had spent yesterday avoiding any radio or streaming station, afraid that the song that had started all the traveling would pop up randomly. She needed time here, and she wasn't taking chances. "The girls are fine, Mom; they're in school. I drove them, which was weird since I had to be surreptitious in getting directions. And then I didn't know at what time they started. Thank goodness for Zelda who seems to know everything about everyone in this house."

"Honey, the real purpose of my call is to wish you luck with Stephanie today. Are you nervous? What will you say? Are you going to ask her about the affair?" Gladys's questions were rapid-fire, not giving Lisa a chance to answer.

"Mom, I have no idea. She asked for the meeting. And I don't know if I'm confronting her about anything. I feel disingenuous questioning her about an affair with the man I know is her husband in my time. But he's my husband now." Lisa dropped her phone. "Aargh! Hold on," she yelled into the air.

Finally dressed, Lisa sat on the blue bench at the foot of the bed. She leaned against the large matching blue pillows, their softness massaging the small of her back. They reminded her of the pillows her mother laid in her room when she was a child, and the fragrance of lavender sachets inside a small basket on the corner of her mother's dresser. She remembered being left with a babysitter on the evenings when her mother worked late. On those occasions, she would sneak into her mother's bedroom and inhale the fragrance as if it could magically transport her mother home. She closed her eyes now, transfixed by the sound of her mother's voice.

"I'm back, Mom."

"You sounded like you were in a war and losing badly. Now, what are you going to say?"

Lisa rolled her eyes. "Why are you so concerned with what I'm going to say?"

"Don't roll your eyes at me!"

"How do you know that? You can't see me!"

"I know you; I know how you react when I ask you a question you don't want to answer. Mothers know their daughters."

Lisa chuckled. "I obviously don't know mine."

"Never mind that. You just need a little more time with them, that's all."

Sighing, Lisa left the bench to check her clothes in the full-length mirror in the corner. "That's the problem. I don't know how much time I have with anything anymore." The woman in the mirror gazed back with a furrowed brow. "Mom, I hate to hang up, but I have to go. I'll call you later."

***

The diner was bustling when Lisa arrived at noon. She couldn't sit at home waiting, so she figured she'd stake out a table to watch Stephanie from afar when she arrived. Lisa wasn't sure what she expected from this conversation. She studied the menu, rapping her fingers rhythmically in between staring at the door.

After what felt like hours, Stephanie appeared at the hostess counter. Lisa saw her say something to the hostess, then step into the main area of the diner, looking around. Lisa stood up and waved her over. She was glad she had been early. This gave her a chance to pick the seat instead of having to take the side that Stephanie didn't want.

Stephanie wore blue jeans, black boots, and a pink blouse with a light pink sweater over her shoulders. Her hair was slicked back in a ponytail, making her look youthful. The pink look was sweet. Her face betrayed the fashion tricks. Her eyes were puffy, despite the makeup she had obviously applied. She smiled at Lisa, but it looked almost shy, half-hearted. Not the cheerful person Lisa knew from the hospital in the past.

Lisa broke the ice. "Hi. It's good to see you again."

"Good to see you too. You look well. How are you feeling?" Lisa sensed sincerity in Stephanie's voice.

"I'm feeling fine. Living the dream."

The waitress cut in. "What do you girls want?"

Lisa leaned into Stephanie and smiled. "I studied the menu before you arrived. The soup special is mushroom barley." She turned to the waitress. "I'll have a chef salad and a cup of soup."

"And you, honey?"

Stephanie took her time in responding. "I'll just have a cup of soup, please." She turned to Lisa. "I'm not very hungry." She added as the waitress walked away, "And a cup of coffee, please. Black."

As the waitress shuffled away, Lisa didn't know where to start. The diner was loud, filled with the lunch crowd. How does one introduce a conversation about traveling through time?

Stephanie interrupted her thoughts. "I'm glad you agreed to meet me. I have something to ask you."

"Ask away."

Stephanie lowered her eyes and picked at the cuticles of her fingers. She spoke slowly. "Are you happy with your husband? I mean, do you have a good life together?"

Lisa was taken aback by the question. She straightened herself and moved the silverware around, so it was perfectly aligned with the plate in the center. Just as she was about to speak, the waitress returned carrying two bowls. "Careful, ladies. It's hot."

"Thank you," they said in unison. Smiling awkwardly, they turned their attention to the soups.

Lisa stirred hers while she thought. "I don't know how to answer that question. I think that my husband is not who I thought he was." She waited for a response, but getting none, she continued. "To be honest, I don't think he's happy with me." She looked at Stephanie, whose head was bent over her soup bowl, yet not touching it. "Why do you ask?"

Stephanie raised her head but averted her eyes. She took a deep breath and looked straight into Lisa's. "Your husband is unfaithful to you. That's why I ask."

Lisa noticed the sound of her breathing as she uttered her next words. "You sound very certain. How do you know?"

With a firm voice, Stephanie responded, "He's my lover." She shook her head. "Was my lover—until last night."

The noises in the diner disappeared as if the world had stopped while Lisa took in the enormous revelation. Even though she knew the truth, facing it was another thing altogether. In some corner of her heart, she had hoped she was wrong, that she had misunderstood Adam's moods, that maybe there was something she could do in this world to make things work the way she wanted them to. Tears sprung to her eyes when she realized she had been holding out for hope.

Stephanie's confession crushed her. She wanted to be home, in her actual home, back where she was the lover, not the recipient of this news. A baby crying at the table next to theirs brought her back to the present. She noticed that Stephanie was still looking at her, not defiantly, but defeated, embarrassed almost. She was wringing her hands and playing with a silver braided ring with a ruby rose on her right hand, twisting it, pulling and pushing it off her finger.

"Did Adam give you that ring?" Lisa's question was barely above a whisper.

"Yes," came the soft reply.

"And you're in love with him?" Lisa wasn't sure why she was asking questions when she felt she should run away, but her own conscience wanted confirmation. Not getting an answer immediately, she pressed on. "Well, are you?"

"Yes. No. I don't know. I don't know anymore." Stephanie played with her napkin, folding it into long rectangles. Lisa stayed quiet while she watched the other woman busy herself, avoiding direct eye contact.

When she had created a complete paper fan, Stephanie spoke again, the words rushing out as if talking would bring her relief. "It started out innocently, just some flirtation. We met at a cocktail bar where I waitressed part-time a few years ago. I was saving money to buy a condo, and the bar hours were flexible with my nursing job. I needed to do something different from nursing on my days off. He came in one night for a drink. We chatted, and he didn't wear a wedding ring, so I thought he was single. I told him my schedule once, and then he started coming on the evenings I worked. I remembered he liked bourbon, neat. He never took a receipt, so I was used to throwing it away. Then one day, he asked for it, gave it back to me, and told me to write my number on it. So, I did. He called me. We met for coffee in another town one afternoon. We had a great time. He walked me to my car, and that's when he kissed me. I was already smitten, but that kiss sealed it for me. I was done for."

Stephanie paused for a drink of water. Lisa waited, knowing there was more to the story.

"We started dating after that, mostly on weeknights because I worked a lot of weekends to earn overtime pay. He convinced me to quit the cocktail bar, so I'd have more time for him, so that delayed my house purchase, but I didn't care. I just wanted to be with him. Several times I asked him to stay over at night, but he never did, and I found that odd, but I didn't question it. As the months passed, I questioned why we couldn't do more things in public. I wanted to introduce him to my family, but he absolutely refused. That's when I started having doubts. Why was this guy so hesitant to be seen with me? When I confronted him, he confessed he was married to you, that he had daughters, that he had a whole other life that I didn't know about."

Again, Stephanie took a sip of water, her hands trembling as she held the glass. "I was devastated. I told him I didn't want to see him anymore. And we didn't…for a while. But I was so lonely without him. He sent me flowers and wrote me poetry. Haiku is his specialty. Did you know that?"

Lisa smirked. "Yes, I'm aware of his poetic prowess."

Stephanie leaned back in her seat. "Yeah, he's quite the romantic. And persistent. I finally bought the townhouse I live in, and I agreed to let him come see me, so we could talk. He said he wanted closure, that he had done a terrible thing lying to me like that, and that he wanted to apologize in person. That he couldn't stop thinking about me. And like I said, I was lonely, and I missed him terribly. So, I put away my pride, and he came over. He was so sincere that night. He told me that the two of you essentially lived separate lives, that he hadn't left you because of the children, that if he divorced, you wouldn't let him see them, that you had told him this once, and that you'd clean him out financially. Swearing he loved only me, he promised that he'd get a divorce as soon as the kids were a little older. They were babies then. He said he had spoken to a lawyer who told him he'd get joint custody if the kids were out of diapers, but that as babies you could deprive him of the right to see them. And that he couldn't bear the thought of losing his children, that I wouldn't want a man who could do that to his daughters. He was right; I wouldn't want someone like that. Then he continued to promise that he loved only me, and that as soon as he could, he'd divorce you, and he'd marry me."

Stephanie stopped, almost out of breath, looked down at her hands again, and continued quietly, "I believed him. I waited and waited, but the kids were getting older, and I was losing my patience. We were having fights frequently, and he convinced me I was crazy with jealousy, irrational, out of my mind."

Lisa didn't want to interrupt, even though she had a million questions. She let Stephanie empty her sadness onto the table between them. "Then you showed up in my hospital, on my floor, in my care. What are the odds of that? I wanted to buy a lottery ticket that day. I was ready for a witch. He had described you that way—cold, heartless, sexless, mean, always putting him down. But you were none of those things. I could tell when I spoke to you, how you talked about him. You didn't know who I was and had no reason to pretend with me. You were genuinely in love with him. And you were sweet.

"He came to my house on the day you were discharged. I knew it was wrong, but I still hoped that he'd tell me he was leaving you. I was waiting. I'd been waiting for years. But that night, something struck a chord in me. I couldn't believe he had left you at home alone after having that terrible diagnosis with the pineal gland. I wondered what kind of man is this? And I threw him out. I did. I really did. You must believe me."

Her eyes and voice pleaded for mercy. "I'm so sorry, but I don't know what else to say. I'm just so sorry."

Lisa felt miserable now, not only for herself, but for this poor wretch of a woman who was baring her soul to her, when she was the one who should be sorry. She knew she was in the wrong, not Stephanie. She'd tampered with time and had ruined this woman's life. Lisa reached out her arm and took Stephanie's hand in her own, squeezed it, and held it there for a while, just looking at her, wondering how she would tell her how she was the guilty one. "It's OK," was the only thing that came to mind. Stephanie smiled through tears and reached out her other hand and took Lisa's. They sat there, holding both hands across the table, the wife and the lover, both in the same role in different times.

Lisa felt warm, and her head was achy, but she didn't want to break the connection just then. Something good had to come out of this mess she had created. But she was feeling nauseous, and she wondered if there was something wrong with the soup. She hadn't touched the salad. That's when she heard it. *I was working as a waitress in a cocktail bar, that much is true.*

That song—it was there again. It got louder with a chorus of voices. She turned; it was coming from a few tables away, where some teenage girls were singing it at the top of their lungs. Stuck here with Stephanie holding her hands, the song playing, and her vision getting blacker, she didn't have enough time to say "Stop" or to let go. She went blank.

Chapter 14

Lisa shook her head to clear the cobwebs. Where were they? She was still in the diner, but it looked different, yet oddly familiar. She had a plate in front of her with a half-eaten cheeseburger and fries covered in ketchup. There was a beer near her, and Emily was at her side, laughing at some joke. How did Emily get here? And where did the cheeseburger come from? She stared at her hands. Smooth, soft, no wrinkles, no ring on her finger. She looked at the greasy napkin next to her plate, then at the window that bore the name of the diner: Tom's Restaurant. That's where they used to go in college. Did they go back in time? Together? How did that happen? Almost in answer to her questions, she heard a voice across from her say, "What the hell is going on?" It was Stephanie, but not the nurse. The college student.

Stephanie complained louder, "I said—what the hell is going on?" She was obviously talking to Lisa. In her spandex and leg warmers, with large hoop earrings that looked like peace symbols, Emily piped in. "What's going on is that you're going to stay away from my friend's boyfriend, that's what."

Lisa and Stephanie looked at each other directly. "Don't get upset, Stephanie, I can explain," said Lisa. "Just calm down."

"Don't tell me to calm down. This is crazy. One minute we're alone in the diner, sipping soup, and now we're in this—whatever this is."

Emily turned to Lisa. "Lisa, what is she talking about?"

Clearly explanations were in order, but Lisa couldn't do that here. She had to get Stephanie to understand. "Listen, let's just get the check and get out of here. I have a terrible headache, but I'll walk you home, Stephanie. So we can get to know each other better." As she said this, Lisa motioned the waitress over. Stephanie dumbly nodded her head.

Emily wasn't as patient. "That's fine. Leave me stranded, why don't you." She giggled then. "Nah, I'm only kidding. I'm not walking anyone but me home. You guys go on and have a crazy night. I'm tired." She climbed over Lisa's lap and onto the floor. "Spot me on this one, Lisa? I only have a dollar on me." With those words, she blew kisses and walked out.

Stephanie watched her intently, then turned to Lisa. "Who the hell is that? She doesn't mince words, does she?"

"No, she never has. That's why we've been friends for twenty years."

"That's all nice and good, but what's going on? You don't look the way you did a moment ago. You're…you're…you're young!"

Stephanie grabbed Lisa's left hand. "Where are your wedding rings? You were wearing a gold band and a diamond ring. Where are they?"

She looked at her own hands. "And what's this? I'm a nurse. I have chapped, cracked hands from washing them a thousand times a day and wearing hot latex gloves. Look at my hands now. They're soft, smooth. And my nails…. This is hot pink nail polish. I haven't worn that color since…since…college."

Stephanie's voice rose to a shriek as she turned her head from side to side looking desperate. "What have you done to me? Where are we? We were just in the diner across from the hospital, and now we're here, but I've no idea how we got here or even where this is. Where are we?"

Lisa wasn't sure how to handle this. She wasn't prepared. She didn't know what to say, and it just didn't seem like the truth was going to work very well in a crowded diner on Broadway. "Stephanie, look, let's get out of here, and I can explain. I think."

The diner was crowded. Lisa heard murmurs, and the people at the next booth gawked at them. One group of guys chanted, "Girl fight! Girl fight!"

Stephanie got louder. "You think? You think you can explain this madness, do you? What have you done to me? Did you give me some kind of drug that's making me hallucinate? Are these people even real?" She flung her arm around as if to encompass everyone. She started wailing, holding her face in her hands. People stopped their chatter and stared at their table. A trickle of sweat poured down Lisa's back. She tried to soothe Stephanie, but the poor woman was distraught and confused. She repeated, "Where are we? What have you done? What's going on?"

Lisa finally paid and got Stephanie out to the street. There was too much going on at once: they had been in a diner, and now Stephanie was here. Something her mother said popped into her head. Butterfly effect. Not only had she come back in time and done who knows what to the universe, now she had brought someone with her, unknowingly. While it seemed like a great idea in theory, in the flesh, she was terrified she had caused some irreversible catastrophe. If they bumped into Adam, what then? She needed to get them somewhere safe to hide before they ran into anyone they knew.

On the corner, Lisa spotted a magazine kiosk. Tears streaked down Stephanie's cheeks. She continued to mutter under her breath as if possessed, but at least she allowed Lisa to guide her. She pulled Stephanie by the hand, and they ran across the street. The newspapers were lined up in stacks. Lisa grabbed the first one, the *Daily News*. There was the date: April 29, 1982.

"Stephanie, where did you live in 1982?"

Stephanie wiped her runny nose with her sleeve before answering. "What do you mean?"

Lisa shook her head and yanked on Stephanie's arm. "Stephanie, focus. We don't have time for many questions right now. Where did you live in 1982, and who lived with you?"

Stammering, Stephanie waved her hands about, "I was in college. I lived on 110th, off Broadway, with some girlfriends." Stephanie spun around appearing incredulous at the sights around her. "How did we get here—to New York, to Broadway?"

Desperate, Lisa grabbed her by the shoulders. "Never mind how we got here. Your college friends—do you think they'll be home now?"

"How the hell am I supposed to know?" Just then, Stephanie looked at another newspaper on the sidewalk stand. The *National Enquirer*. "This says it's 1982. How is that possible?" She held the paper to her face, peering at the date as if she could will it to change. She put that one down and picked up another, the *New York Times*. "Same date. This can't be. What drugs did you give me?" As she reached for yet another, the man inside the kiosk yelled at her. "Hey, stop picking up and throwing down! If you touch, you buy! This isn't the library!"

Lisa grabbed her by the hand and dragged her from the yelling man, the kiosk, the craziness of Broadway, towards the dorm she shared with Emily. "Never mind where you used to live. We're going to where I used to live, and I'll explain everything."

Chapter 15

Stephanie seemed like a zombie as Lisa dragged her the few blocks from Broadway down to Riverside Drive to avoid crowds of people. They headed to the dorm Lisa and Emily shared. Lisa worried that Stephanie might be in shock, so she walked as fast as possible to reach their destination. She figured that Stephanie would be able to recover if she were in a quiet room. Then she could listen to Lisa explain what happened. That is, if Lisa were even able to explain it all. She wasn't sure herself how she had managed to travel back with Stephanie, but here they were. In the back of Lisa's mind, a stray thought lingered: How was she going to take them both back? The enormity of the entanglement frightened Lisa, but she pushed the thoughts away. She had to focus on this first step, and, hopefully, the rest would sort itself out.

Finally in front of the building, Lisa reached into her jeans pocket and found the key to the entrance door. Without stopping to question how that was even possible, Lisa inserted the key and led Stephanie upstairs to the third floor. The suite door was ajar, but Emily wasn't there.

Posters of the Pretenders, Billy Idol, and Pat Benatar covered one wall of the room. On the windowsill sat a blue boom box with piles of cassette tapes around it. In one corner empty bottles of vodka were stacked in the shape of a triangle like an art project, precariously defying gravity. Bunk beds were on the left side, and on the right, two small student desks abutted each other. They each had a green banker's lamp, a typewriter, and piles of books and notebooks. One desk was covered in papers and books in complete disarray as if hurricane winds had blown everything around. An empty bottle with a half-torn label served as a vase for dried baby's breath. On the other desk, papers were neatly stacked, books sat upright as if at attention, and sharpened pencils stood alongside pens in a neat holder. On that same side of the room were two tall narrow closets. The bulk of the clothes hanging haphazardly in one didn't let the door close, so they spilled out like so much garbage in an overflowing trash can.

Stephanie spoke first. "Is this your room?"

"Yes, Emily and I were roommates."

"Were?"

Lisa stammered. "I mean are. We are roommates now."

While Lisa stood in the middle of the room, staring at her former life, and wondering how she was going to explain all this, Stephanie opened the closed closet door to reveal clothes hung in precise order by length and color. "Is this your closet?"

Lisa's eyebrows furrowed at the nonsensical question. "No, that was Emily's."

Stephanie pressed on. "Was?"

"I mean…is. That is her closet."

"The disaster one is yours then? Not very neat, are you?"

"I guess not. I'm not like that anymore."

Stephanie stepped closer to Lisa. "Why do you keep talking in the past tense?"

Lisa wasn't sure how to answer that. "Well, that's what I'm trying to explain."

Stephanie waved her away. "You haven't explained anything. We were in a diner, talking about your husband, and then we're here, in a dorm room, and you're acting weird, we both look different, and I don't understand anything at all. Is this some kind of revenge drug that you put into my coffee to make me feel like I'm crazy because I confessed that your husband is my lover?"

Lisa walked away and sat on the edge of the bunk bed. She motioned to Stephanie to sit down next to her. Stephanie shook her head. "No, I'm fine standing, thank you. I'd just like some answers, so I can go home. Please."

Sunlight filtered through the one window revealing dancing dust motes. Lisa gazed at Pat Benatar on the wall, hoping for some inspiration, for a best shot, but nothing came. The silence in the room was deafening, and she wanted to break it with an explanation, but how was she to explain any of this when she didn't understand it herself? She stared at the zigzag on the area rug beneath her feet, amazed at the awful taste they had in décor in college. Out of the corner of her eye, she saw Stephanie take a seat at Emily's desk and run her index finger along the spine of Emily's books. She paused at the physics book, pulled it out, and thrust it at Lisa.

"Your friend is not just neat; she's also the smart one, I guess?"

Lisa reached out her hand for the book. "I guess so. Why do you say that?"

"Because she's the one with the science and economics books, and your desk is full of…I can't tell what it's full of. It's just a hot mess."

Lisa felt her face get red and retorted, "Yes, fine, my desk is a mess, my closet is a mess. My…my whole life is a mess. Yours isn't much better from your little confession in the diner."

Stephanie slammed her hand on the desk and stormed towards Lisa. "I thought I was doing the right thing in talking to you. And you repay me by drugging me or something. I don't know what you did, but my patience with you is just about done. I'm going to the police to report you. Whatever you did, I'm sure it's criminal." As she turned towards the room door, Lisa pulled her back by the arm. "No, Stephanie, wait. Stay. I'll try to explain."

Stephanie stopped and turned to Lisa, eyes glaring. Lisa whispered, "Please. Sit down."

They each took a chair and sat facing each other. Lisa took a deep breath. "I'm going to tell you a story that will sound crazy. Wait until I'm done before you ask questions, please. Give me a chance to explain, and then I'll answer as best I can. Agreed?"

Stephanie nodded her head, prompting Lisa to continue. "I'm a time traveler."

Jumping up, Stephanie yelled. "You're a what?!"

Lisa put up her hand. "Stop. You agreed to wait until I was done."

Stephanie sat down again, closed her eyes and murmured. "Fine, crazy lady. Go on."

Lisa started again. "I'm something like a time traveler. As you can see, we're here in 1982 because that's when I went to college. So did you, right?"

"Yeah. So what?"

"The *so what* is that you, and me, and Adam, were all in college, in this very same area, at the same time. And I know Adam from the future. I know you from the future too."

"Lisa, you're making no sense at all. Maybe you took the drugs you gave me too?"

"Stephanie, there are no drugs involved. I don't know how this happened. All I know so far is this: In the future, our lives intersect. I traveled back to 1982 because this is where you and Adam met, fell in love, and later got married. In the real future, the one I came from, I was Adam's lover. In that future, you are his wife and work as a nurse. You have two daughters. He told me you were a horrible person, that your marriage was awful, and that he loved me. I was married also to a nice guy, but we grew apart, and I didn't love him anymore. I fell in love with Adam. Hard. I daydreamed that if I could turn back time, I'd meet him in college, and he and I would fall in love and get married, not you and he."

"Lisa, this story is crazy."

"Yes, I realize that, but you agreed to let me finish."

Stephanie waved her hand. "Go on."

Lisa took a deep breath and continued. "He used to tell you that he had late work meetings, so that he and I could meet. I'd pick him up at the train station sometimes. One night, while I was waiting for him, he didn't show up. I was listening to the radio, and the song 'Don't You Want Me' started playing, and I..."

Stephanie interrupted again. "That awful song from the Human League?"

"Yes, that one." Lisa frowned at Stephanie again. "Are you going to let me finish?" Stephanie raised her eyebrows and sighed.

Lisa kept going. "As the song was playing, I got nauseous and blacked out. When I woke up, I was here in 1982, sitting on the Low Library steps, and I met Adam. We started dating, and that was my chance. He hadn't met you yet. I had the opportunity to change the future, to make sure he didn't meet you, to get him to fall in love with me now—I mean in college—so that when we graduated, he and I could get married and have the life that I wanted with him, not the one he had with you in the future."

Lisa paused, concerned that Stephanie had no expression on her face. "Are you OK?"

Stephanie whispered. "Keep going."

"So, we started dating. It all moved very quickly; we were inseparable. And then one day, we went to the Hungarian Pastry Shop, and you were there."

Stephanie's eyes were as large as saucers. She leaned back in the chair. "That's not possible. I met Adam in a bar a few years ago, and he was married to you." She sighed and closed her eyes then shook her head. "No, no, no. This is nuts. I remember the bar, but now I can see us in the pastry shop. How can I remember that too? She closed her eyes again and spoke very slowly. "How can I recall meeting him twice? At the pastry shop, he was with a girl."

Lisa stayed quiet, seeing that Stephanie wanted to continue. "That was you. I could tell he was dating you, but he kept flirting with me with his eyes. You looked at him as if he were your universe. I remember thinking that I wanted a guy like that, a guy that I could look at with such love."

"Yes, that was me. Then we…"

Stephanie interrupted again. "You met me at a diner another day. You confronted me. It's all coming back. You told me to stay away from him. That he was your boyfriend. And I agreed to stay away. That was a very long time ago."

Lisa waited, her knee bobbing up and down. She picked up a pencil and drummed it on the desk while she watched Stephanie gather her thoughts. Lisa absently noticed an ink stain on the rug closest to her desk and wondered if that was from a pen she had dropped carelessly.

"Stephanie, he's really married to you. In the real world, the real future, he's married to you, and I'm his lover. I'm the one who's wrong, the one who cheated. Not you. I changed the future when I traveled back to the past. Don't you see? I took him away from you by going to the past, and then I made a mess of everything. But for nothing because even when I'm married to him, he's cheating on me with you."

Both women were silent for a moment. Lisa's eyes filled with tears. "You're the one he's supposed to be with because no matter what I do, he's always with you. He's either married to you, or he's your lover, but I'm always just on the side."

Stephanie was quiet. She still held the economics book in her hand and absently fanned the pages over and over again while staring out the window with a faraway gaze. "I don't understand how I can remember meeting him twice. I don't understand anything at all." She paused. "But I am noticing something, Lisa. I don't think he's meant to be with me. You're always in the picture too." She sat up straighter in her chair and faced Lisa directly. "Whatever this madness is…I think Adam wants it all. I think he's just a liar, no matter who he's with. I now remember this too. You had a head trauma, some pineal gland problem. I met you in the hospital when you were admitted. You were my patient. It's weird, I don't know how I know that, but I remember feeling like I knew you from somewhere, and I knew that you were messing around with my husband, but then I also remember me being the one messing around with your husband, and it's all a big mess of memories that seem real and not real at the same time. You know what I mean? And around it all, like mosquito netting on a bed, is this feeling that Adam's a liar. That he just takes advantage of me, of you, of both of us. That that's the only thing that's real. It's like he's the common denominator, and he's the one that's holding this circus together. I have this feeling that his lies and deceit cover everything like mold on an old piece of bread, and if we could just get away from him, we'd both be happy and not these sad lonely women that we've grown up to be."

Lisa wasn't sure how to answer all that. "How do you remember all of those things that haven't happened in this life?"

Stephanie smiled. "I don't know. I don't even believe that you time travel, but I don't know how to explain this young body, with The Pretenders staring at me from a dorm room, yet I remember parts of the story you just told me. I remember being Adam's girlfriend, his lover, and his wife and all the times are mixed up together, but I also remember a layer of unhappiness over everything. Something must have happened, and it's completely crazy, but who knows? Maybe your friend Emily can give us answers from this physics book of hers."

Lisa reached over and grabbed Stephanie's hand. They sat in silence, sharing a space of understanding that Lisa hadn't seen before. These worlds she had created by traveling were like a bubbling pot of stew, everything mixed up. Lisa didn't know whether her strange brain had caused it, or whether there was a reason for it, perhaps so she could finally see the truth. Whatever its purpose, she had to figure out how to undo the chaos she had created before there were any more consequences.

Chapter 16

P anting, Emily barged into the room, disrupting Lisa and Stephanie's quiet moment. "You're here? And you're friends again!" Lisa released Stephanie's hands and walked towards the window. She stared out at the street while Emily rummaged through the contents of the messy desk. She pulled a bunch of papers from the top of the typewriter, scrambling to find something. "One of these days I'm going to get organized. I have a poli-sci class in fifteen minutes, and I need my notes! Lisa, have you seen them?"

With her mouth agape, Lisa turned towards Emily. "Why are you looking through my things? That's not your desk."

Emily laughed, "Yeah, I wish, but you're the neat freak, remember?" She scrambled through more notebooks and loose-leaf papers before exclaiming "Aha! Here they are."

"Wait, Em. That's not your stuff." Lisa wasn't sure if Emily was serious or just trying to be funny. In college Emily had nicknamed her "the Tornado" because their room was a chaotic whirlwind of papers and clothes haphazardly covering the floor. Lisa was careless, but Emily was meticulous, a quality Lisa secretly envied. She covered up her guilt at not doing her fair share of cleaning by pretending it was a quirk that Emily should get used to if she really loved her. Friends put up with one another was Lisa's ever-present response.

When Lisa brought Stephanie into the suite, she assumed nothing from the past had changed. She and Emily were still roommates and best friends. Their suite was the same. On the surface, everything looked as she remembered it, as if the past were fixed with no alterations possible. But now? Lisa gnawed at her lower lip realizing this version of the past contained altered personalities and habits. Had this inadvertent return with Stephanie created a different past from the one she remembered? And what would happen if they returned?

Standing with her fists on her hips like a stern mother, Emily brough Lisa back to the conversation. "What's gotten into you? There's a reason why you call me the Tornado." Emily walked towards Lisa, bent close to her, and scrunched her face into a scowl. "What have you two been inhaling that's making you act so weird?"

Lisa felt goosebumps up and down her arms, shuddering. She had caused this turbulence. She had dreamed of altering history by meeting Adam before he met Stephanie, but she hadn't planned on changing her friend.

Stephanie interrupted Lisa's thoughts when she put her hands up and rubbed her temples. "Do you realize that neither of you makes any sense? What are we doing here anyway, Lisa? I agree with Emily. Maybe you gave me some drug, and you don't even realize it? My head is pounding."

"I have a headache too," Lisa whispered. "And no, I didn't drug you. Stop asking such a stupid question. Why would I do such a thing?"

Stephanie shrugged her shoulders.

Emily continued, seemingly unfazed by anything around her. "If you want aspirin, ask Lisa. She's the one who knows where everything is in this place. I've got to get to class. Wanna hang out later? I'll be back in an hour, maybe less depending on whether I can sneak out when the professor has his back to the class." Emily uttered the end of her sentence as she rushed out the door.

Lisa stared at the empty space left by Emily's departure while Stephanie kept her face down. The enormity of the realization that she no longer knew her friend or herself was a lead weight on her conscience. She inched towards the neat desk that was now hers, and there, in the top drawer, in a compact box marked First Aid, she found the bottle of aspirin. Silently, she offered it to Stephanie. "Wait here. I'll get you water."

Walking back from the suite's kitchen, cup in hand, she puzzled what to do about the knot of time she had created. All these decisions made with the singular aim of getting the love of her life had twisted the people in her life into beings she didn't recognize. They had no say in what had happened to them; they didn't even know they were different people from who she knew them to be in the past. But she knew. She was the constant in all these rivers of time.

Lisa returned to the room and handed Stephanie a red plastic cup with water. "Here, this was the only clean thing in the kitchen. Apparently, my note to the others to clean up was ignored."

Stephanie's face was blank, but her eyes were defiant. With ice in her voice she said, "Thanks." After gulping down the aspirin, her voice softened. "You look as out of sorts as I feel. What's wrong with you?"

Thinking for a moment at the gravity of the question, Lisa whispered, "Everything."

Stephanie scoffed. "For whatever reason and through some strange hocus-pocus, you brought me here."

When Lisa didn't answer, Stephanie pressed on. "Lisa, I want answers. I want to know how we got here and…"

Something in Stephanie's litany of complaints gave Lisa a compelling desire to inspect her closet. If this past was all new, it was possible that she'd have something hidden that might explain how this had happened. Lisa opened the closet door. She could see her reflection and Stephanie's in the full-length mirror. They looked youthful and vibrant. It was uncanny to feel the strength in her muscles and the softness in her hands. She noticed that Stephanie caught sight of herself in the mirror also.

Stephanie stopped talking and slammed the red cup on the desk. She rose from her chair in one fluid move as the water spilled onto the desk. Through the mirror Lisa watched the water fall onto the dirty area rug, creating a dark crimson circle. She was mesmerized by the drip, drip, focusing on the sound of the drops as they landed.

Stephanie's gasp startled Lisa. She noticed Stephanie staring at herself in the mirror.

Lisa stared at her too, marveling at watching someone discover her forgotten youth. Stephanie would understand the wonder Lisa felt the first time she saw herself young again. Stephanie was beautiful in that sinewy sense that's reserved for the barely twenty. Her body didn't know long twelve-hour shifts on aching feet. Wind, cold, and gravity hadn't hijacked her skin or her hips yet. Her hair was thick, luscious, and long, cascading below her shoulders with a bounce. Lisa could see the muscles in her thighs and calves that stretched long and lean below her green shorts that she probably bought at the Army-Navy surplus store a few blocks away. That was also where she likely bought the black combat boots she wore with black socks. Her breasts swelled above the V-neck of her white T-shirt.

Stephanie leaned in closer to the mirror and caressed her face whispering, "How is this possible?"

She turned around and continued. "My brain tells me this isn't logical, but it feels real. If you've played a weird mind trick on me, it's working."

"Stephanie, believe me, this isn't a trick. I wish I could explain it."

"Try. A few hours ago, we were sitting in a coffee shop in our normal bodies, with our normal lives, while I confessed that I've been sleeping with your husband. In the whirl of a moment then, we're still sitting in a diner, but we're no longer the same people. Instead, we're these younger versions of ourselves. I mean, look at us! We look like we're what? Nineteen, twenty years old?"

Stephanie thrust her hands out to Lisa, palms down. "My arms are strong; look at these muscles. And see here? That's where I have a scar from a crazy patient who stabbed me with scissors years ago. But the scar's gone. And my knees. They don't hurt at all." Stephanie jumped up and down, laughing. "I feel like I can play basketball again, or volleyball, or...or anything. Nothing hurts!"

But as quickly as she noticed her agility, Stephanie stopped and stared at herself in the mirror again. She slumped onto the floor, her back leaning against the closed room door. "This isn't possible, Lisa. It's simply not possible. Time travel, multiple memories, accidentally bringing me here. This doesn't happen to real people. This is the *Twilight Zone!*"

Lisa let Stephanie vent, not sure how to convince her. "Stephanie, I know it defies all logic, but I'm telling you the truth. I don't know how I do it. Back in my real life, I had a car accident and hit my head. The accident left a small scar on my forehead. An ambulance took me to the hospital because I was unconscious, and after running tests, the doctor said I have an enlarged pineal gland. Maybe that's why I'm able to time travel."

"Why? Because of the accident?"

"No, because of the pineal gland."

"You think that an enlarged pineal gland causes you to travel back in time and then forward again? You're even crazier than I thought!"

Lisa bit her lip trying to explain without sounding like a lunatic. "It's not just the pineal gland. The song has something to do with it too. I get nauseous, and I don't know, feel like I've fallen through a wormhole or something when I hear the song 'Don't You Want Me.'"

Stephanie laughed. "'Don't You Want Me'?"

Lisa shrugged her shoulders. "Yeah, I don't know why that song, or how it happens. It just does. I hear the song, and my world shifts."

Stephanie tapped her head against the door. "Ironic when I'm the one who met Adam in a cocktail bar." Then she dug her nails into her temples. "I'm so confused and angry, and I don't even know what to say to you, and my head just keeps pounding."

With a mixture of guilt and sympathy, Lisa offered an explanation. "I have a headache too. In fact, I get one every time I travel back and forth. For a few minutes after arrival, my brain feels like scrambled eggs." She paused. "Maybe you have an enlarged pineal gland also. Or maybe you came with me because we were holding hands. Remember? In the diner we were holding hands, and the song came on, and then we were here. In this time. In our past. Except that it's not really our past. It's a different one. That's why I feel so confused because things are different. We never were friends in the past; we didn't come to this room together. And Emily was different, and so was I. I think that coming back with you has somehow transformed the past."

Stephanie set her mouth in a straight line and raised her left eyebrow. "Transformed the past? Fine then, Miss Voyager, now what? I want to go home. To my real home. You got me into this mess. Now get me out of it."

"That's the problem. I'm not sure how to get us back." Lisa sighed. "I mean, I think I can transport us to the future from here. We can do like at the diner—hold hands and listen to the song."

Stephanie jumped up from the floor and grabbed Lisa's hand. "Here we go then. Let's do this."

Lisa pulled her hand back. "No, you don't understand. It's not just hold hands. We have to play the song, and…."

Stephanie moved towards the boom box by the window. "Do you have the song here? We can play it and hold hands, and then we're done." She looked at Lisa, one eyebrow lifted in a menacing arc. "Or is it that you've run out of whatever mushrooms you put into my drink, and now we're somehow stuck in a hallucination." She raised her voice again. "Don't just stand there. Say something!"

Lisa took a deep breath. "Stephanie, please listen carefully. It's not just the song and holding hands. The problem is that I'm afraid I don't know to which future we're headed."

"Lisa, there is only one future."

"I don't think so. That's the issue."

"Oh boy, more make-believe stories."

"No, listen. I came from two different futures. I told you before. You were married to Adam, and I was his lover. That's the real future. That's when I came back here the first time. And I met Adam and thought my dream had come true. But we ran into you, and you were in our lives again. He had been flirting with you, and you wanted him to be your boyfriend. I convinced you to give him up. I was rough with you. We had a terrible fight, and you gave him up. You told me you weren't going to see him anymore. And I think that changed everything."

"How?"

"Because when I traveled to the future again, it changed. I was his wife in that future, and you were his lover. And in that future, you met him at a bar, not in college."

Stephanie sighed in exasperation. "That *is* reality, Lisa. That's our real world. You're married to him, you have two little girls, and I'm his mistress...was his mistress. I broke it off." Stephanie slumped her shoulders.

A single tear fell down Lisa's cheek as she uttered her words in acknowledgement and defeat. "This is some mess." Stephanie hugged her, while Lisa poured out all her grief onto her rival's shoulders.

When the sobbing stopped, Stephanie stood back. "Lisa, I believe that you believe all this. I'm not sure if I believe it all. What I do know is that we don't belong here in 1982. We belong in our real lives. That's where you need to take us, back to our reality. If I believe that you got us here, then I have to believe that you can get us back."

Lisa thought hard about Stephanie's suggestion. She paced in the small room thinking of how she could maneuver them back to the real past, the one where she had created all the problems. Stephanie stopped her while she paced. "What are you doing?"'

"I'm thinking about how to fix this."

As she walked, she realized that going back to that life meant she'd lose everything. She stopped at the window again. She closed her eyes and heard the sound of her little girls laughing. She liked being a mother. She had only known them briefly, yet she already missed them. Returning this Stephanie to her rightful place meant giving up what she had discovered that she loved.

And that's when it struck her. A boulder landed on her chest, pressing into it, choking off all ability to breathe. Lisa wrapped her arms around herself, looking for warmth and comfort as she realized she was about to lose everything again. If she returned to Stephanie's real life, Lisa would lose her mother too. Her daughters may have been fictional at some level of that invented world, but her mother was very real.

Her warm, loving, kind mother. How could she bear to lose her again?

Chapter 17

Lost in thought, Lisa touched the boom box on the windowsill, outlining its edges. She fiddled with the buttons, and the cassette player popped open. Curious as to what she and Emily had been listening to, she took out the cassette. The Pretenders. In a messy stash on the windowsill was the pile of cassettes. The Stranglers, David Bowie, Roxy Music. She grabbed cassettes and threw them on the floor until she found the right one. She put the Human League cassette in the player and turned to face Stephanie.

Lisa didn't speak right away, wondering how much of it she should share. It was an idea only, with no guarantees that it would work, but she didn't need to add more stress to the situation by confiding her worries in Stephanie. "I have a plan."

"I'm holding my breath waiting for this marvelous plan of yours."

"We're going back to the diner where we landed this morning. I'll bring this boom box, and when we're sitting at a table, I'm going to play the song. We'll hold hands again."

Stephanie chortled. "That's it? Your plan is that we sit in a diner and hold hands?"

Lisa heard the simplicity of her words. The strategy was basic, cartoonish almost, but it's how they got here, so perhaps it would work in reverse. Until now, the song brought her back and forth involuntarily. What if she focused on her destination? If that worked, she could direct them back to the place they'd just left where Stephanie was Adam's mistress. That life, where she was a mother and where her mother was alive, was now more important than anything else.

With a slight prickle of her conscience, she tried to reason with Stephanie.

"Of course it will work. That's how we got here, so that's how we will return." While she waited for Stephanie to agree or complain, her mind chattered away on its own. *You're taking advantage of this woman. You know you're lying to her. And to yourself.* But this Stephanie knew no other life; she didn't even believe Lisa that there was another life, so it wouldn't hurt her if they went back to that the world where Lisa had a family and her mother. Lisa knew the truth, but the truth was inconvenient right now. She had had a taste of motherhood, even if it was brief. She had had a taste of money and ease. And she had the chance to have her mother in her life. All those lies were worth living with an Adam who didn't love her. It was a small price to pay. And she wasn't hurting Stephanie at all because she was just returning her to the life she remembered. What was wrong with that? A little voice tried to answer her unspoken question, but she shut it down immediately.

Lisa grabbed Stephanie's hand and pulled her. "Let's go. The sooner we get to the diner, the sooner we'll be home where we belong."

***

The diner was busier than earlier in the day. Lisa looked at her watch. Almost five o'clock. The place was filled with old people. As if reading her thoughts, Stephanie chimed in. "Looks like the blue-plate special thing is real."

"Booth or table?" asked the hostess in a bored voice.

"Booth please. As far to the back as possible." Lisa wanted a little bit of quiet, so they could play the music without interruption.

In the back, near the kitchen, an elderly couple ambled slowly out of a booth. The man waited for his wife while she struggled out of her seat, then offered her a hand to get up. They walked down the aisle together, holding hands. Lisa watched them with longing. That's what she had dreamed of: growing old with Adam. She shook her head to erase those thoughts. She had a plan, and she had to focus.

The hostess wiped down the table and said the usual. "Your waitress will be here shortly to take your order." She laid the two menus down and walked away.

Ignoring the menus, Lisa placed the boom box on the table and turned to Stephanie, who was bouncing in her seat, looking around at the other customers and fidgeting with her fingers.

Annoyed, Lisa said, "Why are you so nervous? Stop it. I need to concentrate."

"That's easy for you. You believe this will work. I still have my doubts. I mean, if this is true, and I'm still not sure it is, what if you scramble my brain, and I end up like you, traveling through time when I hear music?"

"It's not just music. It's one specific song. Now focus."

"What am I supposed to focus on?"

"Think of your life, where you live, your friends, your job." Lisa hesitated but threw it out anyway. "Think of Adam."

Stephanie cocked her head to the side like a dog listening intently. "Why are you asking me to think of your husband?"

"I just want you to think of things that are familiar, so that whatever takes us back will put us in the right place." Lisa hoped that explanation would get Stephanie's attention. She didn't add that she hoped that if both of them thought of the same place, perhaps the directions would be clear. But it was merely a theory. She crossed her index and middle fingers under the table before bringing her hands back up.

"The tape is set to the right song. I'll hit Play, then we hold hands and think of our lives, so that we can direct the energy to send us there. Got that?"

"Got it." Stephanie muttered. "This better work."

Lisa hit the button then quickly grabbed Stephanie's hands in her own.

It was an old-fashioned boom box. The latest version for 1982, but Lisa had forgotten how long it took for the cassette player to start. Amid all the noise in the diner, she could hear the whirring as the tape revolved around the plastic knobs. Stephanie's hands were shaking, and her rings banged loudly on the Formica tabletop.

"Close your eyes and focus," hissed Lisa, trying to will the cassette player to start, so she could see if her theory was correct. She heard the seconds ticking in her head as if her brain had an internal grandfather clock. Tick, tick, tick.

The diner seemed to get louder, but she could hear the initial notes of the song. She held Stephanie's hands like a vise.

She sensed the waitress standing next to her before she heard the words, "Did yous decide what you want?"

Darkness came on quickly, no more dots that melted slowly into her vision. The swoosh that flipped her stomach came on more violently than in times past. She tried to slow it all down, but she was under water, images of her pretend life as the mother of Suzette and Natalie floating before her eyes, distorted like in fun house mirrors. She wanted to scream.

With a thud, she landed in her seat, as if she had been flying through the air. She kept her eyes closed, afraid of throwing up but more afraid of what she'd see when she opened them.

Finally brave enough to look, she opened her eyes and saw that Stephanie was still there, with her eyes shut tight. Lisa noticed that her hands hurt from how hard Stephanie was gripping them.

The boom box was gone. They were in the coffee shop. No more diner. They looked their normal age again. Lisa looked down at her clothes. Yes! The same outfit she had been wearing when they traveled back to college. "Open your eyes, Stephanie. It worked."

"I think I'm going to be sick."

"It will pass. Just move slowly."

Lisa smiled in triumph. Stephanie was the same as before: same clothes, same hair, same chapped hands from working as a nurse.

That's when Lisa checked out her own hands. No rings.

Where were her wedding rings? She was wearing them when she met Stephanie at the diner. She was wearing the same clothes; she had the same handbag. She pulled her feet from under the table. Yes, the shoes were the same. Maybe gold and diamonds didn't travel through time?

She opened her purse and took out her cell phone. Stephanie was mumbling about a headache when the waitress returned to their table. "Would you ladies like more coffee?"

Lisa stared at the phone. She scrolled through the contacts. Adam's name wasn't in it. There must be a glitch with the phone.

The waitress had struck up a conversation with Stephanie. Lisa interrupted. "Could we have the check please? We're in a big hurry."

"Lisa, I don't think I can move fast. I'm not feeling well still."

"Walking will make you feel better. We have to go."

When the waitress came back with the check, Lisa slapped a twenty-dollar bill on the table and rushed Stephanie out the door.

"Why are you running? What's the giant hurry?"

"Stephanie, I need to get home. I have to see my kids."

"OK, I get that. But stop. Please. I have to get my bearings." Stephanie stared at the park across the street. "Hey, this isn't the diner where we met before. We weren't in front of a park."

Lisa had been in such a rush to get home that she hadn't noticed that they were in a different diner. This was a busy street, but it wasn't where they met before. Her head was pounding now, and the urgency of getting home grew stronger. They were on a street that appeared to be a block away from her house. She clearly remembered driving to meet Stephanie at the diner across from the hospital, but now everything was off.

"We have to hurry. If this didn't work, we have to do something else. Come with me. I need to see my kids and my mother. They'll be worried about me."

Lisa pulled Stephanie by the hand, practically dragging her behind her. With each step, her dread grew. Her pace quickened to a run. She didn't notice the storefronts where before there had been a neat row of houses.

When she rounded the corner, she was sure that she'd see her house. But what faced her was a huge apartment building with a For Lease sign on the front. She stopped abruptly, making Stephanie bump into her. The once quiet residential area was filled with people walking about, cars honking, tall buildings casting shadows on the street. The grocery store on the corner with displays in the window pretended to be something more than a bodega.

Lisa stepped carefully off the curb to cross the street to the address that was her house. 5905 Hudson Avenue. But that wasn't her house.

"Are you sure you have the right address? I thought you lived in a fancy house?" Stephanie's voice sounded jealously gleeful to Lisa's ears.

They walked together up the steps to the front door of the building. A rectangular metal plate was screwed into the side wall with little slots for the names of the residents and a buzzer for each apartment. Lisa was afraid to look. She was hoping she just had the wrong address. She peered closely, praying not to find it. But there it was. Lisa Coronado.

"This is all wrong, all wrong." Lisa leaned her back against the wall and covered her face with her hands.

Stephanie checked the list also. "Who is Lisa Coronado?"

Lisa sobbed. "Me. Single." The enormity of what had happened started to sink in. She didn't know where she was, and now she was responsible for someone else. She was afraid to think that her daughters were out there somewhere wondering where she was.

Stephanie put her hand on Lisa's shoulder. "Look, I get your distress. But get a grip. Do you have any idea where we are? I don't know this area. I need to get my car. I need to get home too."

Chapter 18

Trying to get a handle on her emotions, Lisa took a few deep breaths, so she could focus on what Stephanie was saying.

"Lisa! I need to find my car and go home. I'm done trying to help you. It's time to help myself."

Sighing, Lisa walked down the few steps to the sidewalk and looked both ways. Nothing seemed familiar, not from the life with children and not from her previous life. Traveling had left everything in shambles, and she had no clue where to go next.

Stephanie tapped her on the shoulder. "We'll go to my house, get a cup of tea, and sort this out."

"How are we going to find your car if we don't even recognize these streets?"

Stephanie grinned. "Because, my friend, while you were busy bemoaning your fate and being messy and confused, I searched my purse and found this." She opened her hand with a flourish. "Voila! A car key."

Stephanie started back towards the diner with long strides while Lisa ran trying to keep up. When they arrived, Stephanie pointed the key in the air and pressed the alarm button.

Within seconds, Lisa heard a blaring siren. Stephanie looked gleeful. "Aha! I knew it would work." She turned off the alarm as they approached what looked like a brand-new shiny metallic gray BMW. The inspection sticker on the windshield had the year 2008 in large dark numbers. "Hmm. This world seems to agree more with me than with you, Lisa." She opened the passenger door and motioned for Lisa to get in.

The car seats boasted a plum-colored soft leather that felt like butter. It even had that new car smell. When Stephanie sat down and closed the driver's side door, the seat moved to accommodate her. When the car started, the audio system turned itself on to a list called "Stephanie's Favorites."

With what Lisa thought was a bit of a smirk, Stephanie remarked, "I guess this is my car after all. Now I get to see what my favorite music is in this world."

Lisa felt defeated. How could this be? It seemed the tables had turned. "This is all very nice, but how are you going to get to your house? You didn't even know this was your car."

Stephanie fiddled with controls on the front panel. "Let's see what this navigation system does." A lighted map appeared, and at the top the banner spelled clearly—Home.

With that, Stephanie turned to Lisa, whose eyebrows were furrowed. "It's good to have nice things, isn't it?" The note of sarcasm didn't escape Lisa.

***

They drove for a few miles until the navigation system brought them to a quiet residential neighborhood with fine houses and tree-lined streets. It looked very similar to where Lisa had last lived. The thought that this Stephanie now had everything that Lisa wanted was more than she could bear, but there it was—evidence that the twists and turns had upended the world even more than before.

Stephanie pulled into the long driveway of a three-story home and stopped the car in front of the three-car garage. "This is amazing. Looks like I've made out in this deal, doesn't it?" She turned to Lisa and grinned from ear to ear. "Maybe I won't want to go back to 'reality,'" as she crooked her fingers with air quotes.

One of the garage doors was open, revealing a red corvette. Lisa couldn't help herself. "Well, isn't that simply cliché?"

Stephanie replied, "Don't be a hater. If what you say is true, you had your turn."

They got out of the car and headed to the front door. Stephanie stopped. "Let's not go in the front door. Let's go through the garage and see what we can find there instead."

They tiptoed quickly across the garage and through a door that was surprisingly open. It led to a hallway with a laundry room on the right. To the left, stone steps led up to an expansive kitchen and family room. The skylights in the vaulted ceilings filled the rooms with sunlight. The kitchen was pristine, with a large center island counter made of marble with a sink in the corner and shelves beneath stacked with cookbooks. The floor was a rust stone that matched perfectly with the hardwood floors in the family room with an enormous sectional sofa of dark brown leather dominating the space. The giant TV screen on the wall and the score of video game consoles on shelves beneath were proof that whoever lived here enjoyed playing. Sliding glass doors behind the sofa led to a patio with an Olympic-sized swimming pool, a colorful and fragrant garden, and a backyard complete with an outside kitchen and tables and chairs for lounging.

On the other side of the kitchen was a large dining room followed by another small living room. A grand staircase flowed from there towards the second and third floors. Standing at the bottom of the stairs, Stephanie and Lisa heard voices from the second floor.

Lisa noticed that all the rooms but one had the doors open. The noise came from the room with the door closed. She strained to hear, but the sounds were muffled.

As Stephanie started up the stairs, Lisa grabbed her arm. "Wait. Are you sure you want to go up there?" Something told Lisa they might regret seeing whatever was happening behind the closed door.

Stephanie shook off Lisa's hand and replied with abrupt shots for words. "Of course—I'm going up there. This is clearly my house. What? Are you jealous?"

Lisa softened her stance. "No. Maybe. OK, yes, I'm jealous. But I'm also scared. I don't know how this happened or how we're in this position now. But what I do know is that whoever's up there, and whatever's going on, will change you and me forever. I'm just wondering if we should lie low and listen first before we go barging in."

Stephanie walked back down the two steps and led Lisa towards the family room. She stopped in front of the sliding glass doors. "Listen up, Lisa. I've spent far too many years of my life watching you have the life I've always wanted with Adam. I didn't believe you at first when you said you traveled through time, but I gave you the benefit of the doubt. So, I played along. And now we're here, and it's clear that I now have what you had before." Stephanie stared out at the expansive garden. "I mean, look at that pool. Look at this whole place. It's gorgeous. You had this when I met you. Now it's mine and not yours. This is what I thought about as we held hands in the diner—that I wanted what you had. Thanks. I'm really grateful for the time traveling tips." She leaned towards Lisa and kissed her on the cheek. "You can leave now. I've no further use for you."

Dumfounded, Lisa watched Stephanie head towards the stairs. Had she been double-crossed? "Stephanie, wait!"

Stephanie stopped in her tracks but didn't turn around. Desperate to find the right words, Lisa pleaded. "Stephanie, none of this is real. I have to explain."

Rolling her eyes, Stephanie faced Lisa. "There's nothing to explain. And it is real." Stephanie pinched her left arm. "See? I can feel that. Whatever you had planned didn't work. Like I said, it's my turn."

At that moment, Lisa heard someone coming downstairs. Before she could alert Stephanie, a tall blonde woman entered the kitchen. She had long straight hair parted down the middle, icy blue eyes and chiseled features and looked like she'd stepped out of a fashion magazine except that she was wearing a man's white collared shirt, unbuttoned, yet opened just enough to show off plenty of cleavage. She was barefoot with bright red polish on her toes that matched that on her long fingernails. Under the shirt she was wearing nothing at all.

She looked startled when she saw Stephanie and Lisa staring at her. "Oh, I didn't know anyone was here." As if this were her home, she walked towards a cabinet and grabbed a drinking glass, then filled it with water from the refrigerator door. "You must be the new cleaning ladies that Adam hired. He didn't tell me you were coming today." She looked around as she put her lips to the edge of the glass. "I guess you're done already." She took another sip. "I must commend you. The place looks spotless, and you were silent." She giggled. "Or maybe we were too busy to hear you." More giggles. As she put the empty glass in the kitchen sink, she remarked, almost casually. "You're way better than Zelda was." She walked back from where she came and threw over her shoulder, "Be darlings and lock the door on your way out. I don't want Adam's wife to catch us by surprise when she comes home from wherever she disappeared to."

***

After the initial shock wore off, Lisa motioned to Stephanie to step outside.

"Listen," said Lisa to Stephanie. "I know you think you were smarter than me, and you got what I had, but this is what results from messing with time." She pointed upstairs. "Up there is your evidence. If you want to catch him in the act, go up. See for yourself."

Her face flushed and with quivering lips, Stephanie replied, "It's not fair. This is just not fair." She punctuated each word with a slap to her thigh. "This is obviously my house. And that woman upstairs is not you, and it's not me. He has yet another woman? This isn't what I wished for."

In that instant, Lisa felt the weight of all that she had tampered with come crashing on her. The cost of her selfish decision to interfere with Stephanie and Adam meeting, marrying, and having a life together was apparently this jumbled mess. Back at the diner, she had tried to steal Stephanie's authentic life by desiring to return to a time when her mother was still alive. But that wasn't real either. Lisa knew that, but she had tried to ignore it, her self-cherishing pursuits having blinded her to the truth.

This was not what she had intended. And this was not the person she wanted to be. Her actual mother would not be proud of her if she knew of Lisa's machinations. And this was the price—she had nothing now. No children, no mother, no husband, not even a lover. She lived in a run-down tenement. If she explored this world any further, who knows what other calamities she'd find?

And worse than that, she had shown Stephanie no mercy when she took advantage of her and switched her life around. The poor woman had not even had a choice in the matter. Watching her cry in front of her, Lisa felt moved to tears herself. She had to undo this mess.

"Stephanie, listen to me. I'm sorry. This is all my fault. I need to tell you the truth."

"What more is there to tell me? That this is just a bad dream? I'm done with your stories and your plans to fix things. Nothing gets fixed. I've been in love with Adam for years, and he'll never be mine. This is just proof of that. Even when he's supposed to be mine, he's not."

Lisa wondered about the truth of that statement. Even though this Stephanie didn't remember their real lives, she was right about one thing. No matter on what plane they were living, Adam was always with someone else. He was the constant lie in their lives.

Lisa walked over to the pool, took off her shoes, and sat down on the border with her feet dangling in the water. It felt cool and refreshing. "Come over here. It feels nice. We might as well enjoy it a little."

Stephanie sat down beside her. She leaned down, placing her hand in the water, and twisting it this way and that, causing ripples to move outward in a circle that got wider with each turn of her hand. Watching the ripples, Lisa played out different scenes in her mind, looking for a way to unravel the knot she had created.

Both women were silent for a while. Stephanie finally spoke up. "I thought really hard about taking everything away from you when we were at the diner. I figured that if this time travel thing were real, I could think about what you had—the big house, the fancy car, and the handsome husband." She smiled at Lisa. "Clearly that backfired."

Lisa replied. "What I do know is that ever since then, nothing's been real. And nothing feels right. And I haven't gotten what I wanted all along anyway. Adam has never been mine to love. Each time I travel back and forth in time, something else changes, but the constant is that he's always messing around with someone else. It backfired because it's not real, because it's based on another lie. The truth is the only thing that's going to get us back to our actual lives. As much as it pains me to lose my children and my mother, they're not real either." Lisa reached for Stephanie's hand. "But yours are. And they're entitled to have their mother."

As Lisa thought out loud, she got excited thinking she might have discovered a way to return things to normal. "I don't know how it works. Maybe because you came with me from a life track where you were Adam's lover and not his wife…. Maybe if we went back to that life first, then we could jump back to the real world."

S tephanie got out of the pool and walked to a lounge chair where a stack of plush towels lay neatly folded. She grabbed a towel, and as she dried her legs, spoke into the air, "This sure is a pleasant way to live, but, if you're right, Lisa, then I have a family waiting for me somewhere."

She continued talking as she walked around the garden with Lisa following her. "How am I supposed to believe you, though? How do I know that you're being honest this time and that you're going to take me back where I belong? I don't remember any of this life you claim I had. How do I know this isn't another trick of yours? Maybe you'll take me somewhere, so that I'll be the one living in a tenement and not in this beautiful house?"

Lisa sighed. "You have no way of knowing if I'm telling you the truth. But I beg you. Search your heart. What does your gut say? That guy upstairs with the blonde…is that what you want? A beautiful house with a man who has no concept of honesty? Who wants that?"

As if on cue, Stephanie and Lisa both glanced up at the house and saw Adam in the window looking down at them. He waved, as if nothing were wrong. Lisa shook her head in disbelief but wasn't surprised.

Feeling like she was moving in slow motion, Lisa reached for Stephanie's hand and grasped it. "What do you say, Steph? Blow this popsicle joint?"

"All right, Lisa, I've got nothing to lose here and no choice but to trust you. Take me home, wherever that may be."

Lisa felt sorry for Stephanie. She had no idea what was going on. She was on this ride because of Lisa, and it wasn't her fault that they were in this predicament. Lisa couldn't even blame her for having twisted the trip with her thoughts of revenge. No, this was all her responsibility, and she had to fix it.

"Stephanie, let's return to the diner where we first arrived here. We'll play the song, so we can get this pretzel untwisted and go home." Lisa crossed her fingers hoping this would send them back.

They left the pool and dried themselves with the plush towels stacked neatly on a lounge chair. With a flourish, they threw the towels in the pool, and laughing, they both looked up towards the window where they had seen Adam. Almost in unison, they gave the house the middle finger and ran back towards the car.

***

Back at the diner, they settled themselves in a booth. The waitress from before returned with her dowdy face. "Can't get enough of this place, huh?"

Lisa chimed quickly. "Just two coffees please. Black."

Once the coffees arrived and the waitress turned her attention to other customers, Stephanie pulled out the phone and found the song. "I've got it." She placed the phone on the table between them, and they reached across and held hands.

Lisa squeezed Stephanie's hands and pleaded with her eyes. "This time, no strategizing or lying, agreed? We're both going to concentrate on returning to the right place. Deal?"

"Yes, yes, we already agreed to that, Lisa."

Stephanie pressed play and returned her hand quickly to Lisa's.

The music started, and Lisa felt the now familiar buzzing and swooshing blackness descend upon her. Her last thought was, *This time it's going to work.*

***

For a few seconds, they kept their eyes closed and their hands tightly clasped. Lisa's hands were hot and sweaty. She opened one eye and looked around the diner but nothing seemed to have changed. They were in the same dreary spot.

"I don't think it worked," she said.

Stephanie opened her eyes and frowned. "Wait a minute. Didn't we have coffee mugs in front of us? They're gone."

Lisa noticed the table was empty except for large diner menus stacked to the side. "We didn't have menus before."

Stephanie moved her hands all over the table as if touching the contents were more reliable than her sight. A no-brand bottle of ketchup with drippings down the side sat at the end towards the wall of the booth. There was also a sugar bowl and a glass bottle of honey. A jukebox was affixed to the wall.

And there was no cell phone in sight.

"Where's the phone, Lisa?"

Lisa patted the table, then looked underneath. "Maybe it fell down." Crumbs and some withered french fries littered the floor beneath. She was surprised she didn't find roaches.

"No phone down here." *Oh, this isn't good. Now where are we?*

Wringing her hands, Stephanie raised her voice. "Now what, Lisa? What mess are we in this time?"

"Let's just relax and be calm. I'm sure we can figure this out." She waved to the waitress, who came over with a pot of coffee in her hand and placed it directly on the table. She wore a pin with her name on it. Mary.

"Are you ready to order?"

Grabbing a menu, Lisa used her sweetest voice. "Hi, Mary. What a lovely name. Actually, my friend and I have a bet going and were wondering if you had a newspaper somewhere?"

"Girls, I've been on my feet for about four hours straight today, and I still have another four to go. You think because you're young and beautiful, I have time for stupid girl bets? If you're ready to order something, order it. If not, then go find someplace else to play your games." Mary held her pen over a small dirty notepad and raised her eyebrows in anticipation.

At hearing the description young, Lisa glanced over at Stephanie. She looked different from when they sat by the pool. Her hair was now in a ponytail, and she wore big-rimmed glasses. She wore a blouse with a frilly loose tie that turned into a bow. Lisa raised her right eyebrow remembering those were all the rage among the office set in the mid-1980s. She wore no rings, and her hands were smooth as silk. Lisa looked down at her own. No rings there either.

"Thanks, Mary," she said slowly. "We need a few more minutes to decide." Mary grabbed the coffee pot in a huff and moved back to the diner's counter.

"Stephanie, I think we're back in the eighties."

"What makes you say that?"

"Look at your hands. Do you have a mirror?"

Stephanie found a mirror in her purse next to her. She pulled it out and gasped. "Oh man, Lisa, you did it again. Take a look."

She handed Lisa the pocket mirror. The face that stared back was a barely older version of her college self. And, of course, a bow tie and very curly high hair.

Turning to the jukebox, Lisa went into action. "Fine. It didn't work perfectly well. That doesn't mean we can't try again. We'll play the song from the jukebox. This time we'll focus on the year also."

She pressed the buttons on the jukebox. Letter D for "Don't You Want Me." Nothing.

Letter "T" for the Human League. Nothing. "It's not here," she whispered to Stephanie.

"What are you talking about?" She called out to the waitress, forgetting all her manners. "Hey, Mary, what year are we in?"

"Aren't you girls too old to be playing games? It's 1984, you idiots."

Stephanie turned back to Lisa. "1984. That song still played in 1984. And it must be in this jukebox. It looks like it hasn't been updated in years."

They were stunned. For one, this time, they traveled back to 1984, not 1982. And two, how could the song not exist?

Lisa sat up straight in her seat. "Do you remember the name of the band leader?"

"Phil Oakey. Why?" answered Stephanie.

Lisa attempted being hopeful. "Because maybe it's catalogued by the singers' names?"

Stephanie searched by O, then by P. Nothing. They finally resorted to going page by page. More nothing.

Tired and scared of being stuck, Lisa thought out loud. "Emily. I have to find Emily. I'm sure she'll have it in one of her mixtapes."

"And where is Emily now, Lisa?"

"In the phone book, of course."

***

On the corner of the street, they found a phone booth with a large yellow book, miraculously intact. "Found her! No phone number but there's an address. 5905 Hudson Street—the same building where we found my name the last time we were here. Maybe it's improved a bit?" Lisa tried to contain her expectations. *This has to work. Emily will have the song, we'll play it, and all will be well.*

The building was exactly the same. She looked at the apartment listing, and this time found both of their names: Lisa Coronado and Emily Martinez—4B. They were roommates, so that was a good sign. Lisa rang the buzzer and were let in without a word.

The building was run-down—the stairs filled with dust and dirt. The elevator had an Out of Service sign, so they headed to the stairs. Up four flights, they found Apartment 4B. From inside they could hear loud music playing, some kind of punk rock mixed with synthesizers. The two women looked at each other with raised eyebrows. Stephanie spoke first, "I guess she's really into music." She knocked on the door several times, each time louder than before.

The door swung open to reveal a slight woman who looked like Emily but wasn't really her. Emily's straight hair hung to her shoulders, her jeans were baggy, her shirt some sort of bohemian style, and a cigarette dangled from her fingers. She raised her arms to hug Lisa. Lisa coughed from the smoke. "Leese, babe, where've you been? You disappeared a few days ago and never called me." Emily stepped back from the embrace and turned back into the apartment. Lisa and Stephanie followed her into a mess. There were empty Chinese food containers everywhere, discarded cans of beer lying around on their sides, and ashtrays overflowing with butts on almost every flat surface. The music was even louder inside than in the hallway.

Lisa stared at everything in disbelief. This is where she and Emily lived? "Can you turn down the volume? We need to talk."

"You always complain that I play the music too loud," Emily turned the knob on the boom box. "Where were you all this time? You grabbed an overnight bag and left in a huff. I thought you were dead or something." Emily stopped talking long enough to stare at Stephanie. "Who's this?"

"This is Stephanie. A friend."

"So, are you coming back to stay, or are you moving in with Stephanie?"

"What do you mean?"

"Don't play games, Lisa. When we were fighting, you said you were moving out. And now you're back with a stranger, so I'm wondering if you're breaching your lease with me. You said you were tired of living in a pigsty." Emily pushed a bunch of clothes off the sofa onto the floor, disturbing the tabby cat that was sleeping in the sunspot on the floor.

Lisa was appalled at the mess. No wonder she left if she was living in this. "Em, I am not moving out. I need to talk to you. We need to talk to you. Is anyone else here?"

"Nope, just me and tabby girl." She picked up the cat to caress her, then dropped her suddenly when the cat scratched her arm. "You're not much of a roommate, tabby cat." She returned her attention to Lisa. "You're not much of a roommate either, Lisa. But I love you, so I'll forgive your inexplicable departure and welcome you home with open arms." She leaned back on the sofa. "Have a seat, ladies. Can I offer you something to drink?"

Out of the corner of her eye, Lisa could see Stephanie try to find a place to sit. Every available chair was full of magazines, books, and clothes. Emily continued, "Don't mind the mess. We fired the cleaning lady." She laughed raucously at her joke. Neither Lisa nor Stephanie even cracked a smile. Lisa just felt sad. Here again, her actions had impacted one of the people dearest to her, and she felt guilty.

"Emily, don't worry about the apartment. We need to talk. But first, I really need to lie down in a dark room and close my eyes. I have an awful headache. You see…." Lisa stopped. How would she even explain time travel to this person she didn't know? She started again but stopped.

"Your bedroom is over there, so just push over the stuff that I threw on the bed, and you can lay down. It's still your room." Emily took another puff of her cigarette. "Just remember that this evening my game group comes over, so we might be a little noisy."

Lisa raised an eyebrow. She leaned forward in her chair. "What game group?"

Emily scoffed. "Lisa, don't fake not remember to impress your friend here. That was another reason for our falling out. You complained I had the apartment full of 'weirdos' who play StarForce: Alpha Centauri every weekend? That we pull all-nighters on Fridays and Saturdays, that we drink and smoke, and play weird music? Any of this ringing a bell?"

Lisa shook her head while scanning the room. "No." She dragged out the word until she noticed a board game on the dining table and walked over to it. "Is this it?"

"Yes. And tonight is Friday. So, if you don't want to be hanging out with my so-called weirdo friends, you might as well take your new friend here with you as you head out the door. Everyone will be here at seven o'clock promptly."

Lisa glanced through the game with a heightened curiosity that seemed strange to her. She felt drawn to the game board, staring at the different worlds depicted on it. She froze when she saw that one of the worlds was called the Human League. Feeling a frisson in her arms and afraid to face the coincidence, she backed away from the table and ended up in the kitchen, which had a window into the living room. From there, Lisa could see Emily and Stephanie ignoring one another. She noticed Stephanie wringing her hands while Emily had her head back and her eyes closed as if asleep. Observing the kitchen, she noted it was as bad as the living room, although strangely enough, the inside of the refrigerator was exceptionally neat with organized plastic cases labeled by type of food. The beer cans and beer bottles were horizontally stacked on the bottom shelf, and a bottle of Sauvignon Blanc stood unopened in the refrigerator door.

"I'm guessing the wine is mine?" Lisa asked.

Emily yawned. "Did you hit your head, Lisa? You're the only one here who drinks wine."

Emily addressed Stephanie, who was still sitting in the living room. "Could you excuse us, uh, Stephanie, is it?"

"Yes, of course."

"Yeah, well, make yourself at home. The bathroom is down the hall, and you can lie on my bed and take a nap if you'd like. I need privacy to talk to my friend over there."

Stephanie walked out of the room, and Emily sauntered to the kitchen. "Lisa, what's going on with you? You're acting all kinds of weird, more than usual, and what's with the chick?"

Lisa wasn't sure how to explain, but she took a deep breath. "Em, something's happened to me, to my memory, and I'm simply trying to understand where we live now, and what's going on. Stephanie is my friend. She's a pleasant person. Be kind to her, please."

"Fine, I'll be kind but, more importantly, what's up with you? You act as if you don't know my routine. For the last two years, since we graduated, every Friday at the end of my mind-numbing receptionist job at the bank down the street, my game friends meet here. You and your friend Susan tend bar on Friday and Saturday nights, so you crash at her apartment above the bar every weekend. You save your tips, so you can eventually go to graduate school. Any of this ring a bell?"

The banana yellow phone on the wall rang. While Emily talked, Lisa stared out the tiny window at the street outside. "What's up my man? You're not bailing out on me tonight, are you?" Lisa heard a mumbled conversation but couldn't distinguish the words. "Phil, Phil. Don't worry about being a little late. We'll just start drinking without you. Just be here as close to seven with your keyboard, and we'll wait for you to start. See you later, my friend."

Lisa turned back to Emily. "Who was that?"

"Oh, nobody. My friend who plays keyboards and sings, and is a nut about this game, it's like Risk or something. He's going to be late tonight."

"I don't remember anyone named Phil in your circle."

"Yes, you do. Phil Oakey. The guy who wants to be a singer, but no one will give him a chance?"

Chapter 19

Lisa froze as she heard Emily speak the name of Philip Oakey. "What do you mean he's your friend?"

Emily pushed up the sleeves of her white sweatshirt splashed with two blue Smurfs characters before she dunked her hands into the kitchen sink to wash dishes. "I'd better clean some of this up with people coming over." Her bright blue feather earrings twisted around as she turned to Lisa. "What's there to explain? I met him in a dive bar that had an open mic night, and we became friends. He's a typical struggling musician, shattered dreams and all that, despite having an amazing voice and magic fingers on the synthesizer. Even with all that talent, his life is...nothing with a capital N. He wrote a song he carries around with him all the time. Tried it out with a few producers, but they said it was boring, or...something like that."

As Emily spoke, Lisa felt as if she were standing on the edge of a swirling vortex looking down, afraid to fall in but drawn to the danger of the precipice. She and Stephanie had been talking about Oakey only a few hours earlier, and now he would be standing in this very room in a short while. This couldn't be the same Oakey, could it? The coincidence would be too great. It was as if he were materializing because they had spoken about him.

Lisa smiled as she tried to make sense of it all. "I'd love to hear him sing. What's the name of that song he tried to sell?"

Emily scrunched her nose. "I think it was 'Sexual Politics' or something like that. I don't remember. He once told me that I reminded him of the woman in the song."

"With a name like that, no wonder it didn't sell." What a disappointment. This obviously wasn't the same Oakey.

Lisa felt her head throbbing again. Emily was her constant connection, her guiding post. Or was Lisa bringing Emily towards her in every time stream she traveled? She put her arm around Emily's back and laid her head on her best friend's shoulder. "Emily, my head is killing me."

Headache in full swing, Lisa was tired of trying to find a way home. She'd work it out tomorrow with a clear mind.

She opened the refrigerator and found dozens of cans of Tab. She pulled one out and, with raised eyebrows, complained, "Emily, this is junk."

Emily turned to face her. "There's no junk in our fridge. What are you talking about?" Lisa waved the can. "This. It causes cancer in rats." Emily shot her a look of daggers. "What a stupid thing to say, Lisa. Tab is the best soda ever. We both drink it for breakfast."

Sighing, Lisa said, "Never mind. I'll just drink water." Emily reached for a glass in the cupboard above and filled it from the tap.

Lisa put the can back and took the glass from Emily. While gulping it down, with her free hand, she saluted Emily, and asked, "Do you have anything for a headache?" Emily wrinkled her nose. "You keep asking for things as if you've never lived here." She opened another cabinet door. "You should know where it is—you're the one who keeps us stocked with meds."

Lisa grabbed the pills and chugged them down. She forced a smile to cover up the strangeness of this mixed-up, unfamiliar, post-college-life past.

She turned to Emily, "So, sloppy girl, while you're busy here, I'll get Stephanie to help me clean up a bit. Does that work for you?"

Emily followed Lisa out of the kitchen and into the living room, where Stephanie seemed engrossed by *MAD* and *People* magazines strewn about, muttering something about not finding anything about English bands. "Stephanie, are you going to sit there all day reading?"

Stephanie glared at Emily. "It's not like there's anything else to do here. I'm searching for some way to go..."

Lisa interrupted her with a shake of the head, "Stephanie, why don't you help me get this place organized? Emily's friends are coming over, and we might find them interesting."

Stephanie stared at Lisa, squinting her eyes and pursing her lips. "Fine. I'll give you a hand."

Emily clapped her hands. "Excellent! Thanks girls!" With that, she bounced back to the kitchen, picking up her bright pink leg warmers falling to her ankles.

Stephanie and Lisa started gathering magazines and books, piling them in a corner. They collected empty bottles of cheap wine and beer and leftover Chinese food containers, throwing them into a garbage bag.

Stephanie whispered through gritted teeth, "You know, Lisa, I didn't travel with you to be a cleaning lady. You got us into this mess, so you should clean it up yourself." She punctuated her words by throwing things into the bag.

"And for God's sake!" Stephanie uncovered something sticking out from behind the sofa. Her eyes glaring, she held it up for Lisa to see. "A ukulele! Who plays the ukelele here?

Lisa pulled it away from Stephanie's hands and strummed on the strings making an awful sound. Stephanie broke into a grin. "Well, that proves it doesn't belong to you. In the past, does Emily even play an instrument?"

Lisa shushed her. "Keep your voice down; Emily doesn't know we're not from here."

Frowning, Stephanie continued. "I don't care. You know what, Lisa. We always have to do things your way. And so far, we've done nothing but entertain your friend, and now we're cleaning up her house. We need to find Phil Oakey, so he can sing the song and send us back."

"Have some patience. We can't do anything tonight. Tomorrow we'll find a way home. For now, let's just concentrate on organizing this place a little."

Thoughts raced while she focused on the task of deciphering what paper was important and what was trash. She had wanted to return to a time when she could meet Adam in their youth, before he became attached to Stephanie, and it had happened. She had wished they could have a family, and that had happened also. Now Emily had a friend named Phil Oakey who was also a musician. What if it were the same guy who hadn't been able to record his song? And was she the one creating this world? The door buzzer interrupted her thoughts.

In a matter of minutes, after a flurry of hellos and hugs, the living room became more chaotic than it was earlier in the day. Lisa and Stephanie had rushed to the bedroom to hide the piles of stuff still laying around the living room. When they returned, a crowd of about five guys and one teenage-looking girl sat around the coffee table in front of the sofa. Everybody had a glass or a bottle of something in hand while Emily put out paper plates with chips and dip on the end tables. Lisa and Stephanie had done a yeoman's job of cleaning up the living room, and Emily had added the finishing touches. One of the guys had brought what looked like a portable electric piano.

A red-headed girl sat on the corner of the sofa, cozied up to a guy with long dark hair and a goatee. She looked bored, her red lipstick matching the color of her hair and perfectly groomed eyebrows. Her emerald dress complemented her big hair in an almost Christmas tree way. Lisa wondered how much was left in the hairspray can when she was done with her hairdo. The redhead revealed cat-green eyes with a thin nose and green eyeshadow and black mascara with sparkles.

She put her arm on the long-haired guy's denim-clad thigh, like a dog marks a tree. Her man was slim, young looking with brown eyes that were soft and sensitive. At the moment they were completely lit up as he arranged pieces on a game board placed in the middle of the coffee table. On the other sofa were three guys wearing mohawks spiking up in the air. Long armed and long legged, they sat next to each other and reminded Lisa of an insect with six legs and arms holding beer bottles. They leaned in towards the game board, throwing out directions for where the pieces belonged.

Emily had made introductions as people walked in with a loud, "Hey, everybody, this is my roommate Lisa. Lisa, this is everybody." Lisa waved absentmindedly, with her eyes glued on the long-haired man. Redhead noticed and spat out softly, "I'm Susan. My friends call me Sulley. Who are you exactly?"

Lisa grabbed a chair and sat down near the sofa, with a smile that didn't reach her eyes. "Hi, Sulley. Nice to meet you."

"I said my friends call me Sulley. You can call me Susan. And you didn't answer my question."

Lisa swallowed hard. Nice attitude, sweetie. You act much older than your years. "Didn't you hear? I'm Lisa, Emily's roommate."

"Right," she said. Pointing to Stephanie, she added, "And who's the other one standing there pouting?"

Emily chimed in. "Oh, that's Stephanie. She's not my roommate—just Lisa's friend."

The long-haired guy snickered and leaned into Sulley's face, giving her a kiss on the cheek. "Claws in, darling." He turned to Lisa, stood up and extended his hand. "Emily's spoken a lot about you. I'm glad to finally meet you." Turning to Stephanie, "And nice to meet you too." His British accent was the most hopeful sound Lisa had heard in a long time. "I'm Phil, by the way."

The hair on Lisa's neck stood on end as she extended her hand.

He had a broad smile, and his eyes crinkled a little. Lisa felt herself staring at him a few seconds more than what was appropriate when she heard him say, "Why don't you join us in our game?"

She turned her attention to the game board on the coffee table. "I don't know how to play. It looks complicated."

"Oh, it's not any more complicated than life, love." He winked at her. "Give it a whirl. I'll teach you how to play."

Lisa cocked her head to one side in disbelief. "Emily says you sometimes play all night long. I don't have that kind of stamina."

Phil laughed and motioned to the other guys to pay attention. "Did you guys hear that? Emily's told Lisa that we sometimes play all night long." The three guys on the other couch laughed in unison, their mohawks bobbing, until Phil resumed. "Don't listen to Emily. She just gets bored with war games." He winked again. "Well, if the game is going longer than Saturday morning, we move it back to my place. Emily usually quits before that. The rest of us sometimes spend several days playing…nonstop." He kicked off his black combat boots with the last word. "Tonight may be the start of one of those rampages."

Lisa shrugged. "I don't understand. How could a game take so long to play?"

Sulley chimed in. "You've obviously never been a fan of imaginary war games with interstellar travel, have you?"

Lisa leaned back in her chair, curious as to this chick's icy commitment to Phil and his board game. "I'm afraid that interstellar travel hasn't been on the top of my list."

Sulley didn't seem fazed by Lisa's sarcasm but rather had a look of ennui. "It's a boy thing. And it's a Phil thing. He thinks this game holds secrets to life." She paused long enough to run her fingers through Phil's hair then resumed speaking to Lisa but never taking her eyes off Phil. "And by life, Phil means music. That's all there is…." She smiled, leaning in closer to his cheek while he joined her, and they said in unison, "To the movement of the world! Music and the game move the world!"

As if on cue, the couch guys started cheering and pumping their fists. Standing in the doorway between the kitchen and the living room, Emily grinned, and Stephanie raised her eyebrows. Lisa wondered how they got themselves into this situation. "Excuse me, Phil. I don't understand this game."

Phil leaned into the game board as if being closer to it would generate his words. "It's very simple. The players move through worlds, battling one another for the position of supreme being. To do that, they destroy one another until there's only one man left standing."

Sulley dug her nails into his arm, in a manner between possessive and aggressive. "Excuse me? Man?"

Gently, Phil removed her hand and kissed it tenderly. "Sorry, love, I meant person." Speaking to Lisa he said, "She gets a smidge uptight when I forget the ladies."

Stephanie elbowed Lisa and piped in. "She has a point. What else happens in this game? Can anyone join at this point, or do we have to wait until you finish destroying one another to jump into the fray?"

Phil focused his charm on Stephanie. "Anyone can join at any time, sweetheart, and you learn the rules as you go along." One of the other guys interjected. "Tell her about the jumping through time, Phil. That's the best part of the strategy."

In a cold, flat voice, Sulley added, "If you tell her, she'll know how to win, you idiots." The couch guys appeared disappointed at being reprimanded.

Lisa noticed that Phil paid close attention to her. She took advantage of the moment, not sure why she felt the need to outwit this Sulley woman. Purring, she directed her full gaze to Phil. "Well, then, you must tell me the strategy if it's going to be a fair game."

Reaching over, Phil removed Sulley's hand from his arm. "The secret, my lady, is that there's one world that allows you to jump from one point in time to another without being detected by your foe."

"Like time travel?"

Phil put his hands behind his head like a man who's just accomplished a great feat. "Exactly. You can go back in time and correct the mistakes, so that you come out victorious in the end."

Sulley interrupted again. "The world that lets you jump in time is called the Human League. But it's not depicted on the game board. You have to visualize it to get to it."

Lisa's hands trembled as she moved closer to the game board. "Did you say the Human League?"

Sulley interjected. "Emily, is your friend deaf?"

Phil waved his hands over the board. "Come on, love, don't be mean. Let's be nice and teach Lisa how to play a game that jumps around in time." Phil leaned forward and flashed dimples at Lisa. "Wanna play?"

Sulley leaned forward, mimicking Lisa's move. "You have to know when to visualize it, then declare it, and your adversaries have to accept that you've jumped to another time. They won't know where you are until you emerge from hiding. By doing so, you may have changed their positions. Everything is up for grabs when you land on the Human League world."

Phil sighed out loud. "I wanted to create a band with that name, but it never worked out."

One of the couch guys stood up to walk to the kitchen and yelled out, "Because the name sucks, that's why."

The other guy chimed in. "Every producer we ever talked to told you the name of the band didn't work, and neither did that stupid song you made us learn."

Lisa had been fiddling with the game pieces when she heard him utter those words. She dropped them on the board and turned to him, eyebrows high up. "You have a band called the Human League?" Her heart pumped faster, so loud she thought the others would hear.

"Had…or rather, tried to have. No matter what I attempted, it always fell apart. We were never able to get it off the ground."

Venom spilled from Sulley's words. "Maybe if you'd written something better than 'Wanting You for Five Years,' you might have had a hit. But no, you wouldn't listen to any of my suggestions about the lyrics or the music. How am I supposed to sing stupid lyrics? That's why it didn't work. It's cursed."

The Human League. The band. Here in this now.

Sulley's outburst silenced the entire room. After a few uncomfortable seconds, Phil stood up. "I'm getting another beer. Who wants one?" He headed to the kitchen without waiting for an answer. On his way there, he spoke to Lisa. "Love, when we're done with the game, and the beers, later, the boys and I can play the song for you. I've brought my synthesizer. Maybe you'll have some suggestions for me since Sulley thinks it's a stupid song."

One of the couch guys, the one they called Julian, took his eyes off the game board and seemed interested in the conversation for the first time. "Damn, Phil, I didn't bring my guitar." The other guy, Alex, chimed in. "I didn't know we were playing tonight. Phil, you're so disorganized. If you'd told us this was going to be a gig, we would've brought equipment." He turned away from Phil and addressed Lisa. "Babe, I wish I'd known. I'm in charge of instruments and equipment. Maybe another time we can do this?"

Stephanie piped in. "Why wait? No time like the present! Play the song now."

Faced with the very real possibility they could leave this place, Lisa's thoughts ran amuck. In all the fury of trying to find the song, she hadn't thought of the details of where to return. Could she even direct where they'd go? She knew this much: returning straight to her real life meant giving up the people she had discovered in the space just prior to coming here. Wherever here was. She knew she had Emily wherever she went. And clearly Stephanie was tied to her side now. There was the question of Adam. No matter what world they were in, his colors didn't change. If she could steer her return with Stephanie, should she choose to return to the life where she was married to Adam? It was clear he was no prize, but that life gave her beautiful children. And it gave Lisa her mother.

Lisa turned back to Phil and the boys. "Stephanie's right, guys. Play for us. We can be your test audience."

As Phil returned from the kitchen, beers in both hands, "If the guys want to play, I'm in. That song was epic, and we were robbed by those asshole music labels that couldn't see our greatness." He took a swig of his beer. "When we play, you'll see the genius in us." He took another swig. "But first, our game."

Stephanie elbowed Lisa, whose "Ow!" came out like a shriek. As Lisa rubbed her arm, she flashed her most charming smile at Phil. "Why wait, Phil? Best to get your audience while they're still sober."

Adrian stood up on long skinny legs, got up on the sofa, and stepped over the back in one fluid move, his necklaces of steel black crosses and feathers jangling as he moved. "Phil, stop stalling. We never have an audience because you're so bloody picky. It's like you're afraid of getting us a music contract." He sauntered to the kitchen, where he disappeared from sight. Lisa could hear cabinet doors opening and closing and pots banging around.

Emily yelled out, "What are you doing in there?" Adrian's head popped up over the kitchen divider. "Just looking for a drum." More clattering followed, and then he reappeared with a metal soup pot and two wooden spoons in hand. "Here," he said as he sat on the floor near the synthesizer in the corner. "I'm ready."

Julian had turned his head towards Adrian, and, with a big cheesy smile, jumped up from his seat. "Oh, so that's the game we're going to play. Shit! I wish I'd brought my guitar." He also headed to the kitchen, rummaged through the cupboards, and yelled out, "Emily! What can I use for a guitar? There's nothing here!"

Emily headed to the kitchen. "Julian, I don't have guitars in the kitchen."

Julian's voice was muffled from inside a cabinet. "There must be something in this house."

Lisa and Stephanie exchanged glances. Stephanie jumped up and ran to the bedroom, yelling, "I know exactly the thing!" She returned, grinning like a Cheshire cat, holding the dusty ukulele.

Julian stepped out of the kitchen, arms outstretched to Stephanie. "Not bad," drawling out the word while his fingers ran over the strings. "I can improvise with this baby."

Alex shook his head. "You're nuts, but let's play." He turned to Phil. "Now, the band has instruments, and everyone's ready. What about you, man? What's holding you back?"

Phil hadn't changed his position, still holding beers in his hands. With a grunt, he handed them out, then flopped down on the sofa with Sulley. "We can't play my song with pots and pans and a ukelele. That's no band, man." He chugged a beer as if it were last call at the bar. Sulley laughed and rubbed his back. "That's right, honey, don't let them bully you into playing that stupid song of yours."

Lisa noticed the iciness in Sulley's words. What was wrong with this girl? She watched Emily fiddle with her hair, appearing bored. Stephanie was the opposite, sitting on the edge of her seat, focused on every word. Lisa decided on another tactic. She moved to the sofa next to Phil and rubbed his arm, putting as much charm in her voice as she could muster. "You know, Phil, your bandmates seem eager to play this song of yours. My friend Stephanie and I won't be here long tonight. Why don't you play for us even with the impromptu instruments? It might be fun." She purred and batted her eyelashes, then added, "Even if Sulley doesn't want you to play."

Lisa noticed Phil enjoyed the extra attention when she heard Sulley laughing. "Oh, go on Phil, be like every other guy, always needing praise to perform." Her laughter was an icy wind through the room. Lisa wasn't sure if it was the veiled insult or her cajoling, but Phil bolted up from his seat and headed to the corner of the room. The guys followed him. As he walked, she could hear Phil mutter, "No woman tells me what to do, you understand Sulley?" He grabbed the synthesizer abruptly before he softly caressed it.

Lisa moved back to her chair next to Stephanie and whispered to her, "Our lives are in the hands of a nut." Stephanie shushed her. "Stop talking and focus; this needs to work."

Lisa's hands were sweaty. She played with her hair, hoping Stephanie was right. She switched from her hair to wiping her palms on her pants. Minutes ticked by slowly until Phil's triumphant "Set. Here we go."

The synthesizer started playing the familiar tune. Adrian and Julian played with their drum and guitar while Alex watched from the back of the room like a typical manager. Lisa noticed Emily had moved next to him, trying to appear as if she weren't staring at him. Amid all this, Sulley pulled out a small vial of lotion and smoothed it on her cuticles. Lisa heard Phil, "OK, mates, this is the best song ever."

Stephanie and Lisa looked at each other, smiling. They grabbed one another's hands and held tightly with eyes closed. It filled Lisa with hope. Hearing the familiar tune, Lisa smiled, eyes now tightly shut lest anything interfere with her vision. This was the one, the right Oakey! This was the song, the music, even with the improvised band. She squeezed Stephanie's hand.

And then Phil sang.

> You were workin' as a typist in a hotel bar
> When I met you

I picked you up, I shook you up and turned you
    around
Turned you into something blue
Now two years later on, you've got the world at your
    feet
Success has been so easy for you
But don't forget, it's me who put you where you are
    now,
And I can put you down there too.
Won't, won't you have me?
You know I can't believe it when I hear that you won't
    see me
Won't, won't you have me?
You know I don't believe it when you say that you
    don't need me
It's much too late to find
To think you've changed your mind
You'd better change it back or we will both be sorry.

Expecting the swirling blackness to take her, Lisa opened her eyes, mouth agape. No! Right music, wrong words. She let Stephanie's hand drop and jumped out of her seat, yelling, "No! You have it all wrong!"

Phil dragged his fingers over the keys on the last bars, out of time and out of tune. He stopped and stared at her, joining everyone who turned to look at her screwed-up face, obviously shaken by her vehement cry. Phil looked crestfallen. "What do you mean, I have it all wrong? You don't like it?"

Adrian and Julian shook their heads and together said, "Man, she hates it."

Lisa stammered, noticing she was creating a scene. "It's not that I don't like it." How does one tell a songwriter whose song doesn't exist yet that his words are wrong because she's heard him sing it before? "It's just that...isn't there more to it?"

Phil slammed his hands on the keys. "Yes, there's another part, but if you don't like the beginning, there's no point in continuing." He shut the cover on the instrument. "Forget it. I knew this was a mistake."

Alex left Emily's side and ran towards Phil. "No, don't say that, man. It's a great song. Why don't you try it again?"

Julian and Adrian chimed in, "Yeah, dude. Let's play. So what if the chicks don't like it?"

This was all horribly wrong. Stephanie stood next to Lisa and whispered in her ear. "The lyrics are off. The music is right, but the lyrics are off."

Lisa didn't mean to shout, but desperation seeped out of her words. "Don't you think I know that?"

Phil was already back at Sulley's side, a beer bottle at his lips, gulping furiously. "Listen, you don't like the song, but you don't have to be crass about it."

Adrian, Julian, and Alex shifted back to their seats in silence, looking defeated. Clearly, Phil directed everything in this show.

Lisa smoothed her hair back behind her ears and put on a fake smile and a soothing tone in her voice. "It's a great song, Phil. I was just expecting different lyrics, that's all. Maybe if you adjust them a little, it might work better."

"Oh, because you're a songwriter now, are you?" He put his attention back on the game board. "We've wasted enough time humiliating me. Let's play StarForce."

In an apparent act of kindness, Sulley rubbed his neck. "Sweetheart, ignore her. She's got no taste either."

Sulley glared at Lisa. "See what you've done? You encouraged him just to throw cold water on his creation."

Lisa moved back to the sofa and cozied up to Phil. Caressing his arm, Lisa felt she was dealing with a two-year-old having a tantrum.

"Phil, the song is beautiful. I just think adjust the lyrics a bit, that's all. Why don't you try them again, and maybe we can change them a little, you know, to make them more marketable?"

"What do you know about selling music, huh?"

Lisa snapped, "I know that you don't sound like Miami Sound Machine, and they've had hit after hit."

Julian wrinkled his nose. "Miami Sound Machine? What the hell is that?" Everyone in the room murmured in agreement. Emily piped in, "Lisa, what's a...what did you call it?"

Lisa pressed on. "Miami Sound Machine, Gloria Estefan? 'Turn the Beat Around'? A woman singing the lead?"

Blank faces stared at her. Julian answered again. "I've no idea what you're talking about."

How could no one know what she was talking about? Then Lisa saw the obvious. "Oh, never mind. It must have been some band I heard in a bar somewhere." She pushed her fingers into her temples and took a deep breath. Get a grip, Lisa, you're screwing things up.

She turned her attention back to Phil and purred to feed his ego. "I'm sorry to throw you off, Phil. You're obviously a brilliant musician. I know talent. And I know what a great song sounds like. I can help you." She rubbed his arm some more, and Sulley pulled him closer to her. "We should leave, Phil. This place is too crowded."

Stephanie joined Lisa. "Please, Phil. Lisa and I have been to lots of concerts, and we know a little about what an audience wants. Think about Madonna. She's had lots of hit songs. Look at Prince. Or Genesis with Phil Collins on the drums. Stephanie gestured to Lisa, "What's the name of that song from Huey Lewis and the News?"

Once again, everyone in the room stared, this time at Stephanie. Emily spoke up. "I have no idea what you're talking about. Who are these singers?"

Stephanie and Lisa raised their eyebrows in unison

Lisa turned her attention to Phil. "What about the Police? They've had some hits, right? I'm sure they collaborated with their friends to create hits."

Julian and Alex groaned and threw out together, "The Police suck!"

Phil shook his head, "The boys are right. You can't compare us to the fucking Police."

Everyone started to talk at once, anger filling the room. This was not what Lisa intended. This was wrong, all wrong.

She tried to smooth talk her way back into the band's graces. "Look, boys, I didn't mean to offend anyone by mentioning the…."

Phil stopped her. "Don't even say the name again."

"Got it." Lisa sighed. "I'm sorry. Let's forget I mentioned anything. I know you're really great. I can feel it in my bones. Why don't you go back to play, and we can listen again? It's the least we can do after all the effort you went through with the drinks and the game. Come on. Give Stephanie and me another chance."

Pouting like a child, Phil shook his head. Julian and Adrian jumped up again and moved back to their makeshift band. Julian spoke, "I suppose we can forgive your terrible taste." He smiled. "Come on Phil, let's give it another whirl. Stop wasting time."

Phil shook his head as he stood up. "Fine. But these lyrics are perfect. You guys just don't know what you're talking about." He took another gulp of his beer. "Plus, you didn't hear the complete song." He swaggered back to the keyboard, his boots clicking on the wood floor.

Lisa and Stephanie smiled conspiratorially. Lisa ventured forth. How to convince a man to follow directions? "Why don't you try using a waitress in a cocktail bar instead of a typist. A waitress is more seductive."

Stephanie chimed in next. "Yes, great idea, Lisa! And how about you add it took five years, instead of two? Five years shows more commitment."

Julian shouted, "No, we chose two years for a reason."

Stephanie snapped her head in his direction. "What reason was that?"

Julian grinned, looked over at Adrian, and replied, "I can't remember."

Alex clapped his hands. "Try what the woman suggested, for God's sake. The song didn't sell the way you wrote it. Maybe it needs a woman's touch."

Back at the synthesizer, Phil crooned with the new words. "That does sound better." Between synthesizer, metal pot and tiny ukulele, the shaky band had potential.

Phil flew his fingers over the keys again. Lisa tried one more time. "Now, how about you change 'won't you have me' to 'don't you want me'? That makes it more forlorn."

Phil balked. "You guys are changing my whole song, you know."

Adrian stopped playing. "No, no, no. That line was mine. You can't change my line."

Oh, brother, Lisa thought. More than one man to convince to change the words. "Listen, guys, the song is great. I don't want to change it, but you said it didn't sell, so why not try what we're offering? Even Alex suggested it needs a woman's touch."

She moved towards Adrian. "Come on, Adrian. Try it." She rubbed his arm, and he winked with a smile. "Lisa, after tonight, will you go out with me?"

Lisa would have gone out with all of them at once if they got her home. "Sure, I'll go out with you if you sing the song the way we suggest." She smiled, hoping it looked sexy and not desperate.

Adrian apparently was convinced. "All right. We've got nothing to lose. It's not like we ever had a number one hit on our hands."

Lisa laughed at the irony. "Excellent! Now, one more time!" She went back to her chair and held Stephanie's hand.

The band played again. The words were right. The music was right. But nothing occurred. She and Stephanie stared at each other, disappointment on their faces. Was this it? Were they stuck here forever?

No, she wasn't giving up. That Phil had materialized and that he had his band with him was too great an opportunity for her to stop now. But what was different? The lyrics were right; the music was right. What could be wrong?

Sulley continued to look bored and annoyed at the same time she scrutinized her fingernails. "I thought it sounded fine the first time. What it needs is a woman to sing, and he won't hear of it."

That was it! Alex had said it. A woman's touch! A woman sang on the original song. Softly, Lisa turned to Sulley. "That's brilliant! Why don't you sing the girl part, Sulley?"

Sulley glared at Phil, pointing her red lacquered fingernail at him. She spit her words out to Lisa. "Because he won't hear of it. And I'm not singing his stupid song until he asks me nicely."

Lisa took a deep breath, angry that her life was in the hands of toddlers. "Phil, why don't you give Sulley a chance? That might make the song more marketable to girls."

Phil crossed his arms and stared at the ceiling. He looked at his bandmates, as if for confirmation, but they suddenly appeared very busy fiddling with their instruments.

Adrian was the first to speak. "I'm not getting in the middle of Phil and his girlfriend."

Stephanie murmured under her breath, "Yeah, that didn't work out so well for John Lennon and Paul McCartney."

Adrian said, "Who?"

Stephanie waved him off, "Oh God, never mind."

Julian shifted in his seat and took a deep breath. "Look, man, we've told you before, and you always get pissed off. Let Sulley sing. We've tried it your way for years with no results. Now we have two more chicks...um...sorry, ladies, asking that she sing, so don't be a hard-ass."

Phil was immovable. Emily walked over to him. "Give Sulley a try. She might have a nice voice." She punched his arm then kissed his cheek. "Go on, be the bigger man."

Phil smiled at Emily. "You can always get your way with me, you know." He put down his arms and faced Sulley. "Fine. Come on, Sulley. Sing for us."

Sulley turned her back to everyone and faced the wall. "No. That's not asking me nicely."

Phil strode over to her in two steps and bent on one knee while Sulley turned her head away from him, nose in the air and arms crossed like a petulant child, mimicking Phil's gesture from moments ago. "My beautiful Sulley, glorious woman in red, please, won't you sing this song with me, just once at least?"

She rolled her eyes and turned to him. "That's not enough." She crooked her head. "Tell me you love me. Maybe then I'll sing with you."

Phil lowered his head and raised his eyes to her. "Sulley, I love you. Please sing with me."

And just like that, she jumped up, reached down to Phil, and took his hand, pulling him towards the keyboard. "That's all I wanted to hear." She trilled, "I'll sing."

Lisa gestured to Stephanie to come sit with her on the sofa. Stephanie crooked her arm in Lisa's, and they closed their eyes, whispering in unison, "Here we go."

The music was right; the lyrics were done; and then Sulley's part arrived, and she sang like a scorned woman.

The synthesizer sounds mixed with the humming of the swirling blackness. Lisa's last thought was her mother's face.

Chapter 20

Noise assaulted Lisa before anything else. Plates clanging, glasses clinking, and loud voices all speaking at once. She smelled burnt coffee and pungent bacon. Hands gripped hers, but she kept her eyes scrunched shut. Her stomach was in a knot as she heard a woman's staccato words intermixed with snapping chewing gum. "Honey, have you decided what you're going to order? I don't have all day, and we're really busy. What do you want?"

Lisa opened one eye and saw Stephanie, holding her breath while sitting across from her. The waitress quick-quick tapped her pen on the pad in her hand.

Lisa loosened her grip, sighing as she leaned back in the booth, the soft plastic crunching against her back. She closed her eyes once more, took a deep breath and, when she reopened them, she put on her cheesiest smile and said to the waitress, "Could we have a couple more minutes please? I'm not sure what I want yet."

Harumphing and mumbling under her breath, the waitress scurried to the next table.

Stephanie leaned forward, mouth agape. "We're back?" Her question sounded more matter of fact than surprised.

Lisa turned her head in all directions, taking in the surroundings. The tablecloth was the same red-and-white checker pattern with little blue sailboats in each square. Buoys and ropes decorated the walls painted sea blue, but the main point of attraction was the huge clock on the wall above the diner counter. Shaped like an anchor and spanning about four feet around, it emitted a sound like a foghorn at the hour and half hour.

It was this blaring sound that assured Lisa they were back in the correct place. They had been sitting in this diner, holding hands, when they traveled into that world without The Human League. Returning to the same diner meant she was married to Adam now, and this Stephanie sitting with her was his mistress. The realization they were back assured her she'd done something right. Now the question was what next? The thought of more traveling through time pierced Lisa's temples. Elbows on the table, she leaned her head into her hands, pushing her palms into her eyes to soothe her head.

"Lisa, are you OK? Did you hear me? Are we back?"

All Lisa could muster for the moment was "I think so." She raised her eyes to Stephanie, who was nearly jumping out of her seat. "I can't believe we did that!" She leaned into the table getting closer to Lisa. In a conspiratorial whisper that was much too loud, she added, "I thought we'd be stuck back there...wherever back there was. But here we are again." She put her hand into her pocket and flashed a wide smile. "Ah, yes. My cell phone." She took it out, typed for a few seconds, and shrieked, "Aha! The Human League. They exist again. We're geniuses. I don't know how, but they've reappeared." She continued to mutter while continuing to search through her phone.

A grumbling stomach reminded Lisa that food might help disappear her headache. She leaned over the side of the booth and called out to the waitress, "We're ready for our order." As she said the words, she wondered if the time traveling were responsible for the headaches. She'd never gotten a final decision from that neurologist who was examining her pineal gland. It felt that had happened in another lifetime, and she wondered if she'd ever return to that.

Nothing waited for her in that life. She had no marriage to speak of, a dead son, and a dead mother. What was the point of returning? Here she had everything she had always dreamed of.

The waitress returned. "It's about time. I'm getting old waiting for you two."

Just as Lisa was about to speak, Stephanie jumped in, talking fast like a little kid. "I'm starving. I'll have a couple of eggs over easy, sliced tomatoes, and rye toast. That's it." She smiled at Lisa. "Oh, and a cup of coffee. Large."

Without skipping a beat, the waitress droned to Lisa. "What about you, honey?"

Lisa watched Stephanie return her attention to her phone. She might have everything she wanted, but this woman had lost everything she had. Guilt choked her just then. Turning to the waitress, she swallowed tears that threatened to escape. "I'll have the same please."

She reached out to Stephanie with a touch of her hand. "We're back in the right time. This is where we started."

Stephanie put down the phone. "You know, Lisa, it's been a whirlwind of a trip. I'd say that it was drug induced almost. But even if I believe that everything I saw was real, I have doubts now about my life. I mean…" She cleared her throat and looked at her hands as a flush rose to her cheeks. "I'm your husband's mistress. I thought we were becoming friends and all, but how can you forgive me? And what do I do with him now? I mean he has been such a faithless creep."

Shaking her head, Lisa leaned back in her seat. "I used to think I was certain about everything I wanted. Now, I'm not so sure."

Stephanie leaned back also, "Looks like we both have some thinking to do."

***

After driving Stephanie to her apartment, Lisa returned to her house. She sat outside in her car, pondering the task ahead of her. She could see the girls through the front bay window, jumping up and down on the furniture. A face appeared, peeking around the curtains. Her beautiful mother.

Lisa got out of the car and walked up the steps to the front door. Before she could turn the knob, the door flew open. Her mother swept her into her arms in a big hug as if she'd been gone forever. "Sweetheart, you're home. How did it go?"

Comforted by her embrace, Lisa didn't move, smelling her mother's hair, noticing the softness of her cheek. Everything was just as she remembered from her youth. Being back in her presence, she realized how very much she had missed her, not just from the past few hours that she was gone, but from all the years after her death. All that time she had pushed down the missing and the grieving to make room for living, but, in this here and now, all she wanted was to stay forever, to settle for a half-life with a husband who was nonexistent and to have a family that would make up for that emptiness. She sighed in contentment and disappointment, tears gathering at her eyes knowing this might be temporary and, certainly, not real.

But was it? Wasn't it possible to simply stay? Who would know the difference anyway?

Lisa pushed herself away and looked straight into her mother's clear eyes. "It went well. I'm back. We can talk later."

Her mother raised an eyebrow in that inimitable way she had, half accusation, half disbelief. "Sure honey. We can talk whenever you're ready." She embraced Lisa again, then stepped back to let her in the door. "In the meantime, go see your daughters. They've been asking for you all day."

Suzette and Natalie came running towards Lisa as she stood in the doorway to the sunny kitchen. "Mommy! Mommy! You're back!" The girls crushed her legs in giant hugs, wrapping themselves around her. Lisa reached her arms down to caress their heads and froze in that instant as feelings of love overwhelmed her. All three of them stood there like a giant tree with roots deep into the ground.

Suzette squealed, "Play Monster!"

Natalie chimed in immediately, "Yes, play Monster Mommy!"

Lisa wasn't sure what they meant and tousled their hair while she tried to imagine a game. "Monster? I don't remember what you're talking about."

Natalie raised her soulful eyes. "Yes, you do. We always play. You pretend you're a monster who's grabbed us and are taking us away to be fed to the wicked witch."

"If I'm the monster, who's the wicked witch?"

As one, the girls shouted, "Grandma!"

Growling from her throat and with deliberate exaggerated movements, Lisa pushed her hands against the girls' backs, so they would hold tightly to her legs. She continued growling and moved in giant steps. "I'm the Mommy Monster, and I'm going to take you naughty girls to the wicked witch, so she can cook you into a hearrrrrty meal for me! Grrrrr! Because I'm a hungrrrrrry monsterrrrr!" She took large bulky steps while the girls hung on squealing with delight and fake fear. "No, please, Monster Mommy, don't hand us to the wicked witch—take us to our real mommy please!"

"Nooooo! You're going to be baked into a pie, so I can eat you up!" With that, they had reached the doorway to the kitchen where Lisa's mother stood watching the whole scene. "Here you go wicked witch! Delicious little girls to be cooked for me!"

"Nooo!" came the peals of laughter.

Lisa's eyes locked with her mother's. With the children laughing as if in the background, the world of Lisa's awful decision came crashing on her. These children loved her even though she didn't deserve them. Her mother loved her too. She had missed this family even though she had never known it. How can one miss something one doesn't know exists? And yet, there it was, alive and palpable, breathing in the form of two towheads hanging on to her legs and one all-consuming maternal love she hadn't been able to enjoy for most of her life. This is what she would be giving up by going back to the emptiness of her "real" world.

Her throat tightened, and her words came out choked as she leaned down to unfurl the children's arms from her. She knelt at their eye level and continued the game that was no longer pretend.

"Oh, my dear sweet children!" she said in a sugary sweet voice. "I've missed you so much! The Monster Mommy is gone. I will save you from the wicked witch." She hugged them to her like a lifeline.

Suzette was the first one to step away from her embrace. "Mommy. Don't be sad." She wiped a tear from Lisa's cheek. "It's only pretend, Mommy, and that's only Grandma. You don't need to cry."

Lisa hugged them again, her heart breaking, and her head exploding in pain.

***

After the girls had a snack, they went to the backyard to play with the dog. As they were skipping out, Suzette yelled "Stop!" Everyone stood still. "I'm going to bring my music box!" She ran to the playroom and came back holding a plastic toy shaped like an old-fashioned television set. "See, Mommy? This plays music." She handed it to Lisa, who looked at the box, not knowing what to do with it. "Look, Mommy. I'll wind it up for you. It will play all by itself. I'm going to put it here on the table, so you and Grandma can talk and listen to nice songs while Natalie and I play with Rufus." Suzette adjusted the plastic knobs and tinny music started playing. She left the box on the table in front of the two Adirondack chairs on the deck and ran off to meet her sister on the ground.

Sipping on a cup of hot tea her mother had made her, Lisa watched them as she leaned in the open doorway. Liminal spaces gave her a place to think. She felt, more than heard, her mother approaching her. The older woman's voice was kind. "They are so joyous, aren't they, dear? So innocent."

Lisa didn't take her eyes away from the children as she spoke. "It's because of that innocence that I'm so torn." She turned to face her mother. "Mom, I don't know what to do now. I want to stay so badly, yet I know that's not the right thing to do."

"Come, let's go outside and breathe in all this warmth we have right now."

Sitting on the deck chairs, they watched the girls play tag with the dog as if the poor beast had any chance at their games. Gladys spoke first. "Sweetheart, I know you keep saying you need to leave, but I'm not really clear what you mean by that. I know you spoke about coming from another place, but I've been wondering if that isn't just all the stress of your husband being…well, you know…being the way he is. When you say you're leaving, are you thinking of leaving him?"

Lisa put her cup of tea down on the left side of her chair and leaned into the right side to be closer to her mother. "Mom, are you saying you don't believe I've been time traveling?"

Gladys moved closer to Lisa and whispered. "Honey, are you really still thinking that you time travel? I thought you were just saying that as a metaphor or something." Gladys looked away from Lisa for a moment and gazed at the girls playing. When she turned to Lisa, she had a quizzical look on her face. "Is the stress of marriage that much? Are you just saying that to make an excuse to leave your husband?" Gladys put her hand to her chest and gasped. "Are you considering leaving the girls behind when you leave Adam?"

Lisa couldn't understand how this conversation had turned so upside down. She thought her mother believed her time travel. Now she doubted again. How did that happen? The sun felt lower in the sky, yet brighter, and dark spots were popping up before her eyes. She felt a sharp pain in her temples as if someone were sticking a nail on each side of her head.

"Mom, I thought you believed me. I'm relying on you."

"Darling, it's not that I don't believe you. It's just that your story is so…well, it's so far-fetched. I mean, Lisa, where do you go when you time travel?"

The truth of her mother's statement reverberated in Lisa's aching head. She wasn't sure where the pain came from, but she felt the insistent throbbing move to the back of her head as if her brain were about to explode. "Mom, my head is pounding, and I can't explain anything to you right now. I can't even think straight. All I know is that at some point I have to leave you and the girls. And yet…." She waved her arm towards the children. "How am I supposed to leave them?" Then she turned her body away from the girls and towards her mother. "How am I supposed to leave you?"

Gladys extended her hand and took Lisa's in hers. The warmth of her mother's hand calmed her. She remembered being a little girl, burning with fever when she was sick once. It was late at night with a full moon that shone right through the curtain in her bedroom. Shadows of tree branches danced on the walls and in her feverish state, Lisa thought they were hideous creature hands coming to get her. Her mother had placed her cool hands on Lisa's forehead, and the scary sights had disappeared.

This time was similar, yet more frightening. Her mother's comforting hand was making the decision even more difficult, and now there was the added complication that her mother didn't believe her. If Lisa decided to time travel again, she was giving up her only source of comfort and safety. But her conscience gnawed at her. While she'd be creating a life she had desperately wanted before, wasn't she taking that same life away from Stephanie? The enormity of her creation bolted Lisa upright in her chair. Her head continued to throb, and she dropped her mother's hand.

She heard the girls' joy while the dog barked as they tormented him with an endless game of fetch. She saw her mother's bright eyes welling up with tears that spoke more loudly than the noises in the yard. And in the midst of it all was this incessant pain in her chest and in her head.

Whether she liked it or not, she didn't belong here. She had to leave to make things right. She had upended everyone's world in her search for a love that was not hers to claim. Her traveling had impacted Emily. She thought of Marcus, living alone somewhere back in reality, abandoned by her through no fault of his own, simply because she had been running away from the sorrow of the loss of their son.

Her sweet infant boy. She had chosen not to think of him because the pain of his loss was too much to bear, and in the process, she had left Marcus to his own despair, the two of them drifting away as easily as they had come together.

The realization of her mistakes weighed heavily on her as the pain now intensified at her temples. Her eyes felt as if they were going to pop out.

She now saw the path she had to take as clear as the sunlight that glinted off her wedding rings. None of this was real. It was all a creation of her imagination, of her own choices, and she had to clean up the mess she had made. Her fear of traveling again battled against the certainty that she couldn't stay here.

The tinny music box had been playing what sounded like children's songs all the time they were outside. Now Lisa noticed that the tunes had changed. They sounded more like pop songs. The notes caught Lisa's attention. She cocked her head, trying to listen more closely.

Metallic and soft, she heard the lyrics. *I was working as a waitress in a cocktail bar.*

She stood up on wobbly legs as her stomach churned from the pain that now radiated to her fingertips. She heard the song, the plastic box bringing forth notes and sounds she already knew by heart. It was a strange feeling, as if she were suspended in air, hearing the music and lyrics and feeling such intense pain in her head. Is this what happens at death? The music box seemed to be playing louder even though there was no volume button. All other thoughts were drowned out. Her mother looked far off, dwindling in bright light. Everything was fuzzy. As she stood there, she felt as if she could see the musical notes floating on air, but she knew that was impossible. Music didn't look like anything. It was a sound. What if this time travel had created a way to actually see music?

She felt a buzzing sound as dark spots appeared before her, swallowing all the light in the yard.

"Mom, I love you, but I can't stay," she said as she tumbled forward and fell in a heap on the deck floor.

In the dimness, she heard Gladys scream.

***

The sound of a beeping machine woke Lisa up. She opened her eyes and slowly adjusted to the bright lights of a hospital room. A woman in white scrubs appeared at her side, fiddling with the machine, and pressing buttons to stop the noise. Lisa felt the woman grab her wrist to take her pulse. She heard the voice ask gently, "Well, hello there. Welcome back. How do you feel?"

As her eyes grew accustomed to the bright light, Lisa noticed her head no longer hurt. She felt a dull pain on her scalp, but the throbbing had ceased, and her stomach was calm. She watched the nurse intently and realized it was Stephanie. Where were they? And, more importantly, when were they?

Stephanie patted Lisa's hand. "Your pulse is fine. This damn machine beeps out of control. It probably needs adjusting again. I'll call a technician." Stephanie squinted at Lisa. "Although I admit I feel compelled to check on you every few minutes, and I'm not sure why."

Lisa struggled with the question uppermost in her mind. She shimmied herself into an upright position in bed. "Stephanie, this is going to sound weird. But how long have I been in here?" Lisa noticed wedding rings on Stephanie's left hand.

"You were brought in yesterday. The notes say a friend of yours drove you after you fainted. You weren't in distress, yet you weren't responsive. Very odd. Obviously, you had to be admitted. Another MRI was done while you were unconscious. The doctor will come later to share the results with you. There seems to be no reason for your fainting, but you do have that pineal gland issue, so perhaps it's related."

"My friend brought me here?"

"That's what the medical record says." Stephanie checked the laptop on the cart that was in the room. "Let me see, the nursing notes also say that they tried to reach your husband, Marcus, but he didn't respond to the calls."

Stephanie moved back closer to the foot of Lisa's bed and spoke kindly. "Are you two separated? It's strange when a husband doesn't reply to a phone call from a hospital."

Lisa stared at her own fingers, noticing her wedding rings. She was back in her own real time. "Strange isn't the word. Estranged is more like it." Lisa gave Stephanie a wan smile, feeling her throat constrict. It was hard to think of Marcus. She had spent so much time thinking of Adam that Marcus was almost like an afterthought, but she sensed him very present in her life here.

After a few moments, she looked up to catch Stephanie staring at her with a quizzical look.

"Why are you estranged? What happened?"

Twisting her wedding ring on her left hand, Lisa answered slowly. "I'm not sure. We lost a baby, and then we lost ourselves." She sighed. "And then I think…I don't know." Lisa hesitated to say more. How could she describe to this woman what she had been doing all along? How could she even come up with an excuse?

Lisa took a deep breath. She saw that Stephanie was still staring at her, waiting for an answer. "My husband and I were so distant, and then I was unfaithful to him."

Stephanie didn't move a muscle. Lisa felt herself shrink under Stephanie's scrutiny, as if there were some unspoken conversations happening. Did Stephanie suspect anything about Adam? Did she have any idea that Lisa was involved with him?

Stephanie was the first to look away. She licked her lips, as if in deep thought, then spoke, barely above a whisper. "I have this uncanny feeling I've been to places with you, but I've been here, at the hospital, all along. I know you've been under my care before, but this feeling is more than that. This feels like…I don't have words for it…like I'm here but not here, and somewhere else where I know I've never been."

Lisa didn't move a muscle. What Stephanie was saying didn't make any logical sense. "What do you mean you feel like you haven't been here?"

"I mean that I feel like I'm remembering things that are not possible, especially when I've been working sixteen-hour shifts for several days straight. Logically, I know I've been here, but I have a sensation that I've been in other places at the same time." Stephanie pulled a chair to Lisa's bedside, facing the door. She leaned in close to whisper to Lisa. "Two nights ago, while I was taking vitals of a new patient, I had a vision of myself with you in a diner, listening to music. And holding your hand. That's not possible because it didn't happen, yet I remember it very clearly."

Lisa sat up straighter in the bed and moved closer to Stephanie. "What exactly do you remember?"

"I'm not sure. It's fuzzy, but there were lots of people, musicians, and a song. Some friend of yours named Emily shows up in this memory." She grew silent for a moment, took a deep breath, and continued. "And I have this scary thought that you're connected to my husband." She paused. "It's more than that. I'm certain you're connected to him, and it's all around these memories of things that haven't occurred."

Lisa grabbed the edge of the bedsheet and pleated it as if she were folding napkins. She did this for a few minutes, not responding to Stephanie's words.

Stephanie leaned in even closer. "You know something about this you're not telling me. You're not just here with a head trauma. I'm not buying this whole 'I'm estranged from my husband' story. What is it that you know about my husband, and how are we connected? Why do I see you and me together in places I've never been?"

Not sure how to answer and struggling with the reality of what was transpiring, Lisa touched her fingertips to her temples that felt tender. And now this revelation from Stephanie. How much was the traveling influencing their lives?

"The truth is, Stephanie, I've been told I have an enlarged pineal gland. It's done something to me I don't understand. There's no logic to it, but I've traveled back in time. It started happening a few days ago, when I was at a train station, when I was waiting for..."

Lisa stopped herself. How did she admit to this woman that she was seeing her husband?

Lisa took a deep breath, wringing her hands to find the right words. "The truth is that I was waiting for your husband at the train station, and then I found myself back at college, before I knew Adam. We connected, and I had this idea that if I met him before you did, I'd be able to change history. I'd be the one he fell in love with and not you."

Stephanie sat back in her chair, a strange smile on her face. "What kind of head trauma did you say you had? Because that is the craziest story I've ever heard, and I've been around hospitals and nutty people for a long time."

"I know it's hard to believe, but it's the truth." Lisa pulled her hair in exasperation at not being able to communicate the truth convincingly. "I went back to that time and met him, but you were there also. It's a long, complicated story, but when I returned, I was the one married to Adam, and you were his mistress."

Stephanie got up from the chair and busied herself looking at Lisa's monitor. She checked the notes on the computer once again. "Listen, Lisa, you look like a nice person. And I get it that you have a problem with your brain and all, but you're making crazy talk now, so I'm going to check when the doctor will be here." She started to walk away. Desperate, Lisa yelled out, "Please! Please stop. I can explain."

Stephanie turned around. "I don't know what kind of game you're playing. You sit here and tell me you're having an affair with my husband, and you go back in time. From what I can see, you're the one in a hospital bed with a brain injury or whatever it is you have. So, I don't know if I should be here with you any longer. I'm leaving to find a doctor."

With that, Stephanie hurried out of the room.

Lisa's eyes welled up with tears. She had made a mess of everything, and now she was here with this pounding headache and no one to talk to. She got up and walked to the window. As she stood looking at the night sky, she heard her cell phone. Marcus.

She couldn't talk to him. How was she supposed to confront yet another thing she had destroyed? She let the call go to voicemail. As she stood pondering what to do next, Stephanie returned.

She stood erect, hands on her hips, appearing decisive. "Listen, I had a few minutes to think. I'm not going to speak to the doctor about your story of going back and forth in time because...well, because I'm not sure who sounds crazier, me or you."

Lisa breathed a sigh of relief. "So, you believe me?"

"It's not so much that I believe you; it's that you have no reason to lie to me at this point, and I have this nagging feeling you're telling the truth." Stephanie shut the door to the room and stood a few feet away from Lisa. "Why don't you sit down and tell me this story of yours, and then we can see what I believe and what I don't."

Lisa sat down on one of the guest chairs across from Stephanie. She straightened out her gown and breathed deeply before speaking.

"I've traveled back in time and out of this reality that we're in. On a couple of those occasions, you've also come with me to several different places. And yes, your husband is the connection between us." She stopped and waited to see Stephanie's reaction. The other woman was stoic, not moving a muscle, as if she had ceased breathing.

Stephanie finally spoke. "Go on. Tell me the truth. I already know it, but I want it confirmed."

Lisa looked away, shame burning her cheeks. "I'm your husband's lover. I have been for some time. And...I don't know how to explain this, but somehow, I've been back to the past when you first met him, and I stopped that relationship, thinking it would make my life perfect. But all it's done is create a mixed-up soup of everything."

Stephanie laughed. Quietly chuckling at first, then louder, enough so that she covered her mouth with her hands. "Oh, my God. I knew it. I've known for years that he's fooling around, but with you? I only suspected that today when I started having these weird feelings."

Lisa's cheeks were pink with embarrassment. "So, you knew all along?"

"Oh, honey, the wife always knows." Stephanie laughed. "But I chose to put up with it because I have my two babies and a nice place to live. I figured I'd let him have his entertainment until the kids are grown." She grew pensive. "But today, this sensation of being elsewhere—it's nagging me. As if you know something I don't." She leaned in towards Lisa again, putting her hand on her arm. "Please. You have to tell me. I know there's a secret. What is it?"

Lisa wasn't sure how much she could tell Stephanie, but she wanted to come clean. She had gotten to know this woman in those other worlds, and now she couldn't just go back to business as usual. But how to admit all this and also have Stephanie believe her?

"Look, Stephanie, Adam isn't as wonderful as he appears. You and I...well, we've been together, outside of this hospital. What you're feeling is true. We've been in other places."

Stephanie didn't seem persuaded by the explanation. "So, you're saying I'm not crazy?"

"Not crazy, but it's not normal at all." Lisa wasn't sure how much to explain. "Let's put it this way. You've traveled with me to places that are not this reality, but are almost, invented, not real yet real." Lisa chewed on her bottom lip before continuing. "I think...wait, I *know*, it's related to this pineal gland enlargement I have. It makes me able to leave this reality and go to another life that's similar yet not the same. The same people are in it, but their personalities aren't, and the worlds are also different."

"What does that have to do with you and Adam?" Stephanie's tone was doubtful but cutting.

"In each world where I'm married to Adam, you're his mistress, and you don't have children. I do. But we both know that's not this world."

Stephanie nodded her head. "Go on."

Lisa walked towards the window again to gather her thoughts. "I think the pineal gland lets me move around these dimensions even while I'm still here. While everyone is still here. It's as if there were several Lisas and Stephanies and Adams living in other places at the same time." Lisa paused and turned around. "The people are a constant. But what's also a constant is that Adam is not a nice person in any of them."

Stephanie stared past Lisa as she appeared to listen intently. "You're saying he's always the same womanizer?"

Lisa put on a half-smile. "It appears so."

Stephanie joined her gazing out the window. The sky was dark that night, and the clouds obscured any stars. "I've always known that," Stephanie said. "I just didn't want to face it."

Lisa put her hand on Stephanie's back in consolation. "I'm so sorry. I had this fantasy of him, but my trips, our trips, showed me that he doesn't value either of us or his family."

They both stayed silent for a few minutes. What to say when dreams are shattered?

Stephanie was the first one to speak. "It's been a long day for me, and this is all a lot to digest. My shift ends in a few minutes, and I'm dog tired. I'm back on duty tomorrow morning. I'll come check on you, and we can talk some more. Maybe with fresh eyes and ears I can make sense of all this."

Without even giving Lisa a chance to say anything else, she left the room.

Lisa stared after her when she heard the buzzing of her phone. Marcus again. This time she picked up the phone. "Hello?"

"Lisa, are you OK? I got a call that you were in the hospital. I can't get a flight back until tomorrow, but I'll be there as soon as I can."

"Don't worry, Marcus. I'll see you tomorrow. I'm not going anywhere for a while."

***

Mornings in a hospital start early, even before the 7:00 a.m. shift. Lisa awoke from a deep slumber to the sounds of laughter in the hallways, rolling carts, people talking loudly. *God, didn't they know there were sick people here who needed rest?* The aide who barged into her room was not apologetic, squeaking a marker on the whiteboard on the wall intended to keep patients abreast of shift changes.

"Good morning, dear. I'm your aide, Mary, and your nurse today is Stephanie. I wrote it on the board in case you forget. People with your condition forget things sometimes." Lisa thought she noticed a condescending smile as Mary handed her a sheet of paper with menu options. "Write down what you'd like for lunch and dinner here. Breakfast is on its way, so you have no choice with that." She opened the blinds on the windows and rearranged the chairs so they'd be lined up against the wall, tidied up Lisa's bedsheets, and fluffed her pillows, all the while humming a tune. "Don't take too long in deciding what to eat. The food isn't all that interesting. You just need something to fill your belly and get you strong, so you can get out of here and go home. I'll be back in a few minutes to collect it." With that pronouncement, she marched out as briskly as she entered, leaving Lisa with the sense a small tornado had passed through the room.

Faced with the truth of morning, Lisa stretched her legs and sat in the chair closest to the window, marking down what to eat as if she were studying the menu at an expensive restaurant. While asleep, she was able to escape all that had been happening to her recently, but the sun shining on her face brought back reality. A gentle knock on the door interrupted her musings.

She sensed more than heard his footsteps, and it was only a matter of seconds before he was at her side.

Staring at the menu as if engrossed in a good book, she whispered, "Hello, Marcus."

He folded his six-foot-three-inch frame to kneel at her side and pressed his forehead against the side of her head. She felt his breath on her cheek, and his dark wavy hair with the shocking patch of white tickled her nose. He needed a haircut. She pulled away and looked at him as if for the first time. His green eyes were brooding. Why did he seem so sad? He'd long ago lost interest in her. Silent, he closed his eyes. In that instant, he seemed like a little boy, and she remembered him telling her that kids made fun of his hair as a child, so he dyed it brown in the summer between eighth grade and high school. His coverup was short-lived as the chlorine in the town pool turned it a freakish purple color; he fixed that by shaving his head.

Marcus interrupted her reverie with rapid-fire questions. "Lisa, I was so worried about you. What happened? Why didn't you call me? What's wrong? How long will you be here?" His questions jarred her. Their marriage had been a pretense for years, two people living under the same roof, miles apart from one another. He tried to hug her, and her muscles tensed. After all this time, now he wanted connection? She raised an eyebrow as she straightened her back. His closeness was too much. She had blocked off the part of herself that had once cherished his affection, and he now threatened the walls she had built, brick by brick, around her feelings for him. She didn't trust his renewed concern.

And yet, a nudge of compassion showed up for this man who looked sad. She had withdrawn from him, unable to sustain intimacy when their grief over the loss of their son sat between them, palpable, immovable, destroying any connection they had enjoyed before. Blame and judgment for the death of the baby were the undercurrent of all their conversations. In the deep of the ocean, the undertow of despair separated them. And if she were honest with herself, her actions in the past had not been fair to him. Marcus's ministrations cast a burning light on the breadth of her deceit to him, to Stephanie, and even to herself. She didn't know where to start, feeling obligated to say something. But not the truth. He'd never believe her. Who would?

He brought a chair over. Lisa raised her head, a thin smile on her face. "I'm sorry to interrupt your business trip. That's why I didn't call. I didn't want to disturb you." The lie tasted sour on her lips.

Concern was written all over his face. He reached out and took her hands in his and kissed them. She noticed the gold wedding band on his finger, remembering when they first got married and how hopeful she had been. She searched for tenderness now and saw, in herself, only regret and sadness where long ago there was joy. She wanted to tell him to leave, to forget her because she wasn't in love with him anymore. She even opened her mouth to speak, but words didn't form. In that moment of hesitation, he pulled her towards him for a hug. She stiffly complied, eyes closed, scarcely breathing, noticing that he didn't let her go.

Marcus buried his face in her neck, and she felt a sensation of wetness. It took her a moment to realize they were tears. It took her another moment to realize they were not just his, but hers also. Almost instinctively, she lifted her arms and wrapped them around his back. She dropped the paper menu on the floor and reached her right hand up to caress the back of his head, noticing the familiarity of his hair. Eons ago, she knew his schedule by the length of his hair. It was very short; he must have gone to the barber recently. She remembered he always did that before a business trip. As if in a trance, she breathed in the smell of his cheek. No other man, not even Adam, exuded a fragrance that persisted in her memory. Lisa relaxed into Marcus's embrace, melting perhaps, into the memory of what they once had.

Marcus finally let her go and sat back, a defeated look on his face. "I'm sorry I wasn't here sooner. Are you in pain?"

"Why do you ask that?" wondering what he'd been told.

His tone was gentle as if speaking with a child. "The person who called said you'd been admitted with a head trauma from a car accident. What happened?"

The questions broke the spell of the embrace. Acting on their own, the fingers of her right hand rubbed against one another, missing the smooth texture of his hair that moments ago caressed her skin. Lisa wrinkled her brow, suddenly empty, as if she had lost something she had only recently found but didn't know had been missing. She sighed, out loud.

"It's a little complicated, Marcus. I've had severe pain in my head, and they tested me. The results are that I have an enlarged pineal gland. It seems to cause...I'm not sure what, but I've been having awful headaches, and...." Her voice drifted off, and she turned her head away from him, not knowing how to tell him about what she'd been experiencing. Or perhaps not wanting to tell him. Shame flushed her cheeks pink.

He reached towards her again, his hand pulling hers into his. "What does all that mean?"

She softened her tone, her guilt casting a shadow over his warmth, "It means they don't know what I have. But it has some effects, I think. I'm not sure yet."

"What kind of effects?"

Wondering how far she should go with her story, Lisa started to answer him, "It's a bit complicated...." She was interrupted by a brisk knock on the door. "Good morning, I'm Dr. Alfonso."

The doctor walked into the room, and Marcus jumped out of his seat. "Oh, Doctor, I'm so glad you're here."

As the men shook hands, Dr. Alfonso said, "I'm assuming you're Mrs. Williams's husband?"

Marcus nodded his head, urging Dr. Alfonso to continue.

"I have some test results to review with you, but first, Mrs. Williams, how are you feeling?"

Lisa sat up in her chair. "My head hurts less. But you said you have some results for me?"

"I do. I'm afraid they're not exactly what we'd hoped for." Dr. Alfonso spoke with authority, but Lisa could see his hands fidgeting with the file of papers he carried. "The fact is, we don't know what's happening with your pineal gland."

Marcus started to interrupt, but Lisa stopped him with a wave of her hand. "Not now, Marcus. I'll explain later." His eagerness at being helpful annoyed and pleased her at the same time.

Lisa focused her attention back to the doctor. "Please continue. What's the problem?"

"We're not sure it's a problem, it's just strange. It's enlarged, much larger than what we find in an average woman. The issue is that it's gotten larger from the last time we checked it. We can't tell why it's so big, or why it's growing. I don't want to scare you before we have some conclusive evidence of the cause, but that's the reason you're having such severe headaches. Any nausea or vomiting? Other than the headache, have you had any other of those symptoms, Mrs. Williams?"

"Some nausea," Lisa answered with hesitation, not wanting to reveal it happened each time she traveled. She was afraid they'd transfer her to the psych ward.

The doctor pulled a small notebook and pen from the breast pocket of his white coat and jotted some notes while explaining. "It makes sense you'd experience nausea. We're scheduling another MRI for this afternoon to see what additional growth there's been. You've already had two MRIs, and each time the gland appears larger, so we're concerned about its rapid growth. The headache is caused by the pressure the gland is having on the two hemispheres of your brain. If it continues to grow, we'll have to intervene before it affects other functions."

Marcus interrupted the conversation. "What does that mean, 'intervene'?"

The doctor cleared his throat, appearing to Lisa as if he were biding time before answering. "When there's a tumor with this progression, surgery is the only answer. In this case, the actual gland is increasing in size. A normal pineal gland is the size of a soybean. Yesterday, your wife's gland was the size of a walnut. The last reading shows it's the size of a clementine. Without question, it's growing rapidly. It's also dense.

I'm afraid that, at this point, the only solution is surgery." He paused. "As soon as possible."

He stopped talking for a moment and crossed his arms. "Mrs. Williams, I don't mean to alarm you, but we've never seen a pineal gland growing so quickly. We've seen tumors that are generally benign, but this is very unusual. Have you noticed any emotional changes at all? The pineal gland affects hormones and fertility. Do you have any symptoms like that?"

Lisa's eyes filled with tears as she covered her face with her hands. Was this happening because of the traveling, or was she able to move in time because of this growth? She couldn't ask the doctor. She felt Marcus's hands on her shoulders, his thumbs making circles around the muscles that were tight. The welcome touch confused her. In that instant, she remembered how very much she'd loved his massages when she was pregnant. His hands felt warm and strong.

She took a deep breath, momentarily relishing the comfort of Marcus's hands. The face of her baby son floated in front of her, and sadness washed over, bringing forth more tears. She shrugged her shoulders abruptly and leaned forward to escape Marcus's touch.

A question for the doctor pressed on her, but she was afraid of asking. With quivering lips, she managed to find words. "Doctor, what do you mean the pineal gland affects fertility?"

"Simply put," the doctor said, "fluctuations in the size of the pineal gland affect a woman's ability to conceive. Have you two been trying to get pregnant?" Lisa felt Marcus touch her shoulders again, but she brushed him off.

Her voice choked. "No. We lost a son a few years ago. We haven't tried to have another baby since."

Dr. Alfonso softened his tone. "I'm sorry for your loss."

The three were quiet for a moment. Dr. Alfonso broke the silence. "So, the next step is to rest, Mrs. Williams. Try not to worry about this until we see the results of the MRI. I'll be back later today to talk with you." He nodded his head and left the room.

Lisa's thoughts swirled. Was this problem with her brain caused by traveling? She had a nagging feeling that something was incomplete, but she couldn't put her finger on it. She wondered about her mother and saying farewell for good, but that idea made her dizzy. She grabbed her head again in pain, certain that she had to act quickly before... before what? She wasn't even sure what could happen, but was she willing to risk not having a possible surgery just to see her mother one more time? What if another trip caused irreversible damage? What if she left and then couldn't return?

Her head pounded, so she relented and leaned back into Marcus's hands while he bent down towards her cheek whispering, "Is there anything I can get for you, babe?" His tone was gentle. His presence was such a comfort; she noticed how his voice soothed her. When was the last time she had felt this way with him? Forever ago, but time didn't have any meaning for her anymore. She took a deep breath again, recognizing how much she'd missed him. *Wait a minute. She missed him?*

He let go of her shoulders. *No, don't stop. Please. Come back.* She felt as if someone else were speaking inside her brain, but she couldn't get the words out of her mouth.

Marcus pressed his lips to her cheek while he pulled a chair closer. "Hey, why I don't run to the dog sitter, get the pup, and sneak him in here, so he can lick your face? Jojo will make you feel much better."

The comfort of his familiar lips made Lisa smile. "That's very nice of you, Marcus. I'd love to see him, but what are you talking about, a dog sitter? Jojo's with Emily. She picked him up when I told her I was in the hospital. Come to think of it, I haven't heard from her today."

Marcus furrowed his brow. "Who's Emily?"

"What do you mean, who's Emily? Marcus, I'm the one with the brain problem, not you. My best friend, silly. We don't know any other Emilys."

"Lisa, honey, I don't know any Emily. And your best friend is Kate, in Chicago. There's no way Kate could have taken Jojo anywhere."

Waving her hand in dismissal and shaking her head, Lisa said, "This is no time for jokes, Marcus. Call Emily."

Marcus frowned. "Lisa, should I call the doctor? I'm telling you: you don't have a friend named Emily. Could you be confusing someone else with that name? Maybe someone from work?"

"Marcus, stop it." Her voice went up an octave. "This isn't funny at all. Call Emily, please."

"Look, sweetheart," he said handing her his phone. Lisa grabbed the phone and searched the contacts. No Emily. She scrolled again. "Hand me my phone," she said in a flat tone.

Marcus found her phone by the bed and gave it to her in slow motion. Lisa clicked through her contacts, over and over again, muttering, "How is this possible? Where is she?"

She looked up at Marcus, raising her voice, "Marcus, where is Emily? I told you this is not funny—not one bit." She punctuated each word.

Marcus only shook his head. "Maybe I should go get the doctor."

Her breath got ragged, and her heartbeat pounded so hard an artery pulsed in her neck. *Emily was gone? How could this be? What happened?* She inhaled deeply and spoke slowly to Marcus starting straight into his eyes. "Marcus, for the last time, and please don't play around. I'm not well, so I'm going to ask you again. Where is my best friend, Emily? The one I've known since freshman year in college, the one you took on one date before you met me, the one who was my maid of honor at our wedding. Where is she?"

Marcus reached for his back pocket and took out his worn brown leather wallet. Beads of cold sweat ran down Lisa's back while he pulled out a small picture. He handed it to her gently. "Take a look, honey. There's Kate."

The wallet-size wedding photo had ragged edges. Lisa noted that Marcus carried their wedding photo with him. But her hands made the picture shake wildly when she saw the stranger who stood in Emily's place, wearing Emily's maid of honor dress.

"See, dear," Marcus continued as if he were talking to a child, "There's Kate. She was your maid of honor."

Tears splattered as Lisa shook her head violently, crying, "No! No! This can't be!" Marcus reached over to her. "Sweetheart, I'll get the doctor. Maybe this has to do with this growth in your head. Don't be upset. Stay right here, and I'll be right back."

Lisa wailed. Who was this stranger? She had lost her Emily. This was not possible. They had been friends for half their lives. They had promised to grow old together. Emily was her compass; she had even given Lisa a plastic toy compass as a gag when she left for graduate school in Chicago. Lisa ran for her purse and fumbled through it. Zipper pocket. It was always there. She opened it, emptying out the contents on the table. Nothing.

She beat her hands on the bed, inconsolable. "How could this happen?" she kept repeating.

Marcus ran out the door, calling for a nurse. A few minutes later, he returned with Stephanie. They found Lisa sitting on the floor, elbows on her knees and hands in her hair. She looked up when Stephanie knelt by her side. "Hey there, why don't you lay down, relax for a minute, while I call the doctor?"

Lisa smiled at her kind voice. This woman, to whom she had been callous and uncaring, was being kind and generous. And for what? For a guy who was deceitful no matter what woman he was with. She had lost her way with Marcus, and now, she had lost her Emily in the process. Stephanie took her hand to help her up from the floor towards the bed.

"I'd rather stay here, if that's OK," Lisa said quietly.

"Whatever you prefer. I'll get you a pillow, so you can at least be more comfortable," said Stephanie. "Mr. Williams, why don't you go get yourself a cup of coffee, and by the time you come back, I'll have called the doctor to see if we can move the tests up a little?"

Marcus looked to Lisa, who waved him off. "Go, please, I want to be alone. I'll be fine." She needed him out of the room to think clearly. His presence served only to confuse her further.

Chapter 21

Stephanie crouched down to the floor to be closer to Lisa. "Hey, what's going on? Do you feel faint?"

Lisa sobbed harder, if that was even possible, at the sound of Stephanie's voice. She allowed Stephanie to grab her by the arm and pull her up to sit on the bed. She felt she'd never stop crying, hoping somehow that her tears would erase the horror of what she'd discovered. How could Emily be erased from this world? Traveling back and forth in time must have altered something, but how? What had she done? How would she undo this tragedy if she didn't even know the source?

An icy fear gripped her chest. She looked up at Stephanie's concerned, worried face. Her throat tightened at the thought she had manipulated time to create something unreal. Yet here she was, alone in this life without her best friend.

"I have to go back. I have to fix this." Lisa said these sentences almost incoherently.

Stephanie rubbed her back, making gentle circles as one does with a colicky baby. The motions were a soothing balm for a brief moment. "Is there anything you need? What do you have to fix? The doctor said you need surgery; don't worry. You'll be in great hands. He's a really good surgeon. Please try to calm down, or I'll have to give you a sedative."

The word sedative brought Lisa back from the abyss. She contorted her face, shook her head, and pushed her hands against

Stephanie's chest. "No! No sedation. I have to think clearly. I have to go back and find her." She bounced off the bed and headed to the tiny hospital room closet to find her street clothes. She stripped the faded blue polka dot hospital gown from her body and furiously dressed herself. "I have to be ready for when it plays, then I can go." Then she grabbed her cell phone from the nightstand and scrolled through until she landed on the music folder. She pressed the song, thanking her past self for having had enough sense to download it.

Stephanie asked, "What do you need? Are you calling your husband?"

Lisa retorted, "No! I'm not calling my husband. This isn't about him. I'm playing the song. God, I hope this works." Lisa stood in the middle of the room with her eyes closed and bouncing up and down on the balls of her feet like a sprinter preparing to hear the gunshot for the start of the race as she listened to the tinny sound of music from her phone.

Stephanie placed herself in front of Lisa and put her hands on Lisa's shoulders. "Lisa, what are you doing? I'm going to have to call someone for assistance if you don't calm down. You're scheduled for surgery tomorrow morning."

"There will be no surgery. Not until I bring her back."

Stephanie picked up the discarded gown and threw it gently on the bed. Even in her frenzy, Lisa noticed how she moved slowly. "Until you bring who back, Lisa?"

Lisa ignored the question. *"You were workin' as a waitress in a cocktail bar, when I met you."* She knew the familiar lyrics and concentrated on the first few lines. She spoke to Stephanie in a calm voice like one does when reasoning with a child. "You're going to see something strange, but please, don't tell anyone. I have to go." She felt the familiar sensation of darkness. She relaxed into it as the swirling starting. She felt, more than heard, Stephanie come close to her and grab her arm. "Lisa, please, what are you doing?"

Stephanie's hand was on her arm, and Lisa tried to swat it away, but as the darkness came upon her, the other woman's hand gripped her arm as if in a vise.

"Don't you want me, baby? Don't you want me ohh?"

There was a whirlwind of sound and lights…and then nothing.

***

Lisa felt pain in her arm and noticed fingers digging into her skin. As if in a dream, she pried Stephanie's hand away and focused her attention on where they stood. The smell of hot dogs and pretzels mixed with rotting garbage from an overflowing trash can on the corner sharpened her senses. Sound returned: cars honking, people talking loudly, a crowd of young adults with bags and books passed by them. Stephanie looked stunned, her eyes wide as she turned around, looking at everything at once. "Where are we?" she whispered.

Lisa spun around, taking in the surroundings. This wasn't the hospital. And Stephanie was with her. She knew exactly where they were. "We're on the Columbia University campus." She grabbed Stephanie's hand, pulled her towards the newspaper stand on the corner, and pointed to the *New York Times* in the pile. With glee, she announced, "It's 1982, Stephanie. It worked."

"What are you blathering about?" Stephanie snatched the newspaper as the vendor yelled. "Pay for that! This isn't the library." Lisa put her hand into the pocket of her jeans, acutely aware that these were not the clothes she was wearing in the hospital. She found a few coins and paid for the paper as the vendor muttered, "Damn college students."

She showed Stephanie the first page, pointing again to the date. "See? April 19, 1982. We're back to the beginning." The news of the day showed the prime minister Margaret Thatcher dealing with the British predicament over the Falklands in Argentina, and the Middle East was still in crisis over the Sinai Peninsula. Closer to home,

President Reagan was dealing with issues over a tax surcharge. Further inside the paper were advertisements for Lord & Taylor Santa Fe dresses, cinched at the waist and flowing out like flowers. And the movie *Raiders of the Lost Ark* had won five Academy Awards.

Stephanie mumbled, "*Raiders of the Lost Ark*? I saw that movie in the theater."

Lisa patted Stephanie on the arm. "Of course you did. In 1982 we had nothing else." She continued softly, "You came with me because you were holding my arm as the song played. I came here to find Emily."

Stephanie shook her head, eyes wide and mouth agape. "Wait. I remember this. We were here before, weren't we? Back in 1982. You did this to me before. That's why we're back here, on Broadway, wearing these ridiculous leg warmers. Oh my God, I'm going insane." She strode away from Lisa, aiming towards the crosswalk, muttering, "I have to go home." Lisa followed her and saw her glance at her wrist. "Where's my watch? What time is it? I have to pick up my kids from school." She paced back and forth, her head spinning around, lips trembling.

Lisa grabbed Stephanie's shoulder and yanked her to a stop. "Stephanie, remember there are no kids in this time. They aren't born yet." Shaking the newspaper at her face, Lisa continued in a gentle voice, trying to soothe the other woman's panic. "Focus, Stephanie. We're here again. See?" She pointed again to the newspaper's date. "It's 1982. We've traveled back in time. You're not married yet. You're still in college, just like me."

Stephanie moved her body in a circle, taking in the surroundings. She stopped, faced Lisa, and gently touched this now-twenty-year-old's hair. "You look so young. Your hair is long and dark." She put her hands out in front of her and turned them palm up and down, brought them close to her face. "My hands, they're so soft, like they were before I became a nurse." She kept staring at her hands. "No wedding rings. And the scar on my left hand, from the accident with a scalpel, it's gone." Mouth agape, she spoke. "How is this possible?" Before Lisa could speak, Stephanie waved her hands in the air. "I have this uncanny feeling I've been here before, like a weird déjà vu. I can't pinpoint it...." She stumbled with her words, her head turning around again. "I recognize this place from the past. This looks like my college street."

She straightened her back and punched Lisa in the arm, her voice strident again. "I don't care what you're up to. I want to go home. Now!" Stephanie pushed Lisa with both hands.

Lisa caught herself before falling backwards, the newspaper flying out of her hand. In a soothing voice, she continued. "Stephanie, I know this is a jolt, and it's...well, I guess it's uncanny, but believe me, it's all true. We've traveled back in time."

Her head cocked to one side like a golden retriever, Stephanie stared at Lisa. "You're crazy, you know that. You're one crazy bitch, and I want you to change whatever you did, so I can go home. In real life, my shift is about to end, and I have to go to my kids' school and pick them up. So whatever shit you pulled, stop it, and get me home. Immediately." She stared at Lisa, defiance in her eyes, until fat tears started rolling down Stephanie's cheeks. She covered her face with her hands. Seeing the woman's despair, Lisa pulled her into a hug and rubbed her back. Stephanie slumped into Lisa's arms, sobbing.

"It's going to be OK, Stephanie. Don't worry. Your girls are fine. Nothing's happened to them. We'll get back home later, and you'll see them again." As Lisa said this, she hoped she was right. Every time she traveled, something changed, and in trying to fix this recent mix-up, what if she made things worse? But what could be worse than losing her best friend? Lisa sighed, the thought of being stuck here scaring her as well. Then she saw Emily's face in her mind's eye and remembered her mission. She had to figure out what to undo so her best friend would return.

While Lisa was lost in thought, Stephanie pulled back from her, her crying more controlled. She straightened up and stared at Lisa. "Fine. We're here. Now what?"

Lisa smiled, putting her arm over Stephanie's shoulder, and held her close. "I promise it's all going to be fine. We have work to do, and I don't know how much time we have. But we're here to find my best friend, Emily. Let's go get a coffee, and I can explain along the way."

***

The two women walked towards the Hungarian Pastry Shop. Lisa wondered what she would find, hoping against all hope that retracing her steps would show her a hint of what had gone wrong with the last trips to the past. She didn't know whether this would help, but she had to start somewhere, and the coffee shop was the last place where she had seen Adam in this time. She intuited Adam had something to do with what had gone wrong. Rather than feeling jittery or excited about seeing him, she felt determination with every step.

As they walked, Lisa summarized her trips to Stephanie. Every few feet, they stopped. "Stephanie, are you getting what I'm saying?"

"Yes, Lisa. I get that you're telling me you've been traveling to the past, and that you find me there. And somehow, I'm remembering things I've never seen. I get the gist of what you're saying, but it makes no sense. It's totally illogical and impossible."

Lisa laughed. "Well, no one said time travel was logical. But here we are." As she said this, they found themselves in front of the pastry shop. The awning was bright and clean, appearing new.

Stephanie gasped at the entrance of the pastry shop. "I used to work here. I had a part-time job while I was in nursing school."

"Precisely, woman. That's why we've come back to this spot—to start from the beginning, so I can fix whatever I screwed up."

"How do you know you screwed up anything?"

"You remember Marcus telling me that my best friend was some girl named…God, I don't even know her name…because she never existed in my life before. My real best friend was Emily. Is Emily. And something I did, or probably something Adam did, has erased her from my life." Lisa opened the door to the shop. "And we're here to sort this out."

Walking into the pastry shop was stepping into the past. Lisa watched Stephanie gaze at everything: the pictures on the walls, askew and dusty, were photos of Leona Helmsley, the Queen of Mean as they called her back then, and old photos of Dean Martin and George Burns. There was a photo of Madonna: young, fresh, and clad in black lace and a pink bow on her head. The small tables lined up close to one another, and the glass case with pastries was the same. Students crowded every table, book bags thrown about, notebooks and textbooks open while ceramic cups lay next to them. Thinking out loud, Lisa said, "It must be finals week. We don't have a lot of time. Students will go home soon, so we'll work fast to find Emily."

Stephanie pulled Lisa's arm. "Wait, if we're back here, that means that I might run into myself, or into someone I know."

Lisa stopped for a moment and stared at Stephanie. "I hadn't considered that. Think quick: what shift did you work?"

Stephanie bit her lip. "I tended to work the evening shift after I was done with classes."

Lisa looked at her wrist and remembered she never wore a watch in college. The clock on the wall caught her eye. One o'clock. "We should be fine. It's still early."

At her words, the manager, a crusty, balding guy with a paunch and a chocolate and grease spattered apron that was once white yelled out. "Stephanie! Glad you're here. We're swamped. Care to work a few extra hours?"

Caught off guard, Stephanie shook her head. "No, no. I'm not here to work. I'm just…. I'm just here to get a cup of coffee."

He dismissed her with a wave of the hand and an audible mumble under his breath, "Useless kids," as he walked towards the cash register.

Stephanie leaned into Lisa's ear and whispered, "At least I won't run into myself." Lisa patted her arm. "Let's not even think about those consequences, shall we?"

They resumed the chore of finding a place to sit when Lisa saw a young girl emerge from the back room, headed towards the manager with a receipt and a few dollar bills in her hand. Lisa couldn't help herself as she shouted, "Emily!"

Emily looked up, appearing startled, her voice raised louder than what Lisa knew from before. "What are you doing here? I told you to leave me alone." She approached Lisa and with gritted teeth and a thin smile said, "Listen, I'm working. I don't want any trouble."

Lisa touched her shoulder. She sighed. "I don't want trouble either. I just want to make things right for us." She winced as Emily pushed away her hand. "You made your choice, Lisa. Not me. I wanted to stay friends, but you refused." With that, Emily resumed her trip to the cash register.

Lisa leaned her hands on the glass case. "Emily, I'm sorry. I don't remember what I did, but whatever it was, I'm sorry. I can't live without you. You're my best friend."

Emily shook her head. "Well, you certainly didn't show that when you refused to accept that Adam is my boyfriend as you threw me out of our dorm room." Lisa opened her eyes wide.

"Oh," added Emily. "You forgot that, did you? Did you also forget you opened the window to our room and threw out my clothes onto the street? You don't remember that?" Emily banged her fingers on the cash register.

Stephanie moved closer to Lisa. "Maybe we should leave? She clearly doesn't want to talk to you."

Emily waved her hand towards Stephanie. "And this one. You bring this one here with you. What? The two of you are friends now?"

"I don't even know you," said Stephanie, stepping back away from the case. People in the restaurant shifted in their seats, their murmurs undulating like waves. "Lisa, we should go. You're making a scene, and everyone is staring at us."

"Let them stare. This is what I came here for." Lisa turned back to Emily. "Emily, I'm sorry. I didn't mean to do any of that."

"Could have fooled me. My clothes dropping on the street didn't seem like an accident."

The manager piped in. "What the hell is going on?" He moved towards Lisa and Stephanie and waved them towards the door. "Look, girls, whatever boy problems are going on here, take them outside. Stephanie, I'll see you later tonight or tomorrow or whenever the hell you're really supposed to be here. And you," pointing at Emily, "get to work. I don't pay you to have girl fights in my shop."

Lisa and Stephanie walked outside and stood by the door. Stephanie broke their silence. "Now what?"

Lisa sighed. "I don't know, but we wait here until her shift is over."

"I don't have time to wait for shifts, Lisa. I have to get back to my kids. You got me here. Now get me back."

As Stephanie was speaking, Emily opened the door and walked towards Lisa. She held her head high and shoved a piece of paper into Lisa's hand. "Listen, I get that you're sorry. But I can't talk here. Meet me later tonight. We can talk then." With that, she walked back inside.

Stephanie ran over to Lisa. "What did she say?"

The paper hung in Lisa's shaking hand. She headed towards the crosswalk with Stephanie at her heels. They reached the benches in the cathedral's garden, and Lisa sat down, paper still in hand.

"What does it say, Lisa?"

With quivering lips, Lisa read slowly. "Come to the party at Fuller Hall tonight. Ten p.m. You'll see what chick Adam's been with since he dumped both of us."

Chapter 22

A fter reading Emily's note, Lisa sat on one of the benches in the park by St. John's Cathedral. Stephanie had gone off by herself to wander the gardens, telling Lisa she needed time to be alone. Lisa could see her pacing back and forth and could only guess what could be on the woman's mind. Several hours before the party started, Lisa wondered where they could go in the meantime. Almost absentmindedly she reached into the pocket of her high-waisted jeans and found a key and an identification card. Her picture stared back at her. For a moment, even though the photo was fuzzy, she didn't recognize the fresh face in it. Her hair was long and brown, and even without makeup she saw the carefree youthfulness in her eyes. The young girl in the picture smiled broadly, seemingly happy to be starting life.

***

It was a long afternoon and evening waiting for ten o'clock to arrive. Lisa's hands shook as she headed towards the Columbia campus with Stephanie. There were more people outside at night than during the day with students hustling towards bars, parties, and whatever else they did after the sun went down. The punk kids with their spiked mohawks mixed with the others totally clad in black protesting life in general. Some students wore brightly colored leg warmers, big hair, and more makeup than Lisa had seen in decades. Spandex, cigarettes, and pot abounded. The lights on the campus walk were bright, and the steps to Low Library were full of kids smoking, laughing, and singing along with songs from boom boxes. Stephanie followed at Lisa's side. "I'd forgotten how alive this place got at night."

Lisa was oblivious to the sounds. She focused on the task before them, wondering when she'd find Emily, hoping the encounter would be the catalyst for returning life to normal.

They arrived at the party in a large hall on campus, loud '80s music assaulting them when they opened the doors. Stephanie waved her hands in front of her face at the rush of cigarettes seemingly everywhere. "God, does everybody smoke here?"

Lisa smiled wryly. "Proof that we're back in time."

The party was jumping with people dancing in the center floor to songs by The Police and Huey Lewis and the News, and others hanging on the sidelines in groups, beer cans in hands. Some were gathered around a keg, waiting for their turn to fill red plastic cups. A large, hulking guy with a mohawk who looked like a football player stopped them. "IDs please. You don't look like Columbia students." Lisa pulled her ID from her pocket, and he grunted in approval. She smiled coquettishly and stood on her tiptoes to lean close to his ear. "Do you know a guy named Adam Scheiner?"

He put his meaty hand on her waist and pulled her towards him. "No, but I can be Adam if you'd like."

Lisa pushed him away with both hands, still smiling. "Never mind. I'll find him myself."

She grabbed Stephanie's hand and strode into the room as if she owned it, all the while scanning for Adam. They walked the periphery of the hall. Chrissie Hynde's mournful voice and her blaring guitar with the Pretenders made talking almost impossible. As they approached one of the corners, Lisa noticed a couple making out. Something about the guy looked familiar, maybe the way he cocked his head to the side when he separated himself from the blonde girl he held by the waist. Stephanie pulled her hand hard and pointed as she leaned into Lisa's ear to shout, "There he is."

"Adam!" said Lisa as she grabbed his shoulder. He turned around with a smirk on his face. His eyes shot wide open when he saw Lisa and Stephanie together. He gulped noticeably and looked confused for a moment before he plastered a fake smile on his face and stretched out his arms. "Ladies! Welcome to the party. Will you join us?"

Stephanie reached out her hand and slapped his face, so hard that it swung to the other side. As everyone stared in shock, Emily showed up from nowhere and stood next to Lisa. "I told you he was scum. But you didn't believe me."

Holding his hand to his face, Adam straightened up and pushed his shoulders back, uttering epithets under his breath. He looked at all three women standing before him, then smiled with a sinister grin that showed all his teeth like a cat about to pounce on prey. With one hand, he grabbed the blonde's waist, and with the other he waved in the general direction of Lisa, Stephanie, and Emily. In a voice meant to be smooth and suave, he said, "Ladies, ladies. No need to fight. There's plenty of me to go around."

Stephanie was the first to respond. "Adam, is this who you really are?"

Still holding on to the other girl, Adam reached over to Stephanie and put his hand on her shoulder. "Come on baby. You know I'm just playing around. I forgive you for the slap. I probably had it coming, but you know, I'm just a guy. Guys have needs, you know what I mean?" he said, pointedly winking his right eye.

Noticing that Stephanie's arm was pulled back aiming to slap him again, Lisa grabbed her hand and yanked her away. "He's not worth it, Stephanie. One more slap, and we'll get ourselves kicked out."

She turned to Adam, vitriol spewing in her words. "We're not interested, asshole. We're through with you." In unison, Lisa, Stephanie, and Emily stepped away from him.

Adam shrugged his shoulders and leaned in closer to Stephanie. "Pity you're so frigid. We could have had fun tonight. You would have been a nice addition to the collection." He turned away from her and slinked closer to the blonde. Lisa heard him whisper, "Come on, Susan. Let's get out of here. This party just got really creepy."

As they walked away, Emily was the first one to speak. "You see, Lisa? For this, you threw our friendship away."

"Emily, I don't know what I did, but I'm so sorry."

"Nah, too late. I'm never forgiving you. I just wanted you here, so you could see for yourself. I'm out of here." She waved Lisa and Stephanie off and headed to the makeshift bar in the back of the room.

Lisa watched her friend disappear into the crowd, regret crushing her chest. Stephanie bumped her hard in the arm. "Listen, forget her. She'll get over it." Stephanie turned around and around, gesticulating with her arms and pointing everywhere, a note of near-hysteria in her voice. "What are we doing here now? You said we could go home. I don't see what any of this has to do with me. I was at work, minding my own business with a husband and a family, and you've ripped it from me in your quest to find your friend. Well, you've found her. Now you saw my husband fooling around, and your friend doesn't want to speak with you, so stop jerking me around here, and take me home." She took a breath and continued, "You know what? I'm going to tell the DJ to play 'Don't You Want Me,' and we can go back to reality."

Lisa only half listened to Stephanie as she walked in the direction Emily had headed. Stephanie continued, "Lisa! Where are you going? We have to leave! Don't test me. I swear to God, I'll have them play that song."

Lisa ignored Stephanie, watching Emily carefully, noticing that she had struck up a conversation with some guys who appeared obviously drunk, even from a distance. Curious as to what could happen next, Lisa continued her path while Stephanie jabbered in her ear about finding the DJ. She stopped in her tracks and yelled at Stephanie. "There's no home without Emily, don't you understand? That's the reason we're here. Adam is inconsequential now. Emily was right. He's garbage. He cheated on you while he was married to you. He cheated on me when I was married to him in the other fake world. He cheats on everybody. But Emily." Lisa stopped and pointed in Emily's direction. "That girl is my best friend. She's the reason I graduated; she's the reason I didn't lose my mind when my son died. And she's the reason we're here now." Lisa paused, insight into her life appearing from nowhere, as if the fog that clouded her view of Adam disappeared.

She continued, breathless and excited. "We have one mission, and that's to save Emily from whatever I did that caused her to disappear." She resumed her march toward the bar, ignoring Stephanie a few steps behind her.

As they got nearer, Lisa noticed the guys surrounding Emily. They were laughing at a joke one of them had just said, and Lisa could see Emily throwing back shots of some liquor. One guy was pouring them and lining up the glasses in a row.

That's when she saw him. Marcus, a younger version of him, with his shock of white hair and his beautiful smile. He was standing to the side away from the guy lining up the drinks.

Lisa stopped in her tracks. She had forgotten how handsome he was in college. She couldn't understand why he was here, at this particular party, but she felt a calm take over her, as if all was now well with the world. He was watching Emily, and he sauntered over to her as if he didn't want to get any attention. Lisa saw him lean down to Emily and whisper in her ear while he took the drinks away from her. He put his arm around her shoulder. Lisa couldn't hear him, but she assumed he was saying something soothing. That was Marcus—always with a soft tone. What had happened to them?

Lisa hurried towards Marcus. "Hi! What are you doing here?"

His eyebrows raised like fuzzy inchworms. "Do I know you?"

Shit! She hadn't met him yet. But this wasn't how they met the first time.

Lisa recovered and added with a smile, "I'm Lisa. This is my friend Emily."

"I know Emily. We work together in the library. Now, if you'll excuse me, I have to take her out of here."

"Do you mind if I go with you?" Lisa heard herself almost purring. Her hands were shaking, and her heartbeat raced. He was intriguing. Maybe this was why Emily got lost? So she could find Marcus again? Questions swirled in Lisa's mind, interrupted by Stephanie tapping her on the shoulder. "Don't test me, Lisa. I'm headed to the DJ."

Lisa heard the threat and grabbed Stephanie's hand. "Give me just a few more minutes. Please. Just a little more time." Stephanie frowned but stayed put.

Marcus returned his attention to Emily and cajoled, half pulled her away, but she got out of his grasp and went back to the guys at the bar. Lisa drew closer and saw one of them whisper in Emily's ear. She giggled and took his hand while he led her outside. Lisa rushed to stop them, but Emily pushed her hand away. "Leave me alone, bitch. We're not friends anymore."

Emily's words were a punch to the gut. Lisa stood motionless, a single tear running down her face. Marcus must have taken pity on her. He bent his head down, gentle eyes staring into hers. He wiped her face with his index finger, as if collecting her tears. "So, your name is Lisa. And you're Emily's friend?"

"We're best friends, even if she doesn't remember right now."

"In that case, best friend, why don't we follow them and save her from herself tonight?"

Stephanie, seeing that Lisa and Marcus were now heading outside, pulled up alongside Lisa. "Time's up. We need to go home."

"Stephanie, I have to see this through. Please, I beg you. Stop. We'll get you home as soon as I get this solved. I promise."

Once outside, Marcus was the first to spot Emily down the block. "Look, there she is—getting into that black Trans Am with that guy. If we run, maybe we can get her to come with us."

Long, sleek legs sprinting, Marcus was the first to reach Emily. She was sprawled in the car with the door still open. As she struggled to reach the door handle, Marcus blocked her. Lisa and Stephanie reached the car as Marcus grabbed Emily's arm. "Come with me, Emily. You can't go with this guy."

Emily yanked her arm away. "Don't you tell me what to do!" The driver yelled at Marcus, "Fuck off, man! She doesn't want you!"

Lisa leaned into the car and pulled Emily by the shoulder, begging, "Emily, please, come with us. He's drunk. You'll get hurt. Let's talk out here." Marcus reached into the car and grabbed Emily's other hand, and between him and Lisa, they stood her up and pushed her to the sidewalk. Marcus slammed the car door. The driver stuck his hand out the driver side window and gave them the middle finger as he peeled away. "You're all a bunch of assholes!"

Emily slumped into Lisa's arms, mumbling incoherently and slurring her words, "You ruined my party. I want to get back in the car."

That's when they heard the screech of tires and the clash of metal on metal loud enough to rise above the regular din of city nightlife. Turning in the direction of the noise, they saw the Trans Am smashed against another small red car and crushed against a light pole. The cars were two heaps of distorted metal blocking the intersection. Everyone in the area stopped to gawk, and traffic ceased moving.

Marcus, Lisa, and Stephanie collectively gasped at the horrifying sight. Stephanie was the first to speak. "Oh, my God, look at those cars!"

Emily, roused by the noise, stared at the accident and pointed: "What's that?"

Lisa was the first to respond. "That is what we just saved you from."

Emily turned her face to Lisa, still holding on to her. "You saved me? That's so nice of you. I think I'm going to be...." And with that, she threw up on the sidewalk, splattering onto Lisa's clothes.

Stephanie grimaced, "That's gross...and I'm a nurse."

Amid the noise of police sirens, ambulances, and people yelling indistinctly, Marcus pulled out a napkin he had shoved in his pocket, took Emily from Lisa's arms, and wiped her face while he murmured. "Let's get you cleaned up a bit and take you home." Still in her stupor, Emily smiled broadly. "You're so kind, but you're not my type. Lisa here—she could like you. You should ask her out." She leaned her head on his shoulder, and he patted her back while smiling at Lisa.

"Maybe she has a point. I should ask you out when this is over."

Lisa noticed how in charge he was, so cool, just as she remembered him. She grabbed Stephanie's hand and turned to thank her for helping her to find Emily when she heard the now-familiar tune. Traffic was stopped everywhere, and a car's radio was loud enough to be heard amidst the noise of the crowd and the sirens.

Don't you want me baby?

Lisa gripped Stephanie's hand and let the notes of the song wash over her. She felt the darkness coming on, a smile on her face this time.

***

The hospital floor felt cold. For a moment Lisa was confused as to why she was sitting there, leaning against the wall, holding her knees and her bare feet on the floor. Stephanie was sitting on the bed a few feet away with a distant look on her face. She was the first to speak. "Are we back?"

Lisa shrugged her shoulders. "Looks like it, but I don't know when this is. Do you have a cell phone to check the date?"

Stephanie reached into her pocket. "It's still the same day; only a few minutes later. It's as if we've been here all along." She dialed home. "Hello, sweetheart!"

Lisa overhead Stephanie, "I'm coming home soon, honey. Really soon. Is Daddy there?"

High pitched giggles could be heard through the phone's tinny speaker. Stephanie's eyebrows went up as she answered, "What do you mean Daddy came to see me?"

More giggles while Stephanie continued, "Oh, it's a surprise. Well, I won't tell Daddy that you told me. It'll be our secret."

And a few seconds later, Stephanie replied, "Bye, my lovelies. I'll see you soon." Stephanie wiped a tear from her cheek. "They're all right. My children are all right." She sighed happily. "I can't wait to go home to hug them!"

Eyes wide open, she continued, "Lisa, how is this all even possible?"

Lisa stood up carefully. "I still don't know how anything is possible. I know only that it happens."

Stephanie walked over to her and checked her pulse. "You're normal. How's your head?"

Lisa gingerly ran her fingers through her hair. "Amazing." She felt her neck and the crown of her head. "It doesn't hurt anymore." She kept prodding around the formerly sore spots. "No pain anywhere. That's weird. I'd gotten used to it."

Stephanie cocked her head to the side, "I wonder if this last trip has something to do with that?" She stepped over to the nurse's computer on a cart in the room. "Oh, good. We didn't miss it. Your MRI is scheduled for fifteen minutes from now. Let's get you there."

Lisa grabbed her phone from the side table. "I have to check on Emily." She scrolled through the contacts, but there was no Emily. "She's not here, Stephanie. I can't find her."

Stephanie took the phone and looked also. She patted Lisa on the shoulder as she said, "Don't worry about that. That only means she's not in your contacts right now. Maybe the phone takes some time to adjust? Maybe it's an Apple thing?" Her words didn't ring true to Lisa, who appeared on the verge of crying again.

Stephanie piped up brightly, "Let's get your MRI done, and by the time you get back, maybe the time glitch will have adjusted the contacts."

Lisa hung her head and let herself be led away like a child, despairing that she had lost her friend, perhaps forever.

***

Back in her hospital room, Lisa paced the floor anxiously waiting for the MRI results. Frustration oozed from her fingers as she repeatedly tried to remember Emily's number without success. She was stuck in this hospital prison with no access to finding out if Emily was back in this world or not. She had tried Marcus, but he didn't answer his phone, and he wasn't responding to texts. Lisa felt utterly alone.

After what seemed like hours, Stephanie walked back in. She had papers in her hand and a broad smile on her face. "I don't know how this happened, but I have your test results here." She handed the report to Lisa. "Pineal gland: normal size."

Lisa raised her eyes in disbelief. "What happened?"

Stephanie put her hands up. "Who knows? Maybe this last trip made it smaller again. Maybe that's why your head doesn't hurt anymore. No one knows. But what I do know is that you can leave. This afternoon. I'll just get your doctor to process your discharge papers."

Lisa clapped with a mixture of glee and worry. Maybe going home would give her answers. From home, she could call Emily.

***

Dressed and ready to leave, Lisa waited impatiently. Stephanie finally returned with the paperwork. "Here you are. These are your instructions for lots of rest, at least for a week. Do you think you can handle that?"

Lisa smirked. "Yes. I just want to get out of here. I can't reach my husband for some reason. Can you call a taxi for me?"

A familiar voice interrupted their conversation. "Hey, hon. They said at the nurse's station that you were here, and I wanted to surprise you." Lisa could recognize Adam's voice anywhere. But she realized he was talking to Stephanie, not to her. He walked towards Stephanie his arms outstretched with a bouquet of flowers.

Stephanie raised her eyebrows and stepped back. She looked at Lisa and mouthed, "What?"

Lisa noticed that Stephanie turned her head when Adam tried to kiss her lips. He appeared stunned at his wife's apparent coldness, and the two of them stood apart for a minute. Stephanie examined his face. Lisa could only imagine what was going through her head as she saw her husband in a new light.

Adam continued. "It's OK I walked in here, right? I'm sorry, miss. I didn't mean to be rude. It's just that it's our anniversary, and I have to leave for a business trip tonight."

He doesn't know me. That's different. Lisa shook her head, "Truly no problem at all. Happy anniversary."

As she uttered the words, she realized she felt nothing about Adam not knowing her. It was as if erasing his memory had erased her obsessive attraction to him. She felt free. Full of possibility. Excited to see what else may have changed, to discover what she could create with this freedom from Adam.

Stephanie wiped her face with her hand and became professional and crisp. Her words brought Lisa back to the present. "Lisa, my shift is over. We could drive you home if you'd like."

Lisa raised her hands in prayer, in thanks. "Yes, my friend. Thank you. That would be lovely."

***

Lisa waved to Adam and Stephanie from her front door. The house was empty and quiet. Her only task was finding Emily's number to call her. She remembered that she kept emergency numbers on a bulletin board by the kitchen sink. She ran there only to find a big heart drawn on a piece of construction paper pinned to an otherwise empty board. Without giving it any thought, she searched the junk drawer for a phone book without success.

The disappointment, the sadness and despair, made her realize she was bone weary. She shuffled her feet to the living room, took off her shoes, and lay down on the sofa, pulling a soft blanket from the back of the couch to cover herself. The throw pillows were warm and comforting, and, before she even noticed, she was fast asleep.

She woke up to the sound of the door unlocking. Disoriented, she sat up on the sofa and peeked towards the door. Striding towards her, Emily squealed. "Oh, my God, you're home! I came here to get you underwear and a fuzzy robe, and then I was going to the hospital to see you. How'd you get here?"

Lisa rolled off the couch, ran to Emily, threw herself into her arms and sobbed. "You're here! Oh, Emily, you're here!"

"Of course I'm here, crazy woman. Where the hell else would I be? I left your dog in my house. I wasn't sure when Marcus would be home tonight, and…." Emily's voice trailed off as she noticed Lisa trembling in her hug. "Listen, I know you love me and all, but it hasn't been that long since we saw each other. I was just at the hospital yesterday."

Lisa stopped her crying. "I know, I just…it just feels like you were missing and…I'm just emotional to be home."

Lisa hugged Emily even harder, mumbling, "I couldn't find you in my phone contacts. I couldn't call you."

Emily laughed. "Silly girl. My phone died, and I got a new one yesterday with a new number, remember? You deleted the old contact."

Lisa looked up in disbelief. "Emily, I was so scared I'd lost you." She snuggled back into her friend's arms.

"OK, crazy lady. Sounds like you're hormonal or something. How about I make us a cup of tea, and you can tell me all about how they set you free from headache central?"

They headed to the kitchen and gabbed as if no time or space had separated them at all. Overjoyed to have her friend back, Lisa stared at her as if she had been away for an eternity.

As the late afternoon turned into early evening, they heard the front door opening. A man's voice boomed. "Hey? Who's home?"

Hearing steps striding along the hardwood floor, Lisa turned in her seat to see Marcus standing in the kitchen doorway. He walked over to her in two steps and hugged her tightly. "You're back," he whispered. "I thought you'd still be in the hospital when I didn't hear from you today." He pressed his nose against her face and kissed her cheek. "I was planning to make us a quick dinner before heading to the hospital to see you."

Lisa leaned away from his embrace and, with a quizzical look, asked "Us?"

That's when she heard him.

A young voice yelling "Mommy!"

She turned in her seat to see a little boy of about nine or ten with curly brown hair running towards her. He jumped onto her lap like a spry kitten and squeezed her, covering her face with kisses. "I missed you soooooo much! Are you happy to see me?" Stunned and speechless, she stared at the child, at Emily and finally at Marcus, who had stepped into the kitchen to stand by the refrigerator.

Was this child in her arms a figment of her imagination or a ghost she had conjured up? Was she dead and this was heaven? Perhaps it was hell when the thought that it could all disappear in an instant occurred to her. But she felt the child's arms on her waist, smelled his scent of air, grass, and little kid sweat. It must be heaven, she thought. Her eyes opened to everything in the house—the kitchen refrigerator magnets holding up crayon drawings, the picture frames full of Marcus, of her, and of their son, the toys strewn around, the paper flowers in a tin can vase. All the signs of a home filled with love.

Marcus leaned down to Lisa and put his lips on her neck. She freed one hand from the child and pulled his head down towards her. She snuggled into him, breathing in his scent. She had missed him. All this time she'd been wandering in her head and across time, this is what she'd missed the most. A family. Marcus. His calm assurance, his generosity, his warmth, and his love. She had blinded herself with grief at losing their son, when all along, she had pushed away the joy that Marcus brought to her life. She had shut him out, not letting him share in their joint sorrow, not seeing that together they might have been able to overcome the pain.

And now, after all the wandering, all the sorrow, all the loss, she had everything she had missed. She had Marcus. By some inexplicable miracle, she also had her son, alive, beautiful, growing. She had her best friend.

Gratitude spilled from her eyes. "Seth?"

He smiled up at her.

She kissed her son's head, breathing in his life and pouring out her love for him. He was here. She was his mother. Still.

Her life was complete.

In a burst of energy, Emily shouted, "Oh you guys! You're making me all sappy and crying. Stop that! Let's have some fun!" She turned to Seth, pulled him from Lisa and twirled him around by the hand. "Auntie Emily is here, Seth. What shall we do for fun tonight?"

With glee, Seth yelled in his high-pitched little boy voice. "Alexa! Play The Human League!"

THE END

Acknowledgments

Everything meaningful that I've created in my life hasn't happened alone, and this book is no different. Countless people loved and supported my dream to have this novel in print, and there isn't enough space here to acknowledge every person whose love has buoyed me over time.

This story started from a dream and languished in a drawer for years. My friend Danny Jiji, who believed in my dreams, introduced me to his cousin, Jeff Ourvan, the owner of *The Write Workshop* in New York City. I am forever grateful to Jeff and his community of beautiful and talented writers whose generous loving critique kept me afloat through the birth pangs of this novel: Beau Karch, Kathleen Scheiner, and Ashley Williams. Without you, *Don't You Want Me* wouldn't exist.

My editor, Adriana Senior of Regalo Press, has been an angel with her talent and generosity.

There are those friends who've been miraculous supporters: Dr. Mayra Alvarez, Georgia Pestana, and Susan Mullane Burke inspired the fun of 1982. We have a history that allows us to travel back in time whenever we meet. Mayra: You're my Emily.

Francie Webb, John DeWees, Cheryl Pearson, Chris Ziccardi, Michael Pirson, and all the people in the Team Management and Leadership Program helped me discover what it's like to live a life creating teams and fulfilling dreams. There are too many of you to name, and my gratitude for each of you is boundless.

My History and English teachers at Memorial High School in West New York, New Jersey, especially Mr. Augustine, Mr. Silvestri, and Mr. Cocuzza, showed me the power of words and paved the way for me to attend Barnard College, Columbia University. This immigrant kid from Cuba thanks you forever.

For the Spell side of my family, especially Deb, Wendy, Denise, and Anne who've been waiting for years to read something in print: Here it is. Endless thanks for your encouragement.

My sister, Damaris Gutiérrez Azan, loves me enough to have read this novel several times with her keen librarian eyes. You are my rock. Without you, my childhood would have been dull and boring.

My dear friend, forever committed colleague, and most stalwart believer of my creativity, Michael Hennessy: Our friendship is joyous. My big creative life dreams don't come true without your love and support.

And last, but never least, I acknowledge my parents, Hermes and Gladys Gutiérrez. They were brave enough to leave their warm tropical home full of family and friends in Havana, Cuba to venture into the unknown of the United States on one summer day in 1968. Without their love and endless belief in me, I would not be a writer. I owe them my life.

About the Author

Derlys Maria Gutiérrez was born in Havana, Cuba and emigrated with her parents in 1968. Raised in a very protective environment, it was a leap of faith for her parents to allow her to attend Barnard College, Columbia University in New York City, from which she graduated in 1984. Gutiérrez then attended and graduated from Rutgers Law School and started her career in private practice as an education and labor and employment attorney representing public school districts. She now works full-time as an Associate General Counsel for the American Museum of Natural History in New York City while writing about and remembering the 1980s.